INITIATION

A huge man walked into the room just then and entered the circle where Margo was lying, curled into a fetal position. He was horrible and looked like a ram—at least his head did. From the neck down she figured he was human even though it was hard to tell because of the white robe he was wearing, but from the neck up he was all animal, with a ram's snout and a wide, full mouth and ram's horns stuck high up on his head. . . .

"Rise," the ram-man said, and she did so because there was something in his voice telling her she'd better do as she was told.

"Don't hurt me," she said in a voice so small it was barely audible.

"I won't," he said. "You won't feel any pain. I promise you there will be no pain. Later, when this is over, your biological father can stand under the sign of the horns in honor, and so can you, Margo. In fact, after this night is over, your real father, Satan, lord of the universe and all therein, will be at your command."

MARGO

DANA REED

LEISURE BOOKS ⬛ NEW YORK CITY

To my family, for their great patience and understanding. And to the real Margo Windsor. May peace be with you.

A LEISURE BOOK

April 1989

Published by

Dorchester Publishing Co., Inc.
276 Fifth Avenue
New York, NY 10001

Printed in the United States of America.

Prologue

LITTLE MARGO WINDSOR was barely five, but smart enough to realize something was wrong. Two men were holding Mommy, and Mommy was screaming "Don't hurt Margo," over and over as if hurting Margo was a reality and not part of the bad dream Margo was having.

Daddy was there, too, only Daddy wasn't trying to stop those bad men. Daddy was dressed like them—a black robe with a hood and sandals on his feet. So it had to be a dream because Daddy wouldn't ever dress like that, and Daddy wouldn't let anyone hurt his Margo.

There were other people in the dream, too, and everything about them was hidden by those same hooded robes, everything but their smiles. Margo stared at their smiles with soft, black eyes gone dull with fright and wondered just what there was to smile about.

When she looked back to see why Mommy's voice had grown quiet, she saw the two men dragging Mommy from the room. Mommy was asleep because her legs were limp and she couldn't stand, so the men had her under the arms and were taking her away. Then someone pushed her, Margo, into the center of a large circle.

Margo looked down at the colorful figures drawn inside the outer rim of the circle and saw hideous creatures; some were shaped like men with parts of animals completing their bodies—tails of reptiles, birds' wings, horses' feet. Then Margo sat down and began to cry. She wanted to wake up now, right this very minute, before the dream got any worse. As she thought about it, she realized the dream was cresting and growing into an overblown nightmare, so she'd wake up soon enough. At least she hoped she would before anything bad happened.

A huge man walked into the room just then and entered the circle where Margo was lying, now curled into a fetal position. He was horrible and looked like a ram—at least his head did. From the neck down she figured he was human even though it was hard to tell because of the white robe he was wearing, but from the neck up he was all animal, with a ram's snout and a wide, full mouth and ram's horns stuck high up on his head. He kept saying the name "Satan" over and over.

Turning his back on Margo, he walked

straight towards a big, black thing resembling an altar in a church. Margo went to church when she could, whenever Mommy was able to sneak her out of the house behind Daddy's back because Daddy didn't like Mommy's church. Anyway, as she watched, the ram-man stepped up to the black, shiny altar and lit two huge, black candles, their scent heavy with the aroma of burnt flesh.

Then he began to talk again, saying some funny sounding words and always ending with Satan's name, while all those smiling people around him yelled "Hosanna" and "Hail Satan." When he turned to face Margo again, the ram-man's eyes were real big and red and sparkling, and he had a long, thin silver knife in one hand. Margo had seen the knife lying on top of a white bowl on the altar. There was a whip curled around the bowl, but she wasn't scared; at least she tried not to be scared because this was a dream, so all of those hurtful, painful things couldn't hurt her, could they?

Margo was still lying in a fetal position, her body covered with a white silk gown Daddy had given her, her long, black hair curled into ringlets. Although she tried not to, she began to shake, her body quivering with the sudden reality that this was no dream. Daddy had made her put the dress on, even though Mommy didn't like it. Then he drove her here, to this frightening place while he and Mommy sat in the front seat of the car and fought and yelled at one another. She remembered the whole thing—

coming into the room a while back, Mommy screaming, and people grabbing Mommy when she told Margo to run.

No, this was no dream.

"Rise," the ram-man said, and she did so because there was something in his voice telling her she'd better do as she was told.

"Don't hurt me," she said in a voice so small it was barely audible.

"I won't," he said. "You won't feel any pain. I promise you there will be no pain. Later, when this is over, your biological father can stand under the sign of the horns in honor, and so can you, Margo. In fact, after this night is over, your real father, Satan, lord of the universe and all therein, will be at your command."

Margo thought about what he'd just said and tried to make sense of it. "Will I be big and strong?" she asked. "Will I be stronger than Daddy?"

"Is strength so important to you?"

"Yes." But only because her Daddy had brought her here, and now she hated him with everything in her.

"You won't be big like me, but there's no doubt you'll be strong."

With this in mind, Margo stood firm and accepted what was to be, her hatred for Daddy turning into a festering, raw madness, like a boil full of untended cancer.

Chapter One

AUBREY SOAMES WAS walking home with his son, Tom, when he stopped to stare at the mansion ahead of him. A dark, gray building made of brick and mortar, it stood three stories high and was surrounded by a tall, wrought iron fence. Tom stood next to him, staring as well. The mansion was a curiosity in these parts, almost as much of a curiosity as was its sole occupant, Margo Windsor.

It was a cool night with hardly any moon, and as they stood still, their attention riveted on the medieval-looking structure, the wind around them began to howl and whip at their bodies. Tall trees, half-dead from the wrath of the coming winter, seemed alive, their long, sharp branches dangling dangerously in the wind. Tom was reminded of witches and claws and wanted to leave, but the allure of the mystery surrounding Margo Windsor kept him nailed to the ground in front of her mansion.

Aubrey was the first to make a move, the first to speak as he came out of his momentary trance. A light had suddenly flashed on in a bedroom window on the third floor, and Aubrey was just barely able to make out the form of Margo Windsor, dressed in a shoulderless, white satin nightgown. Two straps, he knew, were all that was holding the nightgown on, all that was concealing her firm, ample breasts from his prying eyes.

"Let's take a closer peek," he said to his son and moved towards the gate, but Tom didn't follow, mainly because he knew better. Things sometimes happened to people who got too close to Margo Windsor—awful things.

There was the time old Ben Anderson, the smithy, crippled her Arabian by shoeing it wrong. Oh Lord, it was too awful a thing to be dwelling on now, while he was standing outside of Margo's house, barely 50 feet from her grasp. But one night after that, some men were hanging out in front of the general store, opposite Ben's shop, when they saw a lot of smoke, more than normal, coming from Ben's chimney.

When they went to investigate, they found old Ben face down in his blacksmith's hearth, his head burned and blackened and shrunk to nothing. It was rumored that something, or someone invisible, was working the bellows, fanning the flames higher and higher until the heat was unbearable—and old Ben's body exploded, right there in front of everyone.

"Come on, Tom," Aubrey urged, but Tom's legs were atrophied from fear and rooted to the ground. Aubrey gazed at the pallor of his son's face and smiled. "Don'cha wanna see what she looks like? Ain't you curious?" Aubrey was. In fact, he was so anxious he was working the latch on the gate without even realizing it.

"Pa," Tom said when he was finally able to speak, "she's got strange powers. She'll kill ya."

"Bullshit. Come on." But Tom wasn't moving, so Aubrey had to walk back to where he was standing and pull him along. Tom's body was stiff and resistant, but Aubrey got him through the gate and halfway up the path to the mansion, almost up to Margo's front door before he stopped.

Then the two of them stood quite still, their eyes roaming the length of the mansion with its cold, gray exterior. "How the hell does she live here alone?" Tom asked. "How does she take care of the place? It's far from a dump."

Aubrey smiled and saw a chance to scare his son, all in fun of course. "Rumor has it she has all the help she needs."

"What're you talking about? I never see anyone come or go from this place."

"Not the kind of help you can see," Aubrey said and hung on when Tom started to back away. "Course, there's not always a lot of truth in rumors. Maybe she has one of them live-in servants, and we just never saw him—or her."

"Yeah," Tom agreed, something fearful in his voice. The wind was whipping them harder now, making the trees around them dance and throw strange shadows on the outer wall of the mansion. Tom saw something standing in one of the windows on the ground floor, but then he looked real close and realized it was the way the drapes were folded over. Hell, there was no one there. "Yeah," he said again, "maybe she has a servant who stays in and never comes out, 'cause this place sure is well-tended."

"And so is Margo Windsor," Aubrey whispered, as he concentrated his energies on the form in the bedroom on the third floor. "I'm close to fifty, and Margo Windsor was a teenager when I was born."

"She can't be that old," Tom gasped. "Hell, she don't look no older than—"

"Thirty, right?"

As they watched, Margo Windsor passed in front of the window and seemed to stare down at them for a moment. Tom panicked. "She's looking at us, Pa. Let's go."

But Aubrey made no move to leave. Instead he stood where he was, his face beaming with amusement. "She's not staring at us, son. Didn't I ever tell ya? She's blind!"

For the first time Tom noticed the dark glasses Margo wore. Poor thing, he thought, his heart going out to her. Bad enough she was alone, but to be blind as well. . . . Then his mind traveled back to the story of Ben Anderson, the smithy, and how he'd crippled her Arabian. What the hell did a blind woman want with a horse she couldn't ride?

As they continued to watch, Margo crossed the room, sat down in front of a dressing table and removed the glasses. Clad only in a revealing white satin gown, she reached up and released the pins from her hair. Margo usually wore it pulled into a severe bun at the back of her head, but now, as she let it down, her hair fell almost to her waist. Her hair was thick and beautiful, and Tom let out a low, soft whistle of admiration as Aubrey grabbed his arm to silence him.

"Lookit her hair," Aubrey said. "Do you see any gray? Do you see any wrinkles in her skin?"

Tom never answered. He was too busy admiring the creature with the long, black hair and heavy, supple breasts. He was too busy fighting his emotions, trying not to think about how she was 60 something and he was only 30 and much too young for her. Oh God, he wanted this woman and couldn't understand why.

". . . and she never married," Aubrey was saying while Tom was trying his hardest to listen. "She kept herself segregated from the rest of us in town, kept herself secluded in this mansion like a hermit and never married. Has her food and everything else she wants delivered and dropped at the front door. Bills are sent to Dennis Windsapple at the bank. He even has the legal right to sign checks in her name. Yeah, she's a hermit, all right."

"Pa," Tom said, "she's not a hermit. I'd rather call her a recluse."

"What's the difference? Hermit, recluse? It's all the same."

"When I think of a hermit, I think of an old man, dirty and diseased, living in a shack or a cave somewhere. Now, a recluse—that's something else again. Margo Windsor is a recluse."

"Oh hell, boy," Aubrey said, trying to sound carefree, but his voice cracked, and Tom knew he too was scared, scared of the shadows dancing across the face of the mansion and scared of the trees dancing overhead. The night was alive with movement, only not all of the objects that were moving were inanimate, at least not in Tom's mind. Some of them were . . . well, almost as human as he was, with blood flowing in their veins and a murderous rage in their hearts.

"Let's go," he told Aubrey. "It's getting late."

"Later than you think," a voice said, a soft, hollow echo of a voice, something that was there but not really.

"Did you say that?" Tom asked, because he sure as hell didn't, but it was Aubrey who was silent at that point. Aubrey said nothing. Rather, he renewed his grip on Tom's arm and headed back towards the gate and safety. They were almost safely through the gate and back on the main road when it happened. A large hooded figure in a black robe suddenly appeared on the road in front of them and raised its hands so that the two men could see its talons glistening in the glow of a horned, quarter moon.

"Oh, Jesus! Oh, Lord," Aubrey cried out and clutched at his chest because he knew what this creature had said was true—it *was* too late for them to escape, too late for them to ever make it home tonight. But then he thought about the odds. One of them certainly could make it out of here and safely home.

"I'll keep him busy," Aubrey whispered, knowing deep inside what he meant by that phrase. He'd keep the beast busy—probably getting torn apart with those sharp talons—while Tom made a run for it. But at least his son would get away, at least his son would live to tell . . .

"Don't count on it," whispered the hollow echo of a voice.

As Aubrey watched in horrified awe, two large, grisly hounds appeared beside the man-beast; their mouths foamed with saliva, their heavy jaws spiked with enormous teeth. "Now the odds are more to my liking," the voice echoed before the attack and the darkness set in. And Aubrey Soames and his son Tom could neither hear nor see the voluptuous form of Margo Windsor, still brushing her hair while counting out 100 strokes.

Margo Windsor was up to 25 strokes when she heard shouting and muffled screams, but as the sounds grew dim, she tended to ignore them.

There were always sounds of some sort crashing through the night to assault her hearing, and it was ridiculous. In fact, everyone in this town was ridiculous.

By now they should have learned their lesson and known better than to come here at night and spy, peeking in her window like a bunch of common perverts. Imagine those two men staring up at her while she was alone in the privacy of her own bedroom. What a nerve! Imagine them just standing there, drooling at her in her nightgown. Margo heard them discussing her. Margo heard every thought running through their minds, and she didn't like it one damn bit. Well, she thought, Jared took care of it again as usual.

The brush in her hand was soothing against her palm. The feel of the golden handle was reassuring as were the little lumps in it, lumps made by inlaid rubies. She fingered the brush and felt a quiver of excitement. As long as Margo had golden brushes with inlaid rubies she'd never be poor again, never know what it was to do without. And she had her husband to thank for her wealth.

She smiled and laid down the brush, reaching into her jewelry box to finger her wedding band—solid gold and encrusted with diamonds and sapphires. Nothing but the best for Margo.

Then she thought back to the conversation between the two eavesdroppers moments ago. One of them said she'd never married. Well, that showed how much he knew. Margo *was* married. In fact, as far as she could figure, she'd been married close to 50 years now, ever since her 18th birthday. And not one night spent in her husband's arms . . .

Also, one of those men, the same one who swore she was single, also swore she was blind and couldn't see him. Another stupid mistake on his part. One did not have to have eyes to see with, but then explaining this to someone as ignorant as Aubrey Soames would have taken forever and been a useless effort on her part as well.

She picked up her brush and began stroking her hair again, realizing that her hand was shaking. Margo was angry, and it wasn't just over those two men outside. There was more. Thinking back to her marriage, even thinking back to her wedding day, made her shake with anger. Just what was it about her that turned her husband off?

Other men craved her. Why didn't he? Why did he just slip a ring on her finger and leave so abruptly? She recalled her wedding day, still so vivid in her mind's eye after all these years. There she was in the church, wearing a wedding gown and a pearl tiara and a veil with scalloped edges. And she must have been beautiful because as she walked to the altar everyone in the room sighed with admiration.

Of course, she couldn't see their faces. The strange gift of insight—seeing things in her mind the same as others saw with their eyes—hadn't been given to her yet. She couldn't even see the man who stood near the high priest waiting to accept her hand in marriage. Damnit, she thought, stroking her hair with a vengeance, she wished she'd had the ability to see him then, to see the expression on his face when she walked down the aisle.

Maybe then she'd know why he rejected her, why he'd taken her for better or worse and then left, why he hadn't even stayed for the reception. It had been the social event of the season, attended by congressmen, bankers, lawyers, judges, everyone who was anyone.

Margo was led downstairs to the banquet hall by her sister, Valerie, and when Valerie made a gasping sound as they entered the hall, Margo became alarmed. She didn't know if Valerie was frightened or in awe, but, praise her lord, it was the latter. Valerie, who was much younger than Margo, described the banquet hall in a voice half-serious, half-amused, and how lavish it was after the ladies of the Royal Sect of Satan had gotten through with the decorations.

Valerie told Margo about the white streamers with tiny wedding bells strung from the ceiling and about the three-tier wedding cake, with miniature bride and groom sitting in the center of the bridal table up front. Valerie also told Margo about the band dressed in red satin jackets with dark pants.

Despite her anger at her husband for deserting her after the wedding, Margo could still feel the touch of the linen covering the table beneath her hands. She could still feel the cold touch of crystal when she raised a glass of champagne to her lips to acknowledge a toast to the newly married couple by the high priest himself. But then she realized something was wrong. When she reached over to whisper to her husband, she found an empty chair beside her.

No one would tell her why he left, and now, here it was, so many years later and he was still gone. He'd never returned, and Margo always wondered why. It was the strangest thing. She felt he'd surely return later, after the reception, for their wedding night, but he never did. Instead he sent Jared to take his place—in every sense of the word.

She began brushing her hair faster, wanting to finish the 100 strokes before Jared came to her, for surely he must have gotten rid of those two men by now and was ready for her. And oh, she was ready for him, a warm spot deep within her beginning to throb with passion.

Jared had been given to her almost half a century ago as a gift from her husband. His body was as firm and muscular now as it had been the first time he came to her. Margo put down her brush and stared at her form in the mirror. She too was as firm and beautiful as ever. It was curious that neither of them had bothered to take the time or the effort to age.

But it didn't matter, not to her anyway, not when Jared worked such wonderful magic on her body. And to think she'd almost rejected him, but only because she had been afraid. She'd been alone and blind and afraid, and suddenly Jared was there in her life. He came to her on her wedding night and walked into her bedroom as if he owned the place, as if he owned her, and said quite simply, "Your husband sent me."

Margo was afraid of him, for even though his voice was calm and reassuring, there was no mistaking the underlying passion in his husky tone. He wanted her. He'd been sent there to take her, but at the time, she didn't want any part of him. She had a husband. Where the hell was he, she wanted to know.

"He's busy," Jared said and smiled—and Margo could see him smile.

Somehow, miraculously, she could *see* Jared, but still this didn't quell her anger. She didn't want Jared; she wanted her husband! Was her husband so rich and wealthy that it had gone to his head? Did he usually send someone to do his screwing for him?

Margo continued to stare at her reflection in the mirror—at the high cheek bones, the black hair and eyes, the full sensuous mouth—and tried not to laugh. Those questions about her husband had been spoken in outrage, and Jared should have been shocked enough to leave. But he stayed instead—his own dark eyes focused hotly on hers, his passion building to a pitch. As Margo stared back, she became suddenly aware that her body was being drawn to his like metal to a magnet.

Jared approached her bed with a confidence she both hated and admired. He reached out and touched her body with that same confidence. As he began to take his clothing off, she did the same, sliding her nightgown over her head as if the very act were natural, as if going to bed with a stranger was something she often did.

Now, as the memories returned, she wasn't sorry. Jared awakened feelings in her that her husband might not have; Jared turned her on and kept her that way.

Margo came out of her reverie and heard Jared's footsteps coming down the hall. He was obviously finished with those two men and was coming for her. She had to be ready. She reached to the back of her dressing table and lifted a crystal decanter to her face, slowly removing the cap to savor the fragrance inside—essence of Monkshood and Nightshade, Jared's favorite perfume.

Jared had given her her first bottle of this mixture and told her to drench herself in this essence from then on, and drench herself she did. In fact, Margo would have done anything to keep Jared interested, to keep him coming back for more.

She splashed the liquid on her neck and shoulders, putting a dab or two between her breasts, savoring its bittersweet aroma and watching the door behind her open slowly as Jared came into her bedroom, his large, muscular body framed in the doorway. Then she turned and stared at his naked body and began to slide her nightgown slowly up to the top of her head.

* * *

Margo lay in bed with her head on Jared's shoulder after her appetite had been appeased and marveled that he was still able to drive her to the depths of madness after 50 years of making love. His arm, the one she was lying on, was resting gently against her lower back. Every now and then she'd feel his hand twitch against her flesh and she'd want to do it again, to experience the sensation of his lips against hers and his mouth caressing her breasts.

Jared was very adept at reading her thoughts, and at times like these he'd remind her of how wrong it was to overdo a good thing. So she settled back and allowed her mind to wander to the next time he'd come to her as he had tonight, naked and alluring, and simply announce that her husband had sent him.

She pulled the covers up around her neck and closed her eyes, ready to spend her night dreaming of Jared. But he squirmed away from her and pulled himself into a sitting position, his gaze focused on the quarter moon slicing through her bedroom window. She could sense he was troubled, for Jared usually fell asleep along with Margo.

When he was upset, she'd often awaken at night and find him staring out at the moon or hear him wandering the house like an animal in a cage.

"What's wrong?" she asked, but Jared didn't answer. Instead he rose and walked to the window, a sign that whatever it was, it was bad.

Margo threw off the covers and, shivering from the late fall air, grabbed her robe and joined him at the window. "Jared, please," she said, her hand climbing to his shoulder to comfort him, "let's talk about it. Is it something I've done?"

Putting both hands against the window frame, he lowered his head and sighed, then turned to face her. She knew it was an act of resignation, so whatever troubled him, he'd already decided to accept it. Good, she thought. No quarrels, no fights. They'd never had one in 50 years and this was no time to start.

"Your company's due tomorrow," he said, his dark, intense gaze focused on her.

Margo cupped her hands behind his neck and drew his strong, muscular body against hers. "I thought we already discussed this. I mean, why are you so upset? They're only coming for a visit, not to live here."

"Do you remember the prophecy?" he asked, pulling her away to measure her reaction. "Do you know how much it means?"

"Yes," was all she could manage, drawing him close to her once more.

"Margo, I don't exactly approve of giving power to a child." There was something almost fearful in his voice, Margo noticed, and she smiled to make light of his fears.

"They're in their late teens," she said, "hardly what you could consider children."

"You still don't get it, do you?" he asked and pulled away from her again. She wanted to hold him close, to let him feel the love she carried in her heart, but he was having none of it. He wanted to have his say first. "I'm talking about abuse of power—you know, playing it for all its worth."

"And?" This was all so puzzling to her. Jared had never been this disturbed or serious over anything before. So whatever the problem, she either had to alleviate his fears or be willing to send her sister's children packing, not that she was particularly anxious to have them here. Children were more trouble than they were worth at times. Besides, Margo had never had any of her own. "Jared, please don't hold back. Tell me what's bothering you."

He turned back to face her, still with that awful expression on his face, and Margo held her breath until he'd had his say. "I'm bound to protect you. I've sworn an oath. And protect you I will, no matter what. Now do you understand? If the fulfillment of the prophecy endangers your life in any way, I'll have to do something about it—and then, where will that leave us?"

"Nowhere," she said. "You're worrying over nothing. They're coming to stay for a few weeks. Period! Nothing will happen. Hell, before you know it the weeks will fly by, they'll be gone, and things will be back to norm—"

"I hope so," he said with a sudden desperation in his voice. "I really hope you're right, because you seem to have forgotten some of the details connected with the damned prophecy. It's been thirteen years since the first prediction—"

"Thirteen already?" She was beginning to get his point. "I didn't realize—"

"I didn't think you did," he said dryly. "Think of the terms of the prophecy, Margo. Think and you'll recall the details. I figure we have two weeks. I want them out of here before then!"

Jared waited until Margo was sound asleep before he went downstairs and examined his fingers again. Too short, he thought. One, maybe two, were too short. It was getting harder each time to make the transition, harder to hide his physical abnormalities from Margo.

Though she loved him and wouldn't have given a damn how imperfect he was, his pride was at stake here. When he went to her he wanted everything to be perfect. Margo was special and deserved only the best. Besides, her husband wanted it so.

This led to another more pressing, disturbing question. If her husband demanded such perfection, why didn't *he* come here? Why send Jared and let him torture himself trying to look as normal as possible, when a perfect transition was impossible?

Hell, the last time he made love to Margo, one leg was shorter than the other. He had to tell her to lie in bed and turn off the lights, pretending it was more romantic that way, while he waited by the door. Otherwise she would have seen him limping badly.

The time before that he wound up with three testicles instead of the usual two. He had quite a time trying to convince her not to run her hands over his body. Telling Margo he'd banged into the corner of a table and hurt himself, because his thoughts were on her, was a stroke of genius. At least she didn't fondle him and discover his abnormality.

Reaching for his clothing, Jared remembered what a cold night it was and how the wind was howling. Going out was the last thing he cared to do at the moment, but there was the problem of disposing of those two bodies. He couldn't leave them lying around for long, especially not with those damned relatives of Margo's heading here for a visit.

The less they knew of his business the healthier it was for them.

Chapter Two

MONKSHOOD, NEW YORK, so named for the scores of acres where the tiny, cowl-shaped, blue plants grew wild, was like something out of the past. Quiet, quaint and very unassuming, the town—though now in the late 20th century —was barely past the horse and buggy stage, and most of the townspeople preferred it that way. They liked the solitude, the feeling that somehow progress, along with its attendant vileness, had skipped right on by.

There were no drug problems here, no seamy deals consummated in back alleys, no high crime rate, no muggings, no rapes—just nothing—that is if one didn't count Margo Windsor and the countless strange events connected with her.

Dennis Windsapple had left the bank early today. Three of Margo's relatives were coming in on the noon train, and it was up to Dennis to transport them to her home. Margo couldn't drive. Margo was blind and had been since she was five. Since no one else would take them to Margo's, the job was his. Besides, he would do anything for Margo. He would go to any lengths just to be of service, to please her, to earn her gratitude.

Sitting on the platform waiting for the train, he stared at the fields turned blue with an overgrowth of what many would consider a devil's plant. He tried not to dwell on the legacy of Monkshood which had been handed down by an ancestor. Those tiny, hooded plants were their legacy—or punishment. He could never quite get that part of it straight in his mind.

Was it a punishment that those plants should grow in the wilds and thrive and multiply until they choked out everything else? You could cut them, burn them, pull them out by their roots, and still they came back. So was this a punishment, or was it merely their legacy, a reminder of the evil that men do in the name of God?

Dennis mulled it over and still came up dry. There was no answer. The plants were here, and the plants would always be here, having far outlived most of his ancestors and his ancestors' ancestors. Monkshood was a plant associated with witches and evil potions, a plant that could be ground into dust and then used for everything from flight to death. The witches would mix the powder with oils and then rub it on their bodies so they could then ride through the night air like birds.

They would ride through the air on their way to a Black Sabbath Mass where they would consort with devils, and where, it was rumored, they would even unite with devils in intercourse and other foul acts of degradation.

When a witch united with a devil and a child was conceived, the two would then wait until the child was born, at which time they would sacrifice the fruit of their labors, the child, to the master beast—old Satan. Any child born of so unholy a union could not be allowed to survive, especially if old Satan hadn't sanctioned the birth to begin with.

As well as being used for flight, Monkshood was used to kill. A witch could mix powder from the deadly blue plants in her cauldron with other ingredients and wish away a life, wish an offender dead. And because of those foolish rumors about the plant, those foolish old wives' tales, 13 so-called witches were burned at the stake in Monkshood, simultaneously with the Salem witch burnings.

While Dennis had always wondered if there was a connection between what happened here and what happened in Salem, he long ago decided it was a preposterous assumption. There was no way of communicating with Salem in the 17th century that would have taken less than a few months, and therefore no way of spreading the hysteria to Monkshood.

So the good people of the town in days past had simply taken it upon themselves to burn 13 possibly innocent victims to stop the evil from spreading and discourage any future disciples of the devil as well.

Dennis had once gotten hold of a legal volume listing the names of the victims and their crimes. Carl Ruttenberg, the fat and rotund town tailor, had been accused of consorting with devils and dancing in the nude, along with others, to the tune of a demon's flute. Carl was accused of casting spells via his tailoring, of using tainted demon thread to sew his seams thereby causing the death of several of his clients. Carl was also accused of aiding in the human sacrifice of a witch's child.

The town elders sentenced Carl to death, along with his newborn infant daughter, a product of his seed and therefore carrying the same evil in her soul as did her father. Carl took several days to properly burn down because of his weight, but his daughter burned fast, a tiny hood tied down over her head to spare her from the horrors of the fires of damnation!

Oh yes, it made perfectly good sense to burn Carl's child in the name of goodness since Carl had been accused of burning a child in the name of evil. "An eye for an eye," the Bible said, and the town elders took many eyes before their maniacal hunger was satiated.

Witch burnings became a regular Sunday event, something perhaps to break the spell of a long, dull, hot summer. Every Sunday, like clockwork, a witch was damned to hell in the fires in front of town hall.

Stands were even erected by workmen so the

good folks of Monkshood could sit and enjoy the spectacle and picnic while bodies burned and victims prayed for death.

Dennis Windsapple was brought out of his reverie by the approaching sound of a train whistle. The noon train was right on time.

"Still fascinated by 'em I see. Can't keep yer eyes off them plants."

Dennis heard Hank Wallace's voice coming from behind him and, turning, saw the crusty, old station master wiping his hands on a cloth.

"What brings ya here so early in the mornin', Dennis? Got a train to catch?"

"No. One to meet. Some relatives of a friend . . ."

"Well, seein' as how that train ain't comin' into the station for at least ten more minutes, how about joinin' me for a quick belt?"

Hank Wallace had a drinking problem. In fact, Hank Wallace was about as close to being the town drunk as they came. Normally Dennis would've declined, but not today, not after stirring up memories behind those plants. "Sure, but just a quick one. I don't want to keep Margo's people waiting."

"Margo's people! Margo Windsor has visitors comin' in on that train?"

"Yes," Dennis said, wondering if the offer of a drink would now be withdrawn. He looked at Hank, saw the sudden pallor of his skin, the widened, bloodshot eyes and wished he'd mentioned no names, especially not Margo Windsor's.

"Well, that puts things in an entirely different light," Hank said. "Now I'll need a *few* quick belts. Margo Windsor havin' company—Jesus! Come on, Dennis. Let's get it done before that train pulls in."

Jonathan and Joelle Blake, products of a fertilized egg that had split 18 years before, sat side by side and gazed at the fields of blue plants but didn't really see them. Instead, their minds were absorbed by this visit to their mother Valerie's sister, Aunt Margo, the one they hadn't seen in at least ten years.

Aunt Margo had been 50 something then and was older and probably more crochety by now, although the years had been good to her then. She had looked no older than her mid-twenties. Still, since Aunt Margo had never had children of her own, they both wondered how she'd expect them to behave. Would she accept them as young adults, or would she expect them to act her age?

"What pretty flowers," Eve Blake, their younger sister, said, her mind locked in the same dream world she'd been in since birth. It was only because of the damned oxygen, or lack of it, that Eve was an eternal dreamer.

Eve had been brought into the world stillborn and was forced from the jaws of death after three minutes by a dedicated doctor, but too late it seemed for her brain to develop normally. "They are so pretty," she said again.

Jonathan and Joelle glanced briefly at each

other but made no comment to Eve's remark.
The plants were pretty, as Eve had said, but in a
queer sort of way. Pretty overwhelming was
more what Joelle had in mind.

They'd seen these same plants for the past ten
miles or so, and now Joelle found herself
wondering about them. "Where do they end?"
she asked, speaking out loud for the first time
since getting on the train in Philadelphia.

"They must be the state flower," Jonathan
remarked. "Otherwise, why would they plant so
many of them?"

"I wish Daddy was here to take pictures of the
pretty flowers," Eve said, "and not in Europe
taking pictures of some old, rundown
buildings."

"Ruins," Jonathan said, correcting her. "He's
photographing ancient ruins in Greece and
Rome." Jonathan wished he was in Rome,
photographing those same ruins with his father.
Someday, he thought wistfully, it will be me.

"What's the difference? Old buildings are old
buildings."

"Eve," Joelle said, using the same impatient
tone of voice she always did when speaking to
her sister, "this is a big chance for Daddy—a
wonderful opportunity. He's waited years for
this."

"I don't care!" Eve was pouting now, her
lower lip stuck out in such a childish way that it
was hard to believe she was 16. "I don't wanna
go to Aunt Margo's. I wanna go home."

"Well, we can't," Jonathan said. "If

Mommy were alive it would be different. Then we could have stayed home . . .'' His voice faded out as he remembered the endless quarrels between himself and his father, the elder Jonathan Blake. Jonathan had wanted to stay home, too, as did Joelle. They could watch over Eve.

But Jonathan and Joelle had lost and were forced to give in to their father's wishes. Now they were on their way to see Aunt Margo, scary Aunt Margo with the dark glasses hiding the even darker eyes that saw nothing.

"Does she have pretty flowers around her house?" Eve wanted to know with a sigh of resignation.

"I guess so," Jonathan said, quickly adding, "If she doesn't, we'll plant some. That will be your project, Eve—to plant pretty, blue flowers." Eve smiled then as if she'd willingly accepted her fate, just as Jonathan knew she would. Giving her responsibility, no matter how small, usually made Eve more cooperative, and right now she had to be cooperative. It didn't pay to make waves around someone like Aunt Margo.

"How come we haven't seen her in a long time? How come Daddy and Mommy never brought us here to visit?"

Joelle heard the question, and while Joelle didn't know the answer, she really didn't want to. The family had split up years before, around the time the coven had celebrated it's last Black Sabbath. Her parents had fled to Philadelphia, while Aunt Margo came here to New York.

Somehow, keeping the family separated had been part of a master plan involving a secret pact, one that neither Jonathan or Joelle knew anything about. For years there were no letters or phone calls, no contact of any kind between the family members as if their lives depended on this secrecy. Joelle wondered why the code of secrecy was now being violated with this visit to Aunt Margo. Why was it all right for them to meet now, when for the past ten years they'd lived as strangers to each other?

"Are you thinking the same thing I am?" Jonathan asked, knowing full well that she was. As twins, there had always been this certain closeness between them, as if their minds had once been fused only to split like atoms when they were born.

Joelle's eyes were focused on Jonathan's, and it seemed they were talking without words again, talking through their minds. This didn't set well with Eve. She generally became the outsider when the twins locked thoughts as they were doing now. Well, the hell with them, she thought to herself, let them talk their silly mind talk. She preferred concentrating her energies on the pretty blue flowers outside, the same ones she'd plant around Aunt Margo's house when and if they ever got there!

When the train stopped at Monkshood some ten minutes later, Eve was the first to get off, her senses suddenly overwhelmed by the sweet,

sickening smell of thousands of plants. Oh, it
was beautiful, she thought, ignoring Jonathan
and Joelle when they held their noses and
frowned.

"Do you remember her address?" Joelle
asked.

"I have it right here," Jonathan said, pulling
a slip of paper from his jacket pocket.

"Good. Let's hope we don't have to wait long
for a cab," Joelle said, turning up the collar of
her jacket, her long, black hair tucked inside,
warm against her neck. "It's chilly as
anything."

"Yeah, it sure is," Jonathan agreed. "But
wasn't Aunt Margo supposed to send someone
to pick us up?"

"As far as I know she was, but there's nobody
here." Nobody—that was if you didn't count
the row of men seated on a bench in front of the
station.

There were five men, all wearing flannel
jackets and cloth caps, on that bench. Five faces
were pulled tight with anger; five pairs of eyes
narrowed down into threatening slits; five
mouths resembled angry gashes. A strange
bunch, Joelle thought, careful not to stare at
them too closely and thereby risk drawing their
attention. Yet their attention was focused on the
three strangers who'd just emerged from the
train anyway, or so it seemed.

"What the hell are they staring at?" Jonathan
asked, his tone full of a newfound anger to
match the anger directed at them.

"Not at us," Joelle said quickly, fearing any kind of confrontation. "They just happen to be looking in our direction, that's all."

"Well, they'd better stop," he said, staring back to show he wasn't afraid. Joelle walked off the platform and approached a beat up old Chevy that had just pulled into the side of the station.

Jonathan saw a sign taped near the bottom of the driver's door that read, 'Taxi Service,' in huge, scribbled letters and knew that Joelle figured it was better to take a cab to Aunt Margo's than to wait for their ride, especially since those men were watching them in a way that would indicate they weren't members of the local welcoming committee.

Dennis Windsapple was on his third quick belt when he heard a commotion outside, and from the sound of it, it was an ugly exchange. He heard something about not going near "that bitch's house, 'cause things happen to people who get too close to her."

Then he suddenly remembered the reason he'd come to the train station. Quickly downing his drink, he thanked Hank Wallace and ran outside in time to see two young people arguing with several of the locals, while a third one stood with her back turned to the commotion and mutely stared at the fields of flowers running the length of the tracks beside the station.

"She isn't a bitch!" a young man was shouting, while his sister shouted over him,

"Don't talk about our Aunt Margo like that, you bastards!"

Dennis sucked in his breath and approached the crowd. There were five or six men surrounding Margo's relatives, some with their fists clenched. Dennis cleared his throat and started to say something when one of the men spotted him and whispered to the man next to him, who in turn whispered to the next in line. One by one the men quieted down, clearing a path as they did.

Without a word, Dennis walked through the line of angry locals, wincing at the thick air of hatred around him, and stood in front of the young people. "I'm Dennis Windsapple," he said, his voice slightly slurred from drink. "Your Aunt Margo sent me." The young man he was addressing glared at him and started to open his mouth, but Dennis silenced him with an abrupt, "Enough's been said. Let's go!"

Jonathan Blake wanted to drop the whole thing, and yet it gnawed at his insides like vultures picking at a carcass. Why had those men at the train station gotten so violent over the mere mention of Margo Windsor's name? What the hell did Aunt Margo ever do to them to cause such a severe reaction?

He was riding in front with Dennis Windsapple—the two girls were seated in back—and he tried to concentrate on the road they were traveling, but it was impossible. He'd never come across people like this before.

Not true, he thought, suddenly correcting himself. There had been another incident like this—well, almost like this—ten years before. The setting was different, and the men were different, but their intentions were the same. Those axe-wielding sons-of-bitches had wanted to kill him. In fact, they wanted to kill everyone within their reach.

Shoving the axe incident to the far reaches of his mind, Jonathan turned to Dennis and started to ask for an explanation. He wanted an answer, and he deserved one, too. Yet Dennis, who had been half-watching the road and half-watching Jonathan, sensed Jonathan's inner turmoil and cut him off with an abrupt, "Let's talk about it some other time. I can't just now."

Jonathan was offended at first, but then stopped to analyze Dennis' words and the way they'd been spoken. Dennis wasn't dismissing his question; for whatever reason, he just couldn't talk about it at the moment. Jonathan realized his voice had been filled with a pleading quality that was close to desperation. He was asking Jonathan to drop it for now, that's all.

Somehow, Jonathan knew Dennis would bring it up some other time and supply the answers. For now, he'd been drinking and maybe wasn't able to sort it out in his mind. Maybe it was a long story, or maybe he wanted to spare the girls. Whatever his reasoning, Jonathan respected Dennis enough to let it rest.

"So many pretty, blue flowers," Eve said. "I love it here."

"You love it here?" Joelle asked, a tinge of disbelief in her voice.

"Yes, I do," Eve answered defensively. "It's beautiful here."

When Joelle said nothing more, Jonathan knew she'd decided to let it go, the same as he'd dropped his matter with Dennis. But hell, just what did Eve see when she looked at the town of Monkshood that he and Joelle didn't see? The place was downright depressing.

Actually, bleak was a better adjective. Monkshood was bleak and dreary, like the road they were on, for instance. It was bordered on both sides by high trees skirted by those terrible, blue flowers, and the trees weren't like anything he'd seen before. There was no colorful, fall foliage, no leaves done up in various shades of orange and yellow and brown. In fact, there were no leaves at all.

The branches of the trees were barren, as though something had suddenly come up and taken the leaves, as though the wind had blown them off their branches and swept them away with the same vengeful, violent motions those men in town had used towards the three of them.

Yes, it was bleak, he thought, and he looked up at a gray, flat sky with a pathetically pale sun centered in the middle of it and wondered what was wrong with this town.

He shuddered when Dennis pointed to a grim mansion, bordered by high, wrought iron prison gates, and said, "We're here. This is where your Aunt Margo lives."

Of course, Jonathan thought to himself, where else would spooky old Aunt Margo with the dead eyes and aloof mannerisms live? Where else but in a spooky old mansion with windows that resembled dead eyes, and medieval, hand-chiseled eaves that made the whole place look aloof and impersonal? Yes, this is were she'd live all right, and he suddenly wanted to take the girls and run back to Philadelphia.

But it was too late to run, too late to change his mind. Dennis was already turning into the main gate and driving down a road with dead bushes and trees on both sides, as well as those terrible blue flowers.

Jonathan cursed his father for sending them here, and then he cursed his mother, although she was innocent, for dying and not being home. Then he cursed the creature standing by the front window, the one with the short fingers holding back the drapes and watching them in such a way they were unable to watch back. Jonathan couldn't see who it was because it was too dark beyond the drapes.

But it didn't matter. Jonathan had a feeling they'd meet. All he had to do was keep his eyes open and see which one of Aunt Margo's servants had the short fingers. Then he'd know who had been watching.

Chapter Three

MARGO ANSWERED THE door on the second ring. She was nervous about the conversation about the prophecy she had had with Jared the night before. She tried to forget the whole subject this morning when she first got up and Jared came with her coffee.

Jared never said a word, but then he didn't have to. The expression on his face said it all. He was worried about the arrival of her sister's children. Valerie had been her half-sister, not of her father's seed, but they had been so close that at times Margo tended to forget that only her mother's womb tied them together.

One of the three children—or maybe only of the twins since Eve was no contender—was involved in the fulfillment of the prophecy, and Margo really didn't care to know which one it was. After Jared reminded her of those fateful

predictions the night before, she also wanted
them gone as soon as possible. She wanted them
out of her life before the next holy Black
Sabbath, Dagu's Nacht, barely two weeks away.

When the bell rang the first time, she leaned
against the frame of the door and tried to clear
her head, to think of nothing but the children
waiting outside and how they were blood
relatives. She was their Aunt Margo and,
prophecy or no prophecy, she wouldn't let her
annoyance show.

When it rang a second time, Margo opened
the door and pretended to be completely blind
even though she could 'see' Dennis Windsapple
and Jonathan and Joelle and poor, whimsical
Eve. So far Jared was the only person who knew
about her sight, or insight, and it was safer to
keep her secret as it was. Besides, Margo had
sworn an oath on the head of the mighty
Behemoth to reveal her gift to no one.

"Can I help you?" she asked and waited for
Dennis to speak.

"Margo, it's me," he said with a slightly
drunken slur in his voice. "I picked them up."

Margo gazed at the three faces and saw uncertainty written on two of them. Only Eve was
expressionless as usual, but not Jonathan or
Joelle. They looked frightened. They weren't
sure they wanted to visit spooky old Aunt
Margo, as they had referred to her in their minds
moments ago. And Margo heard those words
and wondered how to deal with them. But then
Margo stepped aside, and the three of them
followed Dennis Windsapple in.

Margo didn't move to follow. Instead she stayed behind and studied Jonathan and the way he scanned the interior as though he was searching for someone who had him scared half to death. Joelle, on the other hand, had a completely different reaction. Her attention was glued to the tapestries on the walls, the antique furniture, and the staircase leading to the second floor.

Once in the den, Margo settled into an easy chair near the fireplace and waited for someone to speak. The ice had to be broken. After all, they were spending at least ten days that she knew of—not the original two weeks because of the prophecy. Margo wouldn't have them here on the Sabbath, and at the moment she had no idea where she would send them, or what reason she would give for sending them away.

In the meanwhile, they had to talk, had to communicate.

"I love your dress, Aunt Margo," Eve said in that dreamy way she had about her. "And I love your hair."

As Eve uttered those words, Margo caught the look of surprise and shock registered by Joelle, but said nothing. Obviously Joelle didn't agree, and to be fair, not many would agree with Eve's opinion. Margo was wearing the usual ankle-length, plain black dress, the same type she'd worn for years, and her hair was pulled into a severe bun at the back of her head. Margo never did believe in calling attention to herself, and so she'd chosen the most unglamorous form of dress possible.

"You look really pretty," Eve babbled.

"Thank you," Margo said, not looking at Joelle this time, knowing the shock was still there.

"I can't believe it's been ten years," Jonathan said. "You haven't changed." He was studying her now, disbelief written on his face instead of the fear he'd shown earlier. "Mom always said you were ageless."

Margo adjusted her glasses and remained silent at first. Jonathan had mentioned Valerie, opening a raw wound, but it really wasn't the fact of her death that was so disturbing. It was the way she had died.

"How was your trip up?" Margo asked, changing the subject. "I hope the ride on the train wasn't too uncomfortable."

"It was okay," Joelle said. Joelle sounded like Valerie, while Eve's thin, frail frame reminded Margo of Valerie. Margo wondered how long she could hold it in. Seeing the three of them made her want to cry, to mourn Valerie all over again.

"Would you like something hot to drink? Are you hungry?" Margo asked, sucking in her breath for restraint.

"I am," Eve answered. "I'm awfully hungry."

"We should unpack first," Joelle said, shooting a look at Eve. "You're acting rude."

"Oh, really now," Margo said, dropping her guard. "Eve can be awfully hungry if she wants to. This is me, Aunt Margo, remember? It's not as if we're strangers. Come on," she said, rising to her feet in a graceful motion that made the too-quiet Dennis Windsapple sigh with admiration. "I'll show you to your rooms. You can leave your suitcases there until after lunch. The damned unpacking can wait!"

She was halfway out of the room when something made her stop and turn, something she'd forgotten till now. "Thank you for picking them up, Dennis. Will you stay for lunch?"

"No," he said. "I have to get back to the bank. There's a ton of paperwork on my desk. Perhaps some other time."

Margo noted the reluctance in his voice; he really didn't want to leave, but he was a busy man. "Will you show yourself out?" she asked and left the room, her long, black dress whispering against her body, leaving behind a scent of Monkshood and Nightshade.

Jonathan was the first to follow Margo upstairs. Then came Eve, then Joelle, who was lagging behind because her mind was on all of the mysteries connected with Aunt Margo.

First of all, there was the question of her youth and beauty. Although she tried hiding her beauty behind an old maid's disguise, it didn't work. Margo was breathtaking. She was beautiful, and Dennis Windsapple was obviously in love with her. So why try to hide her looks when it was close to impossible? She had an indescribable something about her. Margo was still an alluring woman.

And why did she look so young, barely 30, when she was in her late sixties? What was her secret? Strong doses of vitamins, perhaps? Hell, Margo had been older than her mother, and Valerie had looked her age. In fact, Valerie had looked older than Margo when she died.

Although Margo was young and beautiful, there was an evil ugliness deep inside of her that marred her beauty, and, at the moment, Joelle felt she was the only one capable of sensing the evil.

Joelle walked quietly up the wide staircase, her hand gliding along a smooth, oak railing, and marveled at the evidences of Margo's great wealth. It was not inherited because Margo's parents had been average, middle-class people. The money didn't come from Joelle's grandparents; if it had, Valerie would have shared in the inheritance and would have been wealthy, too. But that was not the case, so Margo's wealth remained a mystery.

Perhaps the money came from her husband, the man who married Aunt Margo and then deserted her. Valerie had once told Joelle about the wedding, but when Joelle tried to ask about the groom, Valerie became extremely nervous and dropped the whole thing. Now Aunt Margo still carried the name Windsor, her maiden name, and she wore no wedding ring.

Joelle was ankle deep in carpeting before she realized that she had been ushered into her bedroom. Aunt Margo was now awaiting her approval. Joelle scanned the room with its dark paneling and dark, wooden furniture and tried to act impressed. It was beautiful if you were into admiring the sophisticated drabness of a bygone era.

The bed, she noticed, was large enough to accommodate two. Perfect, she thought. Eve would stay with her because Eve had to be watched and taken care of. "It's very nice," she said to Margo, which wasn't a complete lie. Everything about the room was nice and expensive, even if it wasn't to her taste.

Margo smiled at the remark, her mouth pulled into a thin, cold line. Joelle wondered what she was really thinking, but it was so hard to tell with those dark glasses hiding her eyes, hiding her feelings. "I'm glad you like it, Joelle. Now, Eve, I'll show you to your room."

"Uh . . . Eve can stay with me," Joelle blurted out, but Eve stopped her.

"I want my own room. I'm old enough."

"You have to stay in here with me!" Joelle insisted.

But Margo was having none of this. "Her room adjoins yours. All of these rooms are adjoining. So Eve will be right next door." Without waiting for an answer, Margo took Eve's hand and led her out.

Joelle was annoyed because Margo was spoiling Eve, but then everyone spoiled Eve. Everyone felt sorry for the poor child who'd lost three minutes of precious air when she first entered this world. Joelle imagined that they thought spoiling her would erase the pain of

being dumb, but, as Joelle knew, it wouldn't.
Eve felt no pain. Eve dwelled in a land of milk
and honey, her mind locked in eternal happiness, unaware of the struggles of life. Eve
needed no spoiling to exist.

Once Joelle was alone with Jonathan, they
both stared at each other. "How does she find
her way around?" Joelle asked.

"You know what they say about blind people.
They have strong instincts. Their other senses
take over. Besides, she's been living here for a
long time. She just knows her way around,
that's all."

Jonathan's explanation sounded good, and
yet, it still didn't explain why Aunt Margo stared
at them and seemed to be studying them. Of
course she hadn't been around them in ten years,
and they had changed, but Aunt Margo
presumably was blind and supposedly had never
seen them to begin with. So why would any
change in their appearance cause her to stare?

"I don't know," Joelle said uneasily. "There
are a lot of mysteries about her. I hope this visit
goes fast. I don't like it here."

Jonathan was alone in his room—depressingly
antique, like Joelle's—before he allowed her
thoughts to dominate his. She didn't like it here.
Well, he didn't either, but not for the same
reasons. He wasn't concerned with mysteries.
He wasn't as impressed with Aunt Margo's
youth and beauty as Joelle was, something he
sensed when he concentrated his energies on

Joelle's mind. In fact, he wasn't even curious about her alleged husband.

His mind was on the past, and memories that came back to him as a result of seeing Aunt Margo for the first time in ten years. Aunt Margo was connected with these memories —some good, some bad—and while he tried to recall only the good, the bad ones also seeped in.

He recalled going to church every week, a family tradition. There were Grandma, Grandpa, Aunt Margo, his parents, Joelle, Eve and himself, all decked out in their best, going to church together, hand in hand, like your average, ordinary family.

Though Grandma never seemed anxious to go to church, she went. Otherwise, as Grandpa often insisted, the high priest would have been offended by the absence of an important family member. So Grandma went to church and said nothing.

And oh, what a strange church it was!

Jonathan had never been to any church but his own, so he had nothing to use in comparison. Still, he wondered if animal sacrifices were the norm. He wondered if cutting a beast's throat and drinking its blood, or slicing it open and devouring its vital organs, was something done in other churches.

He could remember that the altar was made of black onyx. He could still picture the white bowl on the altar, representing purity, or rather the defilement of it.

Jonathan's suitcases had been miraculously transported up to his room. He placed the bag containing his precious camera equipment on top of his bed and tried not to wonder who'd brought his things here. Was it the creature with the short fingers? Was he the one who carried their bags inside and up the stairs to their rooms?

He shuddered and was lost once again in the memories jostled by the sight of Margo Windsor. In his mind he was looking at the black whip encircling the base of the white porcelain bowl and the black candles on either side of it, candles rumored to be composed of baby's fat from dead, miscarried or stillborn babies. Eve was almost burned and the fat from her body taken for candles—but Eve survived!

Behind and to the side of the altar, there had been a white table that was used for sacrifices. Animals were tied to the table and then carved and sliced by the high priest while he cried for the spirit of their lord, Satan, to bless the gathering and all who were there. Jonathan had never wanted to drink the blood or taste the animals' organs. . . .

Liar!

No, I never did, he told himself again. The truth was, although hard to admit, Jonathan loved the taste of blood and the taste of raw, bloody flesh. He could have lied to himself at any other time and said that this part of it disgusted him, but being here, in Aunt Margo's house, after all of those years, brought the truth to light. He loved the animal sacrifices!

In fact, this was the part he looked forward to each week—his church's version of Holy Communion. Unlike those Christians he'd heard a few things about, his church drank animal blood instead of wine, and his church ate animal flesh instead of bread or host. Otherwise, it was the same; it was Holy Communion.

His church should have stuck to animals, but on the Black Sabbaths things changed. They went to humans instead.

"I remember it, too," Joelle said, her mind locked in on his though he tried to keep his thoughts private.

"Do you remember the young girl and her baby?" Joelle wanted to know.

"Oh, yes. How could I forget?" he answered, but desperately wanted to forget. There was a young girl, the mistress of a priest from one of the lower orders, who had become pregnant, but the pregnancy wasn't sanctioned. So she had to die—and the baby as well.

The priests slaughtered them both on that damned table, while the miracle of birth was taking place. The baby was gutted and its organs consumed while it screamed and flailed its body and shivered with pain. And everyone, Jonathan included, drank the blood and ate the flesh.

Tears formed in Jonathan's eyes then as the memories became too painful to bear, and he became angry because Joelle was there in his mind and knew he was crying and not acting like a man. Out of his anger came the strength to force Joelle back, to keep his thoughts hidden, and it wasn't until his mind was closed to outside forces that he allowed himself to dwell on his own mysteries and not those connected with Margo Windsor.

He found himself wondering if his soul was tainted and hardened by the sights he'd seen as a child. He wondered if Eve had been touched by the same atrocities, or had her wonderful inability to think safeguarded her mind? Or was she as jaded in her thinking as both he and Joelle?

If that were true, then the prophecy could include her as well. For one of them, one of the three Blake children, was destined for greatness, except that none of them knew which was the chosen one, which of them would wield the powers of the coven.

Nonsense, he thought, suddenly dismissing the predictions of the high priest as one of his usual drug-ridden trips. Sure, Nathan took drugs, and his mind went to the Land of Oz. He was nuts when he was on that shit.

Jonathan became aware of someone knocking on the door that separated him from Joelle. It had to be Joelle. She was probably angry with him for shutting her out as he had.

"What do you want?" he asked once the door was open and the barrier between them removed.

"I just thought of something, when you were thinking back to those sacrifices."

"And?" He tried to keep his annoyance from showing in his voice, but it was no use. Joelle sensed it.

"It's important!"

"Yeah! Sure! To you, maybe!"

"No, Jonathan, to all of us at the moment."

"Go on." He really didn't want to hear this, but since Joelle would tell him anyway, he listened.

"Aunt Margo was the only one who stood up and complained when the poor girl was being slaughtered. Do you remember? She said that it was wrong to sacrifice humans when we too were humans and were actually stepping beyond the bounds of our race by practicing cannibalism."

Jonathan concentrated and saw the event in his mind's eye as shown to him by Joelle. He saw the enraged and much respected Margo Windsor challenging the high priest with everything that was in her. He heard the other church members grumbling in anger, only their anger wasn't directed at Margo; it was directed at their holy leader because they felt Margo was right.

Then something terrible happened. The high priest grabbed his staff, directed it at Margo and cursed her with a barren womb. He told her she'd never bear children because she had openly defied his authority, and the other members, who up until then had been on her side, suddenly sided with Nathan, the high priest.

"That's why she never had children of her own," Joelle reminded him. "Because she stood up and challenged Nathan. Also, she defied the highest force in the universe, the force of our lord, Satan."

"You know something?" Jonathan said. "She isn't so bad after all. She may act mean and she may talk mean, but her intentions are good. She's a strong, humane person who cares about others. Maybe we should relax and try to get along with her. Is that what you're trying to say?"

"Hell, no! What I'm pointing out is this—how did she know who or what was being sacrificed? Nobody said anything to her that I can recall, and she's blind. How did she know about the girl and her baby?"

Jonathan couldn't believe he was hearing this. They both just now had remembered something that would help them better understand Aunt Margo and get along with her. The woman had sacrificed her right to bear children because of an ideal she believed in. Hell, she knew she was going to be punished somehow by questioning the highest figure in the church. And here was Joelle, involved in technicalities. "Someone must have said something to her," he argued. "You know, given her a description."

"The only thing that was said was that there were two sacrificial victims this time instead of the usual one."

"Well, what the hell does it matter," Jonathan argued.

Joelle looked at him, her dark eyes full of disgust, and started to leave the room. At the last moment she turned and hissed, "This answers one of our questions about this woman. She can see when she wants to!"

Then she was gone, leaving Jonathan alone. Maybe his Aunt Margo could see when she wanted to. So what? Shrugging off Joelle's words, Jonathan unzipped the camera case and began to examine his equipment for damages possibly caused while they were traveling.

Actually there was no big deal over Margo's ability to see, but Jonathan wasn't impressed with the importance of Joelle's theory. Instead, he was more impressed because Margo Windsor had risked her life for an ideal.

Risked her life, indeed! Margo knew she was safe when she challenged the priest. She was too respected to be attacked. Keeping this in mind, Margo Windsor had stood up and had her way, and from what Joelle knew, this wasn't the first time this boisterous, strong-willed woman opposed the church.

And it didn't even have to involve murder and cannibalism. Hell, Margo fought with anyone who didn't bow to her wishes or jump when she gave a command. Too bad Jonathan was so overcome with her beauty he couldn't see her for what she was—a tyrant who made unreasonable demands on the church.

Joelle recalled an incident that had taken place when she was about six or seven. It seemed Margo was in the conference room arguing with Nathan, the high priest.

When Joelle had been sent to fetch Aunt Margo because the family was ready to leave, she got as far as the conference room and stood outside, not really sure if she should knock and disturb her aunt.

She remembered standing outside that large, oak door and thinking how unfair it was that the knob was so high up. The door was so thick that she'd have to pound on it with everything in her to make herself heard. At first she wasn't really sure Aunt Margo was inside; she couldn't hear a thing, neither Aunt Margo's voice nor Nathan's.

Then one of them, Aunt Margo, began to shout, and her words threw Joelle into temporary shock. Aunt Margo wanted to enter the priesthood! She demanded equal rights as a long-standing member of the coven. Joelle couldn't believe she was hearing this—her aunt a priest! The whole idea was absurd, as Nathan pointed out in a voice laced with impatience.

Joelle turned and went to find her mother. She was not about to interfere when two adults were arguing over something so important as females and the priesthood. She didn't want to knock on the door and catch the brunt of their anger.

Aunt Margo was turned down; her demands had been denied. Aunt Margo would never be allowed to conduct a service, never be allowed to deliver a sermon, never be allowed to lead the members in prayer. And because of this, Aunt Margo bitterly vowed to torment any high priest who crossed her path.

And Jonathan, my dear, if you're listening, this is why Margo Windsor made a scene when that young girl and her newborn baby were being slaughtered. Not because she was being righteously indignant and appalled by an act of cannibalism. No, dear boy, it was because she was a woman scorned, one who could never forget that the priesthood had been placed out of her reach when she so rightly deserved a chance to be a church leader. And if you don't believe me, Joelle thought, too bad!

Joelle went into the bathroom to wash up for lunch while her own private memories of the coven came back to haunt her. In two weeks the Black Sabbath of Dagu's Nacht would become a reality after 13 years of waiting, and one of them would become . . . certainly not the new Messiah or the new anti-Christ.

Certainly nothing as simple as that.

No! She refused to dwell on the rest of it because it was far too awful to think of when she was alone in the bathroom in Aunt Margo's house.

Eve was alone with her memories as well, but, unlike the twins, she could only think back so far and certainly never as clearly as they did. Events would come to her, but those events were usually muddled. Instead of trying to relive the past in detail, she tried to dwell on things that happened only hours or minutes before, instead of years ago.

Standing at the window and glancing down at the pretty, blue flowers below, she thought back to the time she first laid eyes on Aunt Margo after ten years.

Aunt Margo had come to the door to let them in, and when she opened it and stood before them and allowed them to feast their eyes on her, Eve wanted to run. Aunt Margo was older now, even older than she was the last time they saw her, when those men with the axes came.

Aunt Margo had scared her then, as now, with her black dresses and her black glasses and her snow white hair. Bags of wrinkles hung on her face and made it droop, and her chin was almost down to the top of her dress. Yet everyone said Aunt Margo looked young, and while Eve tried to fathom it out, she couldn't.

She looked at Aunt Margo in the same light they did, so why did Eve see her differently? But then Eve's mind was weak. Maybe Aunt Margo was young and beautiful, and Eve was seeing a distorted image of her. At least this is what Eve came up with while sitting in the den with Aunt Margo.

Not wanting to appear rude, or stupid even, Eve had told Aunt Margo how much she loved her dress and how much she loved her hair, but it was a lie. The truth was Aunt Margo was hideous!

But then old people, the real old ones, always struck Eve as being hideous, mainly because they seemed to be walking in the shadow of death. Death was around them and in them, taken into their bodies when they sucked in air and exhaled when they let it out. Death lived in their eyes and in the expressions on their faces. And oh, lord Satan, Eve was afraid of death.

Eve shuddered then and tried to gather enough strength to go down and face Aunt

Margo over lunch and not throw up from the sight of her, but it wouldn't be easy.

Eve's attention was suddenly drawn away from the flowers below and from thinking about Aunt Margo when she spotted the man from the train, the one who'd followed them from Philadelphia. It was the same man she tried telling Jonathan and Joelle about, but they wouldn't listen to her.

Anyway, he was standing near some trees in the front driveway. Eve knew she'd seen him before, only she couldn't remember where. It had been ten years ago, and now she was frustrated as she tried to recall if he'd been one of the men with the axes, or one of the men who tried to *stop* the men with the axes. The incident had taken place so long ago that it was hard for her to remember which side he was on.

In spite of her inner turmoil, she did manage a slight smile and a wave when he raised his hand in greeting. He wasn't really a bad man, Eve imagined. At least he didn't look evil. He was tall and thin with broad shoulders and a heavy chest. If the man wasn't following them, what was he doing here now? Why had he come to Aunt Margo's?

And who was the man with his back to Eve who was walking up to her friend? Whoever he was, he'd just come from inside of Aunt Margo's house, and it seemed as though he was threatening the other man.

As Eve watched, the two men spoke for several minutes, the one who'd come from Aunt

Margo's house waving a hand that had a few
very short fingers. Eve felt sorry for him because
he was deformed, but then her friend, the one
who'd followed her from the train, had one arm
that was shorter than the other. They were both
handicapped, poor things!

Eve knew what it was like to be different, to
be mocked and scorned because you weren't the
same as everyone else. She waved to get their
attention, hoping to invite at least one of them
to lunch with Aunt Margo. Aunt Margo
certainly wouldn't mind. She was hideous
looking, so she was handicapped in a way.

But the two men ignored her. Then the one
from the train turned and left, but not before
waving good-bye. The one with the short fingers
glanced up at Eve and scowled before entering
the house. Eve turned and went downstairs for
lunch.

Jared was livid. He knew that bastard and
knew him well. A so-called member of their
coven from the past, he'd followed Margo's
relatives there to keep them safe. But who would
keep *him* safe? Jared asked himself and laughed.

The men said he had been sent there by
Nathan, to make sure nothing went wrong and
that the three young adults would be protected.

Sent there by Nathan indeed, the lying
bastard! Jared was tempted to ask him how old
Nathan was, but he didn't because the bastard
would have lied again and said that Nathan was
doing fine.

Only Nathan wasn't doing fine—far from it—and Jared knew this better than anyone else because old Nathan lived upstairs, in a room down the hall from Margo's. Old Nathan had very little to say at the moment, mainly because old Nathan was in no condition to talk.

Chapter Four

MARGO'S THOUGHTS WERE filled with the past. Seeing Johathan and Joelle and Eve after all of these years had brought it all back, and try as she would to keep her mind occupied solely on the present, she was waging a losing battle.

The one thing preying on her the most, the one thing coming back to torment her, was the memory of dear, sweet Valerie, with the innocent eyes and the eternal enthusiasm for life and the family scene that Margo could never quite fit into. But then, to be absolutely fair, Valerie's husband didn't disappear after they were married.

No, the senior Jonathan Blake stuck it out and stood by her, even joining the coven when he didn't believe in such nonsense. But then Jonathan was an agnostic and didn't believe in much of anything, not their lord, Satan, and certainly not his antithesis known as God.

Despite his beliefs—or lack of them—Valerie married him and defended his right to believe in nothing other than what he could see and hear.

Margo had returned to the den to wait while Jared made lunch. She was sitting quite still, listening to the crackling of the logs in the fireplace, when the door opened and Jared stood before her in all of his magnificent glory; his tall, slender body was framed by the door in a way she found to be both exhilarating and sexy.

Raising an arm, she motioned for him to come and sit by her. She needed the touch of him for reassurance. She felt overwhelmed by the presence of Valerie's children and wanted the warmth and comfort Jared usually gave her.

Jared came willingly. His hands thrust into his pockets, he sat on a stool near her feet. He was smiling, his eyes hot with love and tenderness, and it made her feel warm inside. Yet there was something about him that said he was disturbed because he knew the three intruders upstairs had caused her mind to wander back over the years. Jared lived in the present and wanted her to do the same.

"If you want to talk about it, I'm listening," he said, although he wasn't really up to playing psychiatrist to Margo at the moment.

Margo said nothing at first. Instead she ran the backs of her fingers through his hair and wished they were alone in the house, but since they weren't, she had to let the memories run their course. Otherwise she'd keep them inside and become totally depressed.

"I remember when the twins were born," Margo began. "Valerie was in her mid-forties, too old to be having children, but the coven ordered it. Nathan told Valerie that she'd been chosen to bear a child of greatness, but Valerie was scared."

"Of what?" Jared asked, but he already knew the answer. Yet Margo had to talk and get this out of herself.

"Valerie knew there were risks involved in bearing children when you were over forty. Anything could go wrong. The child could have been born deformed or retarded, and Valerie could have died giving birth. But the coven promised that everything would be all right, and yet it wasn't. Look what happened when she gave birth to Eve two years later. Eve wasn't breathing—she was born dead—and now her mind is not what it should be. She can't function as well as the twins." Margo stopped talking, but Jared knew she wasn't finished. So he kept quiet and waited.

"And Mother was there as always," Margo said, a catch in her voice, "my wonderful, supportive mother. The night the twins were born, she came to the hospital with my father—or rather, my step-father. My own father died years before."

As Margo continued, Jared wondered why Margo never discussed her father's death, other than to skip lightly over the event as though it were unimportant. Yet Jared knew better.

Killing her father had been one of Margo's goals after she was blinded by Nathan, but then, Margo didn't actually kill him herself. She didn't choke the life from his body and watch him go.

No, it was much worse than that. Margo was directly responsible for his death, but she never touched him. She was only five and a half when it happened.

"There we were," Margo said, "all of us sitting in the hospital lounge drinking gallons of coffee and wringing our hands because we were worried about Valerie. You couldn't come that night, and for the life of me I can't rememeber why." He started to answer her, to tell her why, but she didn't wait. "It doesn't really matter what excuse you gave. I've learned to live with your shyness—"

"With my what?"

"Your shyness, poor dear," she said, again stroking his hair. "Every time someone comes around—and it doesn't matter who—you conveniently find other things to do in order to avoid contact. You avoid people, and when it comes to going anywhere, you stay home. You make some silly excuse to stay home to avoid meeting anyone, and, for whatever it's worth, I've learned over the years to accept your shyness. In fact, I don't even expect you to make an appearance while the children are here."

"Oh, good," Jared said, forcing a sigh. "That's a relief!"

Margo removed her glasses and smiled, her

dark eyes focused on his. "You know I'd never do anything to make you feel uncomfortable. It's just that there are times I miss you, times I need you near me to lend emotional support—like when Valerie had the twins. Mother made such a scene in the hospital. She had everyone upset.

"She kept bitching about the coven and about how Valerie would never have endangered her life by bearing children at her age, if it wasn't for them. Valerie, as you know, had problems. The twins had to be delivered by Caesarian section, and that's dangerous. Mother used that fact to try and discredit the coven. She went on for the longest time, with all of us just listening to her inane chatter and saying nothing.

"She even brought up my disfigurement, as she termed it, and how I was blinded by Nathan. Then we all tried ignoring her because Mother was such a mousy, little person, never speaking up when it really mattered, never telling the coven members or Nathan how she felt. The only time she had something to say was when we were alone somewhere, away from the eyes and ears of the coven.

"Finally I told her to shut up because I was so worried about Valerie and her nonsense made things worse. Our worries were all for nothing. Oh, Jared, you should have been there. When Jonathan and Joelle were born, it was a miracle. They were so beautiful. And to think about how and why children are born is a miracle in itself—the mixing of seeds of two people in love.

Jonathan Senior, my brother-in-law, really did love Valerie! There was no doubting it.

"And oh, it was such a miracle we all just about cried, but then Mother spoiled things as usual. That woman was a bitch at the wrong times. Imagine this! She wanted to examine the babies. She insisted on seeing their naked bodies, insisted on counting their fingers and their toes."

"What the hell for?" Jared asked. "You never mentioned this part of it before."

"Well, Mother had this theory. She claimed that if the coven wanted Valerie to have children to fulfill a prophecy, then perhaps those children would be demons when they were born."

"Demons?"

"Yes," Margo said and laughed. "Isn't it the silliest thing you ever heard? She felt that perhaps the coven had manipulated the conception of the twins by substituting a demon for Jonathan in bed. In other words, she believed Valerie was screwed by some demon or other, and so there was Mother, counting fingers and toes and checking to see if one arm was as long as the other and that the legs were equal in length."

"Why?" Jared asked. He already knew the answer, but the idea was to see if Margo knew as well.

"Because demons who take on human form cannot duplicate us as perfectly as they'd like to. Something is usually wrong. Either they're missing a vital part of their bodies, or their limbs are uneven. This way we, humans, can tell who's really one of us and who isn't.''

She'd said it so simply that the explanation had seemed false, but to Jared's horror, Margo understood. All this time he'd been hiding his obvious imperfections, such as his short fingers, to keep her from thinking he was anything but perfect.

Now his abnormalities had to be kept hidden for another, more important reason. Margo had always believed he was human. What would she do when she discovered he wasn't?

"And then when Eve was born," Margo said, "Mother went through the same routine. And you know, Jared, when Eve was born dead, or almost dead, I remembered Mother's words and the bitterness aimed at Nathan for talking Valerie into having children. For a moment there, I hated him about as much as she did, because Valerie was so sensitive that losing a child in birth would have driven her mad."

Jared wanted to say something to Margo, but, at the moment, he could do nothing other than think about how she knew the truth and always had about his failed transitions. He shoved his short fingers deeper into his pockets and tried to listen to Margo rather than the scratching noises at the door. Someone was out there listening, one of the three intruders no doubt.

He knew he should have been enraged, but he wasn't. He was too busy worrying about Margo and her knowledge of satanic matters to care that someone was listening.

"The most wonderful part of all was watching those children grow and mature," Margo said, oblivious to Jared's fears and to the intruder outside as well. "Watching them go from being toddlers to school age was the most wonderful experience of my life. It made me wish I'd had children of my own, but I didn't. Nathan made sure of that as well as other things, too. It was Nathan who made sure I was torn from the children for the past ten years."

"It wasn't Nathan's fault," Jared said quietly. He wanted to make a point, but he didn't want to argue with her.

"Oh, yes, I remember now," Margo went on, her voice sounding bitter and sardonic. "Nathan made us separate because of the prophecy. He said it was for the good of the coven."

"He did it because our lives were in danger, Margo, and for no other reason."

"He was the one who came up with the stupid idea of the prophecy to begin with, and no one ever challenged him or checked it out because it was Nathan who did the predicting. So, on the whimsy of a drunken drug addict, all of our lives were disrupted."

"We had to leave. We had no choice."

"And Valerie was killed! I missed seeing those children grow into young adults and Valerie was killed!"

"It had to be. Do you remember what happened? Do you remember an angry mob?"

"Probably hired by Nathan to get his own way. Nathan would do anything to win a point."

"Margo," Jared said, his voice now edged with annoyance, "when you go back and relive the past, you usually end up emotionally drained, and you're hurting no one but yourself. Now, I suggest you let it lie—permanently! If you can't do anything to change it, why let it torment you?"

Margo listened to his words and put her glasses back on to hide the tears of bitterness welling up inside. Jared was right. Why dwell on something she had no control over? She bent forward and brushed his forehead with her lips to let him know she agreed. Then she rose and waited while he did the same. It was time to call the children down for lunch.

"Now, take in a couple of deep breaths and smile," he said, quickly removing a hand from his pocket to slip around her waist. "Those three are scared of you as it is, and if you look depressed when they come down . . ."

"You're worried about them. You're worried about what they think," she said.

"No, I'm worried about what you think. If you have a bad time while they're here, it'll haunt you as much as the memories of the past do."

They were halfway to the door when she turned and kissed him, again wanting the warmth from his body to give her the strength she needed, the strength to face the children and make their visit here as pleasant as possible.

Eve was in the hall outside, sitting on the steps leading upstairs, when Margo left the den. Jared stepped back into the shadows when Margo spoke to Eve. Jared, she knew, would keep himself hidden, and Margo had to respect his right to privacy or risk losing him. So she quickly closed the door behind her as she entered the hall.

"Are you hungry?" she asked Eve.

"A little," Eve replied. She was crouched, with her knees pulled up against her chest. When Margo attempted to go nearer to where she was sitting, Eve shuddered and pulled her body into a tighter ball for protection.

I used to change your diapers, you bitch, Margo wanted to shout, but didn't. Eve was afraid of her, and the twins were afraid of her as well. It wasn't fair, none of it. She was their aunt. She was there when they were born; she watched them grow. Now, because of the passage of ten years, they were afraid of her.

"Go get the twins!" Margo commanded when she was able to speak. "Tell them lunch is ready." While Margo watched, Eve released her knees and bolted up the stairs, leaving behind an awful stillness. Margo was alone in the hall, listening to the wind outside whipping the trees in a frenzy.

The trees were dead, she knew, their leaves gone and with them the colors of the fall foliage. She wanted to see the leaves turn. She wanted to see the last, dying breath of summer shriek and protest in a splash of browns and yellows and reds. She wanted to see fall enter with all of its grace and dignity, for it brought back such happy memories.

To Margo, fall was a time of pumpkins and holidays and frost in the air, a time for homecoming football games and bonfires, a time for sitting in front of a roaring fireplace, sipping hot chocolate and waiting for the festival of Bael to begin. Fall was also a time for killing Daddy, because Daddy took her eyes by giving her to the coven. Daddy had robbed her of the sight of the foliage when she was five and had been a dreamer, the same as Eve.

Now Margo wondered who was to blame this year. Who was responsible for taking her memories away? Was it those two men—Aubrey Soames and his son, Tom? Or was it those hateful bastards who inhabited the town? Were they the ones who'd taken the leaves and robbed her of the memories she needed to survive? She had little else. How could the past rise up in her mind to dull the sharp edges of the coming winter, when there were no colorful leaves for stimulation? Only dead branches and dead tree trunks remained, skirted by those damned, blue flowers—Monkshood!

They grew and survived, but they also gave her a fragrance to splash on her body to drive Jared wild.

"Aunt Margo, are you all right?"

Margo came out of her trance and gazed up at the stairs. Joelle was there, standing beside Jonathan. Eve was hiding behind the two of them, and their faces were a mixture of fear and curiosity. Margo grew angry again. She wanted to see only the curiosity and not the fear, but at this point, she didn't know how to break the spell of a decade's worth of separation.

"I'm fine," she said and led them to the dining room, her dress rustling around her ankles, leaving behind the strange, perfumed odor of Monkshood and Nightshade.

Lunch was overwhelming. The three young Blakes entered the dining room to discover that a buffet had been carefully laid out on a table running the length of one wall. The twins stared at each other, neither of them hiding their surprise, while Eve grabbed a plate and dug in.

Jonathan scanned the table and saw meats and cheeses heaped high on platters, along with freshly cut melons and other fruit. There was also scrambled eggs and bacon and tiny sausages and ham, and there was bread lying next to a sliced layer cake in case they wanted sandwiches. As he stared at the food, he started to wonder if spooky old Aunt Margo with the dead eyes had made lunch herself when Joelle poked him in the ribs and handed him a plate.

"I didn't know if you had breakfast," Margo said quickly, "so I made a sort of brunch."

"Oh, it's wonderful," Eve said. "Everything looks so good." Eve was halfway down the table, her plate loaded with food, when Margo suggested she lay one plate on the dining room table and take another. "This way you'll have room for everything," Margo said.

Jonathan thought he detected amusement in Margo's voice, then he dismissed the whole idea. Aunt Margo had no sense of humor. If she had, she wouldn't be living in this tomb she called a house. Now, as he looked at her, he noticed the edges of her mouth and the way they seemed to be drawn into a sort of semi-smile. He wondered if Joelle had been right when she said that Margo could see when she wanted to.

Margo watched the three of them choosing their lunch from the buffet table for a moment longer, then turned away. If she stared at them for too long they might start to wonder if she could see, and that was no good. What if they asked her outright if she could see? What would Margo say then? She'd sworn an oath not to tell anyone.

Nathan, the bastard, made her swear an oath!

Nathan was forever going into trances and revealing a truth, or at least what the other coven members called a truth or a revelation, but then, Nathan was a drunk, and Nathan took drugs. Nathan was on drugs when he went into a trance and predicted a prophecy that now tore at Margo's heart, a prophecy that had separated her family for the past decade.

"Death was a tired soul," Nathan had said when he first announced his revelation of horror, his eyes misted over from whatever it was he was on.

Margo remembered him standing at the altar in front of the coven members, wearing his ceremonial whites. Nathan had two sets of robes, one black, and one white. Whenever he conducted just a plain, everyday service, he wore his black robes.

They all wore black robes to the services, and so Nathan felt he was being democratic when he too wore black. But when he wore the white robes edged with pure gold, then he was Nathan, their leader, and everyone listened well, because nothing he said was unimportant.

Nathan had been wearing his ceremonial whites for the services the evening he went into one of his so-called trances and made a startling prediction about one of Valerie's unborn children.

"Death is a tired soul. Death, the creature who comes in the night and gathers the old and the sick and the infirm, is tired," Nathan said, his voice slurred from drugs, while the coven members stood in mesmerized silence.

But Margo wasn't mesmerized. Margo's mind kept repeating his words over and over again as though she were trying to analyze them and thereby keep one step ahead of her drugged leader. Death, she knew, was a fabled creature who came for you when it was your time to go. Although she'd never thought much about his existence up to that point, Nathan's words fired up her imagination.

She recalled stories she'd heard as a child, stories about a creature who dressed in black and was nothing more than a gaunt, skeletal figure riding a stallion on the crest of the night winds, searching for victims to claim. She could see him, a monk's cowl pulled over his head, his skeletal mouth drawn back into a sneer as he called out the names of the dead and beckoned to them to follow.

She recalled other stories as well about foreign beliefs on the subject of Death and its many forms.

Sometimes Death came in the form of a snarling, howling dog, and so when the angry howl of a hound rose in the night to shatter their nerves, villagers in Sweden bolted and locked their doors to keep Death out. If some poor soul was caught on the road at night, hurrying for the comfort and safety of home, and the hound showed up . . . There was no way to outrun the Hound of Death.

Sometimes Death took on the form of a human creature—a young girl, innocent and alluring, one who would tempt you away from your loved ones if you stared into her eyes for too long a time. Villagers in Russia would be sure to keep their shutters locked at night, otherwise the young Maiden of Death might gaze into their homes and hypnotize them into following her.

It was also rumored that Death had the ability to imitate someone you'd already lost—a parent or a spouse or even perhaps a child. By imitating the dead, the creature would freely enter your home and talk you into leaving with it.

Margo, however, unlike others, preferred the stories of the gaunt, skeletal figure riding the wind at night. In fact, she even tried to picture him in her mind's eye as he might really look when he came for his victims. Riding a fierce, snarling stallion, with angry puffs of smoke kicking up around its hooves, Death rode a terrible path, his flight made easier by the force of winds carrying him forth on his journey. Oh yes, she loved that vision because it was both frightening and nonsensical.

Death wasn't a creature to Margo, not really. Rather, Death, like birth, was a state of being. You were born, you lived, and you died, and no creature was responsible for that. No creature could take credit for a simple biological act, a bodily function, something that happened when you were old and spent and finished.

So, with this in mind, Margo listened as Nathan went on with his so-called prediction. Death, he said, was worn and had to be replaced, and only a very special child of their lord, Satan, would do.

But there were two parts to the prophecy!

That special child was to gather souls and to reap the dead, but there was something else as well, something so vile and so frightening that Margo tried hard not to listen as Nathan was speaking. Though she tried not to remember, the second part of the prophecy came forth—No! She refused to remember! She forced it back, to the dark recesses of her mind, and concentrated on the children.

She looked at Jonathan and Joelle and Eve and tried to guess which one was the child of the prophecy, which one would wield the power. Was it Jonathan, with his wide black eyes and dark hair and deep sensitivities? Was it Joelle, Jonathan's double, a flower blooming with life? And Eve—Oh, Satan, Margo prayed, don't let it be Eve! If the prophecy is true, let it be one of the twins, someone intelligent enough to use the power wisely.

"Aunt Margo," Eve said and smiled, "aren't you hungry?"

"No, dear, I'm not," Margo answered, trying to hide the tightness in her voice. She wasn't hungry, not now, not when the truth of the prophecy had come back to haunt her in full force. Although she wanted to dismiss it as another of Nathan's drug-ridden trips, she couldn't. What if Nathan was right?

What if it really happened after 13 years? In two weeks the Black Sabbath of Dagu's Nacht would fall on the night of a full moon as Nathan predicted. He was right about that. Dagu's Nacht would fall on the night when all of the witches and warlocks and Satanists would be in their glory, for they worshipped the fullness of the moon as the key to the universe, and as a sign that their lord was alive and in control.

What if it really happened on that night of nights, when the power of the moon was at its peak and was able to lend an extra measure of power to the child of the prophecy? Margo shuddered. She had to believe Nathan now, as she never had before, because not believing him was too risky. She had to believe Nathan in order to take steps to prevent the prophecy from fulfilling itself.

If she didn't, then she didn't want to be around when a force of pure energy, a force of power so strong it couldn't be stopped, was unleashed in the world.

Chapter Five

DINNER THAT EVENING was almost the same as lunch, but the selection of food had changed. There were no more chafing dishes full of eggs and bacon and ham. Now there were platters of prime rib and lobster tails and lamb with mint jelly.

Margo again studied the expressions on their faces and wondered if they'd quarrel over who'd prepared the food this time. She'd been in the hall outside of their rooms after lunch, though not really listening, at least not with her ears. Rather, she was using her mind to scan theirs, because the doors in this cursed place were so damned thick she wouldn't have heard them otherwise.

They were in Jonathan's room when she found them, arguing. Jonathan was telling his sisters about a short-fingered person who'd been watching them from the window when they first arrived. While Jonathan wasn't able to see the person behind the fingers, he wondered if this person had made lunch.

This was so puzzling to Margo. Nobody in this house had short fingers. Besides, there was only herself and Jared, and Jared was normal in every sense of the word. So, Margo surmised, Jonathan had to be imagining the whole thing.

Then Eve said something as puzzling. She told Jonathan she'd seen the man with the short fingers speaking to some man with a short arm who had followed them from Philadelphia. Joelle, meanwhile, who'd been quiet until then, lost her temper and shouted, "Short fingers. Short arms. What're you two—obsessed with short limbs?"

Margo forced herself to stop listening at that point because she remembered something her mother had said when Valerie's children were born. Her mother had examined the children to see if their bodies were complete, because she suspected the children of being products of a union between Valerie and a demon, and everyone knows that demons cannot duplicate our bodies perfectly. Something is usually abnormally wrong, especially concerning limbs. If Jonathan saw someone with short fingers watching them from the front window, then that someone had to be Jared! Margo had come downstairs to find him at the window.

If Jared had short fingers—No! Jared was as human as she was. After half a century of togetherness, she would know if he were human or not, wouldn't she?

"Jonathan," Margo said, attempting to get her mind off Jared, "did you bring your camera?" Of course she knew he did, but this was another of her attempts at feigning blindness. Jonathan, his mouth full of food, nodded his head and smiled. "Good! Then you can take family pictures while you're here. I really don't have any recent photos of you or your sisters."

"But, Aunt Margo," Eve said in her whimsical fashion, "why would you want pictures of us when you're blind? You can't look at them."

"I want them to show around," Margo said tightly.

"But to who?" Eve asked insistently. "You don't have any friends. No one's come here since we—"

"Eve, you're being rude again!" Joelle hissed. "Just keep quiet!"

"Don't hafta!" Eve pouted.

"Eve," Jonathan said, jumping in with a firm but gentle tone, "eat your dinner and you can go and pick some of those pretty blue flowers for Aunt Margo."

"Okay," Eve said and concentrated on her plate while Margo breathed a sigh of relief. Eve was simple-minded, and that was a problem. Simple-minded people often noticed the smallest, seemingly unimportant yet significant details, and they played them to death.

It was Eve who picked up on *blind* Aunt Margo's request for photographs while Jonathan and Joelle had let it slide. Either the twins were being polite by not asking the same questions, or else they hadn't given it a second thought. But not Eve. Eve could only concentrate on one subject at a time, and Aunt Margo's blindness was it.

"I mentioned the camera, Jonathan, because your father told me in his letter that you're following in his footsteps. You want to become a professional photographer."

"Yes, Aunt Margo," Jonathan said. "It's a really good field—and rewarding, financially and otherwise. I mean, when I hold my camera in my hands and photograph something, I'm saving a beautiful sight for all time to come. I'm trapping it on film so that others can see it through me."

"Well, I must say I'm impressed with your attitude. Most photographers, the really good ones, feel the same as you do. It's not just a job. It's a form of art, the same as painting—"

"Daddy's in Europe taking pictures of old, rundown buildings," Eve said, interrupting.

"Eve!" Joelle hissed again, but Margo stopped her from scolding Eve further.

"She only wants to be a part of the conversation." With that, she turned to Eve and tried a little psychology. "I have a white vase somewhere in the kitchen, and it's empty now. My flowers died."

"Don't worry, Aunt Margo," Eve said, "I'll

eat fast and get you some more.''

"It's amazes me how well you handle her,''
Joelle said suddenly, her eyes narrowing as
though she were being coy. "And what also
amazes me is how Daddy asked you, of all
people, to watch us while he was gone.''

"What's so amazing?'' Margo asked, her lips
drawn tightly over her teeth. "I'm your aunt,
and as such, I'm still a blood relative even
though we haven't seen each other in ten years.
So what's so amazing?''

"Well,'' Joelle began, "the time span is what
I'm having problems with. There's been no
communication between you and the rest of the
family in years—no cards, no letters, no phone
calls. An imposed silence. And now it's been
broken.''

"Joelle, what you're really asking is what
separated the family to begin with. What code of
the coven forced us apart and forced the
subsequent silence between us as well? And why
is it now all right to act as though it never
happened? Are these the questions you're
seeking answers to, Joelle?'' While Margo was
speaking she kept her hands on her lap beneath
the table to hide her white-knuckled fists.

"Those are the answers I'm looking for,''
Joelle said, not backing down in the face of
Margo's anger.

"Well, that's a very long, complicated story,
and I don't have time for it right now,'' Margo
lied. The truth was that the prophecy had
separated them, along with the men with the

axes and the need for protecting the children. Margo wasn't sure just how much they remembered of the past, and she wasn't about to fill in the answers. If none of the three were aware of the prophecy, fighting its fulfillment would be that much easier.

Jonathan, like Eve, had been quietly devouring his dinner while Joelle sparred with Margo, but now he sensed a horrible silence and wanted to break it. He felt it would be better to bring the conversation back to its previous light, airy tone than to let it lay dead with gloom.

"You know," he said, directing his thoughts to Margo in between bites, "the woods behind your house are fascinating. I mean, the trees have no leaves to brighten up the scenery, but they still have this stark sort of something. Maybe the girls and I can take pictures there—you know, those family pictures you requested."

"Sure," Margo said, relaxing her fists. "And we can take some indoor shots in the den in front of the fireplace."

"And we can shoot Aunt Margo with the pretty blue flowers I'm gonna pick," Eve said, excusing herself from the table.

"Don't go any further than the front of the house," Joelle called after her, then she turned back to Margo. "Jonathan brought his own developing equipment."

"Oh, wonderful! This way we can see the pictures right away, without waiting for some slow deadbeat from town to develop them. And, speaking of this town, I'd appreciate it if you three would stick close to home and not mingle with the locals. I'm not too popular around here, and I don't want these bastards taking their feelings for me out on you."

"We already found that out the hard way," Jonathan said without thinking. After he'd spoken, he noticed the tightness around Margo's mouth again. "We had some problems at the train station, but nothing serious. Just some name calling."

"Then you know what I'm talking about," Margo said, forcing a smile. "Now, Jonathan . . . about your developing equipment. Will you need an entire room?"

"No, Aunt Margo," he answered, "just the top of the counter in my bathroom will do. Things have changed in the last few years. Developing isn't as messy or complicated as it used to be."

"Good. You can get started with your photography first thing in the morning—after breakfast, that is—and then we can all lend a hand with the developing." Margo saw Jonathan and Joelle exchanging glances and realized what they were thinking. If she were really blind, how could she help? "I can more or less feel my way through it," Margo said suddenly. "When you've been blind for as long as I have, you find ways to cope. Otherwise you're always left out. I can help if you just tell me what to do."

* * *

Dinner had been over for hours, and the pretty blue flowers picked, by the time Eve settled down in her room. What a beautiful room it was, Eve thought, as she lay across her bed and looked around.

Flipping on her stomach and crawling to the edge where her feet belonged, Eve admired the carpeting—thick and luxurious and dark. The colors were all dark, as was the furniture and the walls. Eve liked dark things; they were easier to keep clean when you had fumbling fingers and dropped a lot of stuff.

Back home the carpet in her room was beige, and Eve was forever dropping messy stuff on it. People were forever yelling at her, saying she had ruined it with stains, but Eve didn't mean to drop stuff. It just happened, that's all.

Eve couldn't help it. Sometimes she had trouble controlling her hands. Things slipped right out and fell, and now she was having trouble with her eyes, too. Aunt Margo was still old and ugly, yet Jonathan and Joelle remarked at the dinner table about how stunning she looked, her dark hair all sparkling and shiny from the light of the chandelier.

Try as she might, Eve couldn't see any dark, shiny hair on Aunt Margo's head—only whiter than white hair, looking scary and awful against her white skin and those terrible glasses with the black lenses.

That was why Eve rushed out after dinner to pick those flowers, not because she'd already promised. That was only part of it. Mainly it was because she wanted to get as far away from the gruesome sight of Margo Windsor as she could. Aunt Margo was a horror!

Eve flipped on her back then and stared up at the chandelier, ignoring the rustling noises her drapes were making and the creaking noises of the trees outside being whipped by the wind. It was spooky here—beautiful but spooky. If Eve didn't control her emotions, she'd be tempted to leave this house tonight.

But Daddy said she had to stay for two weeks, and so she had to try and not be scared. She had to shut her ears to those noises, and she had to shut out the sight of the face she maybe saw at the window just now. Eve had seen a baldheaded creature with a round face and no ears and large dark eyes staring at her through the window.

It was a man, and he had a muscular body, she knew, because he wasn't wearing a shirt. She thought the whole thing had to be made up in her mind. She was on the second floor, and nobody was tall enough to stand with their hands on their hips and look in your window when you were on the second floor.

There sure were a lot of strange things going on here, she thought to herself. When she'd gone out to pick those flowers, the man from the train was standing on the road outside of Aunt Margo's big, prison gate. He waved at Eve, then he disappeared—right into thin air—and Eve was watching him the whole time while tiny goose bumps lumped her flesh. She knew she wasn't imagining it, just as she wasn't imagining the man at the window staring at her again.

Eve heard tapping at the window and ignored it. She'd already worked herself into a nervous frenzy and couldn't deal with someone two stories tall who had no ears. Instead, she tried to concentrate on tomorrow, when she and Jonathan and Joelle would take pictures in the woods. Eve loved to walk in the woods back home.

If Aunt Margo's woods were anything like those, there'd be plenty of tiny creatures scurrying up trees or running to hide behind bushes, and maybe there'd be deer, too. Eve could have fun chasing after the squirrels and the raccoons and the deer, if there were any. But then there had to be; woods were woods, and all woods had creatures.

The tall man with no ears was still tapping at the window, and Eve was still doing a good job of ignoring him. Besides, what could she do about him? If she called Joelle, her sister would scream in her face and tell her she was imagining things again. Then Joelle would make Eve sleep in her room, and Eve loved having her own room. Eve rose and started to unpack, deliberately oblivious to the man at the window.

"Eve," he called softly, while Eve put her hands over her ears and refused to listen. But she could still hear him. Now he was saying something about coming there to watch over her and Jonathan and Joelle, but it couldn't be, because the man from the train had come there for the same reason.

Eve put her hands to her sides and stared at the window for the first time since she'd caught a glimpse of the man standing there. It *was* the man from the train, only now, in addition to his short arm, his hair and his ears were gone! He was falling apart.

"Don't worry, Eve," he said and smiled. "Just go to sleep. I'll be here all night to watch over the three of you."

And Eve, being the obedient child she was, changed into her nightgown and crawled into bed to let visions of blue flowers dance in her head.

Jonathan was the eternal procrastinator, so he decided to turn in early and leave the unpacking for tomorrow. As he lay in bed and pulled the covers up around his chin, he listened to the sound of the trees outside, their branches being tossed and pummeled by the wind, and started to doze off when another sound made him sit straight up and pay attention.

Someone was walking the hall outside of his room. At first he thought it might have been Joelle or Eve or Aunt Margo, but these footfalls were much too heavy.

With his heart pumping loudly in his ears, he wondered if a prowler had broken in. If so, then it was his job, as the only male present, to defend the women. Rising slowly from the bed, he walked barefoot to the door and listened.

He couldn't hear much coming from the hall other than the steady rhythm of someone walking—but to where?

It wasn't until he heard those same footsteps thumping up the stairs that he realized this stranger was headed for Aunt Margo's room, and Aunt Margo was blind and helpless. But he was only 18, he kept telling himself, and not sure he was up to a confrontation with an unknown person.

What if the intruder had a gun or a knife?

But Aunt Margo was blind!

Turning back to grab his robe and slippers, Jonathan stiffened his back, opened the door and stepped out into the dark hall. Jonathan couldn't see two feet in front of him, so he stopped for a moment and listened for the sound of the footsteps. If they were still on the stairs, then he had a chance. The intruder still didn't know that Jonathan was after him. But if the footsteps had stopped, then the intruder had heard Jonathan's door open and close and was waiting for him to make a move.

The footsteps were growing weaker, which meant the intruder was getting closer to Aunt Margo's room upstairs. The intruder was unaware of Jonathan's presence, so Jonathan felt he had the element of surprise on his side. Even if the intruder was armed, Jonathan could probably get the drop on him at this point.

Jonathan was walking towards the stairs when a cold, shaky hand reached out of the darkness behind him and touched his shoulder. He wanted to scream as a thousand crazy thoughts ran through his mind. Mainly he wondered if somehow the intruder had doubled back and was now behind him, ready to strike.

He sucked in his breath, and turned to face the danger. "Who are you," he demanded, hating the crack in his voice.

"It's me, Joelle. Who were you expecting?" a voice answered, while he fell back against the wall and tried to get his nerves together. "You heard it, too. Right, Jonathan?"

"Yeah," he whispered with the same crack in his voice. "Whoever it is, he's headed for Aunt Margo's room."

"We oughta go back inside and let him have her."

"Joelle! She's blind. And she's our aunt, besides!"

"She's a cruel, evil bitch. Maybe it's someone she crossed. Maybe she picked the wrong person to start with this time."

Jonathan felt anger replacing his fear. Joelle had gone through a strange transformation once they entered this house. She had been a kind, compassionate, sensitive individual until that door downstairs closed behind her this afternoon. Now she was mean and uncaring. Well, she could stay here and bitch if she wanted to, but he was going up to save Aunt Margo. And from the sound he now heard, or rather the lack of it, there was little time to waste. The intruder was already inside Margo's bedroom.

Without a word, he rushed down the hall and climbed the stairs, with, to his amazement, Joelle following close behind. Once on the top landing, he saw a light cracking under Aunt Margo's door and knew the intruder was inside. Aunt Margo had no reason to turn on the lights, but the intruder did.

"What do we do now?" Joelle whispered. "Do we go bursting into her room, or do we wait until she screams?"

Jonathan's lips were drawn back in anger when he answered. Joelle was behaving like the worst kind of fool possible. "We bust in."

"We have nothing to defend ourselves with."

"We have the element of surprise on our side. He doesn't expect us."

"But—"

"Listen, Joelle, you can wait outside if you want to, but I'm going in there. Hell, by the time she screams, it'll be all over!"

Jonathan walked swiftly to the door to Margo's room and had the knob in his hand, but he couldn't make himself turn the knob. For some reason, the hand holding the knob wouldn't listen to the command from his brain, telling him to go in there and face the danger head on. But he had to!

Turning the knob slowly, he began to push in on the door, trying to be as quiet as possible. There were noises coming from inside, and instead of forcing the door open, he stopped to listen.

He heard a woman's voice, moaning softly, and yet it wasn't the sound of someone in pain. She was moaning with pleasure. But that was impossible, he thought. Aunt Margo was in there, and she was hardly the type to be passionate with an intruder.

"What's wrong?" Joelle asked, coming from behind and startling him.

He backed away from the door and pulled Joelle with him. "I don't know how to explain this, but she's in there having a good time."

"Having a what?"

"A good time. You know."

"You mean screwing?"

"Joelle!"

Clacking her tongue with disgust, Joelle approached the door and listened. When the same moaning sounds came to her, she listened a moment longer and walked back to where Jonathan was standing. "Let's go."

"Why?" Jonathan asked, not sure they should leave. What if they were wrong?

"Because I just heard something that man said to her, and believe me she's not in any danger. Far from it."

"How can you be so sure? What did he say?" Jonathan asked all in one breath.

"He said, 'Your husband sent me,' so she's in no danger because she was expecting him. Come on, let's go back to bed and try to get a good night's sleep."

As Jonathan followed his sister down the steps, he couldn't help but think about her last words and how they were spoken. Joelle's voice had been laced with bitterness, and again he remembered how she'd changed when they entered this house.

Jonathan was halfway down the stairs behind Joelle when something odd caught his attention. He looked up and saw another door with light showing beneath it. The room was at the end of the hall, beyond Aunt Margo's, yet she was the only one who lived up here. So why was there a light on in that room?

Reaching out to grab Joelle, he lifted her chin until her vision was in line with the mysterious room, then whispered to her and told her to follow him.

"What for?"

"Because I wanna take a look up there."

"And what if Aunt Margo and her boyfriend should happen to hear us? How do we explain it? You know, being up there where we don't belong."

"They're taken up with other things," Jonathan insisted. "They'll never hear us. Take my word for it."

"Oh sure, take your word for it. You never slept with anyone in your whole life. How do you know they won't hear us?"

"Will you just stop arguing and let's go?" Jonathan was already halfway up the stairs before Joelle made up her mind to follow him. Passing Margo's room, they both walked as quietly as possible, their attention focused on the mysterious room at the end of the hall.

Joelle didn't like this. It was still dark, and they could hardly see much. What if someone lived in that room? What if someone as evil as Margo Windsor opened the door and they had to run for their lives? What then? They could barely see two feet in front of them and were using the light under the door as a guide.

Before Jonathan reached the door, Joelle grabbed his arm and reminded him of how scared he was a moment ago when he thought he was facing a prowler. Now, here he was, boldly investigating a mysterious room in this spooky, old mansion. Where did he suddenly find his courage?

"Look, Joelle, this is different. I was up against someone who was real a few minutes ago, and I didn't know if he was armed or not."

"Oh, sure, I can see your point," she answered sarcastically. "Now it's much different because now we don't know what the hell we're facing."

"Joelle! It's just an empty room."

"Then why is the light on? I mean if the room's empty . . ."

Jonathan pulled away from her and stopped outside of the door to the mysterious room. What Joelle didn't know, and what he couldn't tell her, was that he was still scared.

"Now what?" Joelle asked, coming up from behind again.

"Will you stop doing that?" he hissed.

"Doing what? What the hell am I doing?" she asked indignantly.

"Sneaking up on me, that's what. One minute you're over there and the next you're here. Make some noise when you walk."

"You said to be quiet because of Aunt Margo and her boy—"

"Oh, never mind. Just be quiet." Once she'd stopped whispering, Jonathan put his ear to the door. He wasn't sure he'd hear anything because the damned doors in this house were so thick, but at least leaning against the door gave him a chance to calm down. Joelle scared the hell out of him, sneaking up the way she did.

"Do you hear anything?" she asked, a tinge of impatience in her voice.

"No!"

"Now what?"

"I'm gonna take a peek through the keyhole. Maybe I'll be able to see inside." He started down on his knees, but stopped when Joelle spoke up.

"What if someone pokes your eye out from the other side? They could stick a knife or something sharp through—"

"Joelle!"

"What?"

"Keep quiet!" He got down on his knees and tried to see the inside of the room from a distance of a foot or more. Joelle's warning had him more scared than he cared to admit, but he couldn't see anything from that distance, so he moved closer and was shocked by what he saw. There was an altar on the far side of the room and a white bowl on the altar, encircled by a black whip and black candles on either side of the bowl.

Aunt Margo had built herself a house complete with a chapel.

"What's in there? What do you see?" Joelle asked, dropping to her knees beside him, but Jonathan couldn't answer. She pushed him away and stared through the keyhole. "It's like our church back home." Joelle should have stopped there. She should have taken Jonathan and gone on downstairs, but she didn't. Instead, she tried to see what else was inside. "This damn keyhole is so small. You can't see a thing," she complained. Then Jonathan felt her body tense up beside him and heard something awful in her voice. "Oh, I don't believe it! How cruel!"

"What is?"

"Jonathan," she whispered dully, "did you ever wonder what happened to Nathan when the coven scattered? Well, take a look for yourself."

Slowly Jonathan took Joelle's place at the keyhole. When he saw what Joelle was upset about, he wanted to scream or faint or do something other than what he was doing—staring at a corpse with its mouth hung open like a damned fool!

There was a ceremonial chair to one side of the altar, and in that chair was a man—or at least what was left of him—wearing Nathan's white, gold-encrusted robe and a cowl pulled over his skeletal face. His eyes were empty sockets, his bony mouth seemingly stretched into a leering grin. The long, pointed sleeves of the robe were not quite covering his long, fleshless hands—

"What the hell do you think you're doing? Get up from there at once!"

Jonathan froze and Joelle gasped as the harsh voice of Margo Windsor came blaring from somewhere out of the darkness. Jonathan sat down, turning his back to the door, and listened to the rustle of her robe coming towards them. He inhaled deeply and recognized the odor of her strange perfume. Without seeing her, without being able to say she was there for certain, he knew she'd seen them looking through the keyhole.

He wondered if Joelle had been correct in her evaluation of Aunt Margo's blindness. Now, on top of the gruesome sight on the other side of the door, the one he was trying to forget as fast as he could, he also had to deal with another gruesome sight—Margo Windsor staring down at them with dead eyes that weren't as dead as she pretended, Margo Windsor with the pinholes in her pupils where Nathan's knife had penetrated.

Oh yes, she'd surely had her revenge on Nathan!

Just as she'd had her revenge on her father for giving her to Nathan over 60 years ago!

"Get down to your rooms. I'll deal with you in the morning!" she commanded. They both moved, Joelle scampering like a small, frightened animal and Jonathan, half-walking, half-running, not caring if he fell in the dark, passed her room and wondered if her boyfriend was mad at them, too.

If so, would they have to deal with him in the morning? Or would it be tonight? Would he come for them when their eyes were closed and their brains at rest, when they were helpless and alone? And if he came, would he put them in that room upstairs? Would he lock them in with

Nathan and let them die the same way Nathan had?

"Oh, Satan, keep us safe this night," he prayed, and ran until the knob of his door was in his hand and turning.

Jonathan had drifted into a troubled sleep, his dreams filled with horror. He dreamed of the coven and their ceremonies, he dreamed of eating flesh and drinking blood, and he dreamed of Nathan—only it wasn't the old Nathan they knew and loved. The one in his dreams was a scary Nathan with a thin, skeletal body and a fleshless face with a bony, leering mouth.

Nathan was leading the mass, praying to their lord, Satan, with his face practically fused to Jonathan's. Nathan was cursing Margo Windsor, and telling Jonathan, as well as the others, how she killed him! "Therefore," Nathan concluded, "Margo Windsor has to be punished for her act of murder, and, by the decree of our master, the sentence is death!"

Jonathan woke up, his body beaded with sweat. He was scared because the dream had been real enough so that he could still feel the heat of Nathan's breath on his face and taste Nathan's hatred for Margo.

He wasn't sure then if it was the wind whipping the trees outside, but he thought he heard a voice calling to someone. He sat up in bed, straining to hear the words, but he couldn't hear it clearly.

Then he heard something else clear enough,

and wished he hadn't.

He heard a body brush up against his door. He heard someone breathing. He heard a hand applying pressure to the knob. Then he rose and waited and wondered if Aunt Margo's boyfriend was the someone who was breaking into his room.

He thought about what was happening and tried to be rational. There were two doors to his room—one leading to the hall outside and one leading to Joelle's room. If the door to Joelle's room opened, then it was his pain-in-the-ass sister coming to disturb his sleep. If it was the other, the door to the hall, then it had to be Aunt Margo's boyfriend.

After what seemed like an eternity, he heard the door open and quickly scanned the darkness around him to see which one it was. Thank you, Satan, it was the door to Joelle's room, and so it had to be Joelle, didn't it?

Then again, what if Aunt Margo's boyfriend had started with Joelle? What if he had punished her first? Then Jonathan would be next.

He stood quite still and waited.

"Jonathan?"

He sighed heavily and reached out to Joelle. He grabbed her and held on, never thinking for a moment he'd ever be this happy to see his sister.

"What's wrong?" she asked, her voice muffled against his chest.

"Nothing," he said, not willing to admit to his fears. "I was just worried about you, that's all. I had a bad dream."

"So did I," she said, pulling away. "But something woke me up. I heard a voice, and when I got up to see where it was coming from . . . Come here, Jonathan. Look out the window . . . down by the front gate."

Jonathan looked and saw a man, his features hidden by darkness, standing on the road outside of the gate. "I thought it was the wind making those sounds."

"No, he's real. And you want to know what he's saying?"

Jonathan didn't answer right away, mainly because he wasn't sure he wanted to hear this. So much had happened since they'd walked through that front door downstairs, and so many bad memories had returned. Now he just wanted to rest.

But Joelle didn't wait for him to respond. Instead, she just went on. "It seems he's looking for some guys named Aubrey, I think, and Tom. Aubrey is his father because he keeps saying something like, 'Aubrey, it's me, your son, Matthew.' Then he calls him, 'Pa.' "

Jonathan tried to listen while Joelle explained what she'd heard, yet his attention was riveted on still another figure in the darkness below. He saw someone moving forward in the shadows of the bushes, towards the man at the gate. Obviously, whoever it was didn't care to be seen. All this person seemed to have in mind at the moment was the idea of getting close enough to the gate to identify the man standing there.

It was such a small figure, the one creeping towards the gate, and it cast such a small shadow that for a moment Jonathan wondered if it was a woman, and if so, could it possibly be his blind Aunt Margo?

Chapter Six

MARGO WINDSOR WAS having coffee in the dining room, waiting for the three Blake youngsters to come down, when her mind drifted back to the night before and what really disturbed her about it.

Their snooping was only part of the problem. After all, young people do have a natural curiosity, so she kind of expected to find them where they didn't belong. No, it wasn't that. The problem here was the very real possibility of their having seen Nathan and how she would explain it to them.

When she found them spying around the chapel, she also realized they had passed her bedroom door to get there, and in doing so, there was the possibility that they'd heard Jared making love to her. Now, what did they think of their Aunt Margo? Did they believe she had human emotions, or would this discovery be something to laugh and joke about?

Jared had been right. She should never have allowed them to come here, not even for a short, two-week visit. Now her life had changed drastically. Not only did she have to be careful about her relationship with Jared, she now had to explain her secrets so they wouldn't think poorly of her. And Margo Windsor had never explained anything in her life!

She lived alone, and did as she damn well pleased.

But this was different. Now she had these relatives staying with her, watching her every move. Damnit! Jared had been right all along. Why the hell didn't she listen when he warned her?

She never dreamed that Jonathan could be right about Jared and his short fingers—and yet he was. Jonathan was right. Last night when Jared had made love to her, he was like an animal, caressing every part of her body, running his hands from head to toe. While he had been so uninhibited, he was also careless, and Margo had felt his short fingers, something she maybe never would have noticed if Jonathan hadn't mentioned them. Now she wondered if Jared were human.

Margo raised her cup to her lips but didn't sip her coffee. Instead, she laughed so hard she had to put the cup down. Was Jared human? What a stupid question. Of course he was. Jared had been driving her to the brink of sexual ecstasy for half a century now, and had been her constant companion as well.

Oh, Jared was human all right. He more than fit the picture of what humanity is all about. So he had short fingers, so what? Everything else was in direct proportion to his size, and if the man had managed to hide this one abnormality from Margo for five decades, then she had to applaud his effort.

She also had to wait and see if his fingers returned to normal, and if some other part of his anatomy became short in their place. Making the transition from beast to human was never easy. The next time his fingers might be normal, but some other part of him might not be fully human.

Oh, Satan, please let him be human, she prayed, while tears misted her eyes. Please don't let Jared turn out to be a disappointment along with the others.

"Good morning, Aunt Margo."

Margo sucked in her breath and then said good morning. Jonathan had come through the door first, followed by Joelle and finally Eve. Margo watched them sit down without helping themselves to the buffet table and knew they were waiting for her to scold them, but she couldn't. She was too upset over Jared to be concerned with their snooping.

They were leaving in less than two weeks and would probably forget what they'd seen as soon as their lives returned to normal. Why bawl them out when it wasn't necessary?

"We're sorry about last night," Jonathan said. "It was wrong, the way we spied into your personal life, and it won't happen again."

Margo was thrown off guard by his confession, but then again, she expected nothing less from Valerie's children. "All right. Then we can forget about it." And no explanations are needed, she thought to herself, especially about Nathan. "Are you hungry?" she asked, smiling when their faces lit up. "Well, what are we waiting for? The food's out. Let's eat."

Jonathan didn't have expensive photographic equipment as yet, but a 35mm with a high-powered, zoom lens was enough for now. What he saw at the moment pleased him immensely.

He remembered telling Aunt Margo about wanting to photograph the woods behind her house and how they had a stark beauty. Now he stood transfixed and examined those woods with Joelle and Eve at his side.

Yes, there was a stark, prematurely dead, beauty that was so appealing it took his breath away. Why, just the angle of the bare branches of the tree in front of him, reaching desperately to touch the sky, struck him profoundly.

Yet, as with all beautiful things, there was a flaw, but not anything you could see and point to and say it was ugly. No, it was nothing as simple as that. In this instance it was some disturbing noises that broke their concentration and made them shudder and pull their collars up higher around their necks. It wouldn't have bothered them so much if it had been an ordinary outdoors, wind-blowing-through-the-trees, kind of noise, but it wasn't.

It was an awful wailing, mournful and painful, and it made them want to pack up and run back to Philly as soon as possible.

"It's coming from behind us," Eve said in her whimsical fashion. "From back over there by that small house."

"Those are stables, Eve," Joelle said dully. "Not a house."

"So what! I don't care what it's called. The noise is coming from there." Before either of the twins could stop her, Eve headed for the stables.

"But Eve," Jonathan argued, "we both think the noises are coming from the woods."

"Don't care," she called over her shoulder. "Don't care what you think!"

The twins watched her small, thin body moving away, her black hair partly covered by a wool hat, and knew she was determined to have it her way. "Come on, Jonathan," Joelle sighed, "let's follow her. She might get hurt."

Reluctantly, the twins followed behind Eve as the idea of a blind woman having stables for horses crossed their minds. "Was this house built for her, or did she buy it as is?" Joelle wanted to know.

"Beats the hell outta me," Jonathan answered, only he was lying. He now recalled a moment when one of his parents mentioned how it must have been nice to have money, because Margo was building herself a mansion in New York.

Eve was in the stable by the time they reached

her side, scrutinizing each and every stall in turn. She seemed fascinated by them, as well as by the nameplates above each bearing the individual horse's name. She paused in front of one and stared at the nameplate—Chrysaor, Arabian Male.

The wailing sounds were louder in here except that it didn't bother Eve as much as it did the twins. Eve was too concerned with the stalls and the nameplates to pay much attention to those hideous noises. "Chrysaor," Jonathan said. "What a strange name."

"Not really. He was the mythological playmate of Pegasus."

"How'dya know?" he asked.

"Because we studied it in school. Poseidon created them both from the blood of Medusa when she was decapitated and her head fell into the sea."

"Man, you are so deep!" Jonathan kidded. He tried to get his mind off the wailing horses, but they were growing louder with each step he took towards the center of the stable.

"Jonathan, take a picture of me here in front of Chrysaor's stall," Eve requested.

Jonathan didn't answer her a first. He was trying to identify the noises assaulting his senses. And for the life of him, he didn't want to recognize them for what they were—sounds generally made by horses in pain!

"Jonathan!" Eve howled. She was starting to get upset. She wanted her picture taken, and he just wasn't paying attention. "Please!"

"All right," he said, releasing the lever on the automatic flash. "Smile, Eve."

At his command, Eve stood under the horse's nameplate, in the middle of the stall, and smiled. Jonathan peered through the viewer and was about to snap her picture when something inside of the camera made him pause, something that shouldn't have been there. He stopped what he was doing and turned the camera around and examined the lens which looked clear. So what was causing the problem?

"What's wrong?" Eve asked.

But Jonathan didn't answer her right away, mainly because he didn't know how to. There was something covering the lens, something that was maybe there, then again, maybe wasn't. He considered wiping the lens down, but he'd cleaned it only an hour or so before.

"Are you gonna take my picture or not?" Eve asked, impatiently.

Without thinking about the problem, Jonathan snapped first one shot, then another, and was about to take his sisters and leave when Joelle's startled voice broke through the air.

"Over here, you two! Oh, it's awful!"

Eve went first while Jonathan lagged behind.

"What is it?" he asked, studying the shocked expressions on his sisters' faces, their eyes big and wide, their mouths frozen open. Following their gaze through a dirt-encrusted window, he saw huge graves out back with headstones, and those headstones had names written on them. Without checking, he just knew those were the names of the horses in this stable.

Chrysaor was among them.

And all had died on the same day.

The wailing was coming from those graves!

Their walk through the woods wasn't as wonderful as the three had imagined it would be. The gruesome discovery behind the stables had left them sullen and depressed, all except Eve, that is. Eve was only slightly bothered by the deaths of those horses, but then, even considering her limited intelligence, Eve was a fatalist at times.

She felt that you were born to die, and since the three of them were alive and healthy, they shouldn't spend too much time worrying about those horses and how they died.

Maybe Eve was right, Jonathan thought, as he watched her on the path ahead, chasing squirrels and squealing with delight. Eve was simple-minded, but Eve wasn't tortured inside the way he and Joelle were. Eve forgot most of what they managed to recall, because Eve couldn't remember, or she figured nothing was important enough to keep you awake nights.

"Yeah, maybe she's right," Joelle said aloud, repeating his thoughts. "But you know, Jonathan, sometimes it's no good to shove things away and pretend they didn't happen. You wind up dropping your guard, and that's no good."

"Joelle, let's take the damn pictures and get back to the house."

"You're doing it again."

"Doing what?"

Joelle stopped for a moment and faced him. She wasn't exasperated or angry the way she usually got when he didn't understand what she was trying to say. There was a disturbing calmness in her. "Because," she began, "you're not giving us a chance to talk this out—and we have to."

"I just wanna forget what's happened," he answered quietly. "We're going home the week after next, and I'd rather think about that."

"But what if we're in danger?" she wanted to know. "What then?"

"Danger? Joelle, what the hell are you talking about?"

Joelle turned away from him for a moment to look after Eve, standing under a tree calling to a squirrel who'd just crawled into a hole near the upper branches.

"Joelle?"

"It's just that everything seems to die here. We found Nathan last night and the horses this morning." She turned back to face him, and he saw the irritating calmness again.

Then he sucked in his breath and tried to stem his growing anger. Joelle had mentioned Nathan, while he'd been trying to forget the gruesome sight they'd discovered in Aunt Margo's chapel. "We don't know it's Nathan for sure."

"What?"

"Well, we don't! It was just a skeleton with

no meat on its bones. It could have been anyone
for all we know.''

"Wearing Nathan's robes?" she asked.

"Nathan wasn't the only one who ever owned
a set of white robes," he reasoned. "So it could
have been anyone."

"True," she conceded, "but I think it was
Nathan. He was up there in her chapel—dead!
And I want to know how he died, and how those
horses died. It's strange—the dates on those
tombstones are all the same."

"The horses probably died from some
common disease."

"All on the same day?"

"Joelle, look, I don't know what you're
trying to say. So would you please just say it and
let me take my pictures?"

Joelle turned quickly to check on Eve again
and then turned back to Jonathan, but before
she had a chance to say anything, she caught
something he was thinking. It was cold out there
in those woods, the kind of cold that chills your
brain along with your body. It was a
combination of things that made it so—the hard
earth beneath their feet, the barren trees, their
bark turned white in premature death . . . and
the dark figure of a man who Jonathan thought
was following them.

"Did Aunt Margo kill Nathan and the
horses?" she asked with a crack in her voice,
while managing to ignore what he was thinking.

Jonathan clucked his tongue, and that said it
all. Joelle was allowing her imagination to run

wild. But then Joelle shot something back into his mind, and Jonathan uttered, "Touché!" What she'd transmitted was this: at least *she* wasn't seeing things, such as dark men hiding behind trees.

"Maybe it's just being here," he said and sighed. "The whole damn place, including the town, is eerie. Nothing's normal here. I don't think Aunt Margo killed anyone."

"You wouldn't! You're much too taken with her beauty."

For the first time since stopping there on the path, Jonathan smiled because the old Joelle was back. Slightly nasty, slightly catty, but not cold and uncaring as she was in her feelings towards Aunt Margo last night. And certainly not quiet and subdued as she'd been moments before.

"Anyway," she said, not finished with him yet, "I think we should keep alert and on guard."

"To what?"

"To the possibility that maybe you're wrong and maybe Aunt Margo *is* a killer!"

"I want my picture taken here, under this tree by the squirrels," Eve shouted, shattering their attention like broken glass.

"Okay," Jonathan said and hurried on ahead, anxious to get away from Joelle and her feelings about Aunt Margo, anxious to begin taking pictures where everything was white and dead and starkly beautiful—white, that is, if you didn't count the dark figure he'd just seen ducking behind a tree.

"Maybe the squirrel will come out for my picture." Eve was looking up at the overhead branches again, her face full of childlike awe. "He was a pretty squirrel, but he had awful teeth."

The last part of what she'd said brought Jonathan's attention away from the dark figure and back to Eve. "How do you know he had awful teeth?" he asked.

"Because he growled at me when I tried to grab him."

"Did he bite you?" Jonathan asked in growing panic. Squirrels were mostly rabid, and if he bit Eve, she'd have to have at least a dozen shots in her abdomen.

"No, he didn't, but I saw his teeth."

Jonathan felt relieved, then guilty. If he and Joelle had been paying closer attention to her instead of arguing back there, this wouldn't have happened.

"Is this a good place to take a picture?" she asked. "I know I want it taken here, but if it's no good . . ."

"One spot's as good as another," Joelle said, coming up behind them. "It all looks the same—dead trees and bushes."

"But no pretty blue flowers," Eve added sadly. "They don't grow here."

"That's right. They don't grow here!" Jonathan was amazed to think they'd found one place in this whole damned town that wasn't full of those damned blue flowers. Then he wondered why. Those flowers grew wild, but they weren't here in these woods, and he couldn't understand why.

Ignoring Eve and Joelle, he turned in all directions, looking for the blue flowers, but there just weren't any.

"Maybe they sprayed the woods with weed killer," Joelle said, her voice sounding as wistful as Eve's.

"They're not weeds. They're flowers," Eve insisted.

Speaking in her mind, Joelle was discussing the absence of the flowers with Jonathan, and how odd it was that they were missing from the woods. Then she went on to say how she'd read somewhere that blue was the color of evil. If they weren't here, then perhaps this was safe ground.

Jonathan almost laughed when he heard the last part. Someone was following them, so how safe could it be here? And who was it? Aunt Margo's boyfriend, perhaps? Did he mean them harm? They had no protection, no weapons of their own. Then he thought about heading back to the house without taking any more pictures.

Neither Eve nor Joelle had seen the dark figure ducking behind the trees, so how was he going to convince them to leave? How would he tell them it wasn't safe here despite the absence of the evil blue flowers? Joelle would go into one of her usual rages, and Eve . . . well, Eve had a mind of her own lately.

"Let's take the pictures and get out of here,"

Jonathan said. "Okay, first I want a single shot of Eve by the tree where her squirrel lives. Then I want a single shot of you, Joelle, in the same place. Then a few shots of the two of you on the path."

"Jonathan, we have to take pictures over there on those big, white roots," Joelle said.

Jonathan followed her lead and saw a large oak tree, its roots pushed up through the soil in a hideous way, as though they feared the darkness below ground. Those roots had continued growing, it seemed, and were now intertwined in such a maze of white bark it was hard to tell where they'd started from or where they ended. It was hideous, but hideous in a starkly beautiful way.

"And Jonathan," Joelle said, "if you show me how to work the camera, I can take pictures of you. Otherwise we won't have any."

Normally Jonathan didn't let anyone besides his father touch his equipment, but Joelle had a point.

"All right. Let's do Eve first, then you. Then I'll show you how to work this thing." Looking through the viewer at the top of his camera, Jonathan motioned for Eve to turn her head one way and her body another while he fooled with the zoom lens and tried to get her best angle.

Jonathan hit the proper button and heard a whirring sound and knew at least one more photo was out of the way. He was a little sad at the moment, because he'd taken a good look at Eve for the first time in a long time. Her beauty seemed wasted because she was so simple-minded and could never have a normal life. What a sin!

He was also sad or scared or whatever because something was still covering his lens, and he didn't know how to get rid of it.

"I'm next. Do you want me to pose like Eve did?" Joelle asked and waited.

"Yes . . . uh . . . no! I want you to pose like Eve did with your head turned slightly to one side, but I want you to look at the camera out of the corner of your eye. Got it?"

"I wanna pose like that too," Eve wailed.

Jonathan was patient, as always, when he answered her. "You can, but let me take your sister's picture first. Then I'll take another of you over there, sitting on those heavy roots, okay?"

"Okay."

Jonathan peered through the viewer again. He'd taken three pictures so far, and all three had been a chore because something was covering his lens—a strange blue mist. While he didn't know how to get rid of it, he did know that it wasn't normal.

And neither was the figure of the dark man standing behind the wide base of the tree Joelle was posing in front of.

Jonathan tried his best to shoot a picture of Joelle and forget about the blue mist and how it was the same shade of blue as those cursed flowers.

He tried to forget the other things torturing

his mind as well, such as the deaths of Nathan and the horses, and the eerie absence of those evil, blue flowers. He'd tried adjusting his zoom lens. He'd tried fooling with the lighting.

Shit! Just as he was about to take the picture, there was this man, so close to Joelle that Jonathan's breath caught in his throat.

"Hello!" Eve suddenly shouted, leaving his side to duck behind the tree. Jonathan watched her while his brain screamed at her to stop, but no words passed between his lips. Joelle, however, gave out a cry of alarm and ran after Eve. "I know him," Eve shouted over her shoulder. "From Aunt Margo's house."

As Eve spoke, Jonathan found his legs and found himself around the other side of the tree in seconds flat. There was a tall, dark-haired man wearing a black cap and dark trousers and shirt—and he had Eve by the arm. Joelle was standing nearby, kind of studying the situation.

"I mean you no harm," he said, his voice harsh and gruff. "I just came to warn you."

"Who are you?" Jonathan demanded. He was afraid of this man, afraid of what was happening. Digging his heels into the ground to keep the trembling in his body from taking over, he stiffened his jaw and asked another question. "What do you want with us?"

The man had a scar on his jaw and looked dangerous. "I came to warn you about Margo Windsor! You can't trust her. Things happen to people who get too close to her."

"Okay," Joelle shouted, "so you warned us. Let Eve go!"

Jonathan wanted to haul off and slap Joelle as hard as he could. This was no time to be giving orders, but the man never acknowledged her words. Instead, he kept talking and kept saying awful things about Margo Windsor.

"My father, Aubrey Soames, disappeared a few nights ago. He had my brother, Tom, with him. Both gone! And they had to pass her place to get home."

"What does that have to do with anything?" Jonathan asked.

"Twenty-one people have disappeared in the ten years since she came to Monkshood. And it ain't no coincidence that they all had something to do with that woman!"

"And just what did your father and brother have to do with my aunt?" Joelle asked. "Did they work for her?"

"No, but they mighta snooped on her property—outta curiosity."

"So you can't prove what you're saying!"

Joelle was keeping the guy's attention away from Jonathan, who saw an opportunity to reach out and grab Eve. Then, as if he'd read Jonathan's mind, the man let go of Eve. Joelle caught her by the collar of her jacket and stepped in front of her.

"Look," the man continued, "like I said, I mean you no harm. I'm just trying to warn you. She's dangerous. I'm still looking for my kin and I ain't found them yet, which means she mighta done away with them."

" 'Might' isn't the same as saying she positively did," Jonathan said, breathing with

relief. The expression in the man's eyes had
changed from hatred to desperation.

"You got a point there, son, but all's I can do
is warn you. The rest is up to you." He started
to walk away through the woods, but he turned
and made one final statement before he was
gone from sight. "My name's Matthew Soames.
You hear anything about my kin, I'd appreciate
you lettin' me know."

The three of them stood where they were for a
long time and said nothing, almost as if they
were waiting for him to come back. Joelle's
mind was racing in circles and she tried to tell her
feelings to Jonathan, but he closed his mind to
her babbling. Joelle still felt that Margo
Windsor was an evil creature as well as a
murderess. Now this man, this Matthew
Soames, had practically cemented her theories
into concrete evidence with his accusations.

But Jonathan was having none of this. He still
had faith in Aunt Margo. She was harsh and
firm at times, but that didn't mean she was a
killer.

Eve was the first to recover. She was a bit sad
about what the man had said. It was hard losing
someone. Eve still remembered losing Mommy,
but you were born to die, she reminded the
twins. And so, she wondered, were they still
going to take the rest of the pictures?

"Eve, how can you stand there and expect us
to act as though nothing's happened?" Joelle
wanted to know.

"Because, nothing's happened. We're all

okay. He didn't hurt us. And Aunt Margo wants pictures.''

"You're something!" Joelle shouted.

"And you're stupid!" Eve shot back.

"All right! All right!" Jonathan shouted. "Everybody back on the path! Let's get this damned picture-taking over with and get the hell back to the house as fast as we can."

"Yeah, sure," Joelle said with a hint of sarcasm in her voice. "We'll be real safe once we get back to the house."

"We don't have much of a choice now, do we?" Jonathan said, more to himself than anyone else. And Joelle had to agree. They were stuck there for two more weeks and had no place to go but Aunt Margo's.

"Matthew Soames is gonna protect us," Eve was saying once the picture-taking was finished and they were headed back towards Aunt Margo's house. "Do you think Nathan sent him?"

"No! Believe me, Eve, Nathan didn't send him!"

Jonathan heard Joelle's words and cautioned her with his mind. Eve hadn't seen what they had in Margo's chapel, so there was no use in alarming her.

"Then who sent him if Nathan didn't? He's real nice."

"Oh, he's wonderful!" Joelle said in exasperation.

"Forget it, Joelle," Jonathan said, lugging the camera that suddenly weighed 100 pounds or more. "He didn't intend to hurt us. I mean, look at how he just walked away."

"Maybe he felt outnumbered!"

"Oh sure, he was afraid of three kids," Jonathan added sarcastically. Then he turned his attention on Eve because he'd just remembered something important. "By the way, Miss Friendliness, you said something when you ran around the tree to where Soames was standing. You said you knew him from Aunt Margo's. How?"

But Eve didn't answer. Her attention span was short, as always, and she wanted no more of this. She wanted to chase squirrels and play on the way back to Aunt Margo's. Yet Jonathan persisted.

"I seen him at Aunt Margo's, that's all."

"Where?" Joelle asked tensely.

Eve looked over Joelle's shoulder, her mind transfixed on a bare branch of white, oak bark. Joelle felt she'd lost her at this point and clutched her shoulders to bring her back.

"What do you want?" Eve whined.

"You said you saw Matthew Soames at Aunt Margo's house. Where? Where did you see him?"

"He looked like the man who was standing outside of Aunt Margo's house last night. You know, the man who was hollering. He was following us through the woods. I saw him ducking behind trees, but you didn't because you never look."

"Eve, are you sure he's the same man who

was outside of Aunt Margo's house?'' Joelle asked.

"Yes. And you should, too. You musta heard what he said, those men he called to by name last night. Those were the same men he asked about now.''

Joelle stared at Jonathan, their minds locked in on the same channel. They also had seen a man outside of the gate last night, and he was hollering for his father, Aubrey Soames, and for his brother, Tom. But neither of the twins saw his face which was mostly hidden in darkness. The next question was, how did Eve know what he looked like?

Joelle took the lead and asked her outright, while Jonathan's mind wandered back to the small figure he'd seen hidden in the bushes, sneaking up on Matthew Soames and trying to get a look at his face. It couldn't have been Eve, he thought.

"How do you know it was him for sure?'' Joelle asked.

Eve sighed heavily, obviously tired of the game. They heard it in her voice when she answered. "Because, I went down near the gate and looked at him.''

"Eve, what's the matter with you? Now you're leaving the house at night to look at lunatics on the road. Jonathan, we have got to get her back home and fast!''

"I know,'' Jonathan quietly agreed, "but we have to stay here for two weeks. You know how it goes.''

"Well, we just can't. Eve has to be protected. Either we leave or Eve has to sleep in my room."

"No!"

"Eve, listen to me," Joelle half-shouted. Her fingers were biting into Eve's shoulder, but she didn't care. She had to hang onto Eve's attention. "What you've done is dangerous. Something bad could have happened to you when you left the house last—"

"Then I'll stay in my room and not let anyone in, but I won't sleep with you, Joelle!"

After she spoke, she shook herself free of Joelle's grasp and walked on down the path ahead of the twins. Joelle stared after her, while Jonathan stepped up to his sister and took her under the arm. "Come on," he said, "let's get back. I'll keep a closer eye on her, I promise. At least now we know she's growing up."

"Growing up! Jonathan, she's still a child up here," Joelle said, tapping the side of her head.

"She may still be a child in her thinking, but she's developing a mind of her own, and that's something new. Like I said, I'll keep a closer eye on her and take some of the responsibility off your back."

"Great," Joelle said with a lack of enthusiasm. "That'll give me more time to dwell on the dead man in Aunt Margo's chapel and the dead horses and the lack of blue flowers here in the woods. Also, I can now spend my spare time wondering when that Soames man will grab us again. This is all so great, Jonathan."

But Jonathan heard little of what she said. He

was thinking about the same things Joelle was except for the additional mystery in his life, something Joelle knew nothing about—the blue mist covering the lens of his camera! What had caused it, and just how would this abnormality effect the pictures he'd taken?

"Are you slowpokes coming?" Eve wanted to know, and the answer was yes. The twins were coming, only now they weren't walking with the athletic gait usually associated with teenagers. Rather, they were trailing behind like two very old, very tired people who'd suffered through one helluva bad day so far.

"By the way, Jonathan, did you happen to catch what Eve said about staying in her room and not letting anyone in? Who's she been letting in? Or was it just a figure of speech?"

Chapter Seven

MEMORIES OF THE past were still coming back to Margo, her mind stimulated by the presence of Valerie's children. Of course she'd relived the past even when they weren't there, because, as she saw it, her past was all she had. She was much too old for a future, and so, it didn't take a lot for Margo to relive the painful memories she harbored in her heart.

Yet it had been easier to hold those memories back, especially the ugly ones, when it was just Jared and herself living alone. Now, since the three Blake youngsters had arrived, the pain returned to torment her, and there was no way she could drown it out.

Margo could now recall in detail the first time she visited her father's church, the night she was blinded. Sitting alone in the den in front of a crackling fire, she rose to stir the ashes and let her gaze become lost in the burning embers.

Margo remembered that Daddy had given her a white satin dress to wear to his church. At the time it was the most beautiful dress she'd ever owned. After she put it on, some lady from Daddy's church came to the house and curled her long, black hair into ringlets, joined at the top with a bow that matched the dress. Oh, Margo did look stunning, as the nice lady said she did. But Mommy didn't think so.

Mommy was upset. Mommy rolled her hands into balls and begged Daddy to stop this madness while Margo was being dressed for church. She kept asking Daddy if he really intended to go through with this. "Go through with what?" Margo wanted to know, only Mommy wouldn't tell her. Then Mommy reminded Daddy that Margo was of his flesh. "Oh, God, you have to be insane," Mommy insisted.

But Daddy didn't listen. He just walked Margo out to the car and tried to drive away without Mommy coming along, but Mommy hopped into the front seat, and they fought all the way to the church. This was around the time Margo began to feel scared.

Once they were in Daddy's church, Margo began to feel at ease because nothing bad happened in churches, except that this church wasn't a bit like hers, the First Baptist Church. The building was different. It was a flat, one story kind of thing with no windows and no crosses on the roof. It looked more like a warehouse than anything, and the inside was different, too. Margo was used to sitting in a pew and studying the pretty, stained-glass windows.

But there were no windows in Daddy's church. It was really strange. And the walls weren't made of white plaster. In fact, she couldn't see the walls at all because they were covered with blood-red drapes, and there were no pews. The parishioners had no place to sit, but they didn't seem to mind. They just stood around in a circle and smiled a lot.

They were dressed funny, too.

As Margo was studying their black robes, Daddy pulled her away and took her to a place called the nursery where she met other children, some younger than her and some older. That's when she really felt better, when she had someone to play with. Despite her amazement at the differences in churches, she figured this one wasn't half bad, not if she could play with kids.

Only these kids were strange, too, strange like the church.

They laughed at Margo and told her horrible stories. They told her something bad would happen to her, and one of them, a boy barely two years older than herself, pointed to two babies lying side by side in a crib. When Margo went to play with the babies, this boy told Margo they were going to die and be eaten!

She recalled balling up her fists and giving him a good punch for trying to scare her. She told the boy that she'd read about Hansel and Gretel and the wicked, old witch in the Gingerbread House. So if he was using the same kind of story to scare her, he'd better forget it. Things like that didn't happen in real life.

But, as Margo later discovered, he wasn't trying to scare her with his stories. He was telling the truth.

Margo came out of her reverie and stabbed the burning logs with a poker, turning them with a vengeance. How naive she'd been! How very childish! And how very old those children in the nursery were—old in their thinking. Hell, they'd seen it all. They were beyond shock. She should have listened, and she should have run. But she stayed, only to discover that, besides those two babies, she was the feature attraction that night.

Returning to the past, while tears misted her eyes, she remembered being taken back outside, where the adults were. She remembered standing in the center of a pentagram, staring at pictures of mutated creatures on the floor near her feet. Some of them were unspeakably horrible, while others, the ones with human faces, were only a little scary.

Then she remembered how she'd spoken to Nathan when he entered the room, and how she'd listened to him and his promises of power. He had promised that there would be no pain as he wielded his ceremonial dagger, and she remembered trying to be brave, keeping her hands at her sides while her vision wandered from Nathan's face to the table behind the altar, where she saw the remains of the two babies. They both had been gutted!

And oh, she should have run then . . .

But she was only five and scared . . .

And full of hatred for Daddy . . .

And full of desire for the power she was promised.

So, when Nathan stuck the tip of the dagger into each eye, right smack into the center of each pupil, and robbed Margo of her sight, she took it like a little soldier and felt no pain as Nathan had promised, because Nathan had her hypnotized. No, she felt no pain, only that lingering, festering, inner rage at Daddy.

But she got even. She fixed Daddy really good!

Realizing she was getting ahead of herself, she stopped and went back to the night she was blinded. After Nathan stuck her, she felt something hot and wet on her face, flowing from her eyes. If only she'd known it was her blood, but she was blind by this time and couldn't tell what it was.

Being concerned about spoiling her pretty dress, she raised her hands quickly to catch some of it before it dripped, and she felt Nathan press something cold against her face as he slapped her hands away. It was a cup. She felt the rim of it against her flesh. Nathan wanted her blood, wanted it for the coven to consume.

"And now, child," he said, "you have the right to stand under the sign of the horns. You have the right to call yourself a child of the beast."

Margo had no idea what he was talking about, but the others did, those people in the black

robes with the smiles on their faces, the smiles
she'd seen before everything went black. They
knew what he was saying. Margo heard them
singing hosannas. Then Margo went to a party
somewhere in the church. She was led down a
flight of steps to a room, and she was sat down
at a table and fed cake and ice cream.

Someone let Mommy in to sit by Margo, only
Mommy didn't sit. At first Mommy just
screamed and screamed and screamed.

Later, after the party was over, Daddy and
Mommy took Margo home. Daddy was so
happy, carrying on about what an honor it was,
this gift he'd given to the coven, but Mommy
still wasn't happy because Mommy had very
little to say. In fact, Mommy had very little to
say for the rest of her life, unless, of course, she
was away from the coven and its members. Then
Mommy had a whole lot to say, but it was too
late. Margo was already blind!

Daddy was happy for a while until he came to
realize that Margo's hatred of him wasn't something that would ever go away. He figured
Margo was angry because he'd given her eyes
and her blood to the coven, and that after a
while she'd outgrow it. However, after six
months went by and Margo was still angry at
him, he became sullen and depressed.

He took to staying in his bedroom near the
back of the house for days at a time with the
door locked, as if he were afraid to come out.
Margo would hear him rocking in his rocker by
the window, talking to himself and praying to

someone named Satan for deliverance from the child.

Every once in a while, Mommy would get tired of him being locked in his room and tired of lugging meals to him, and Daddy would come out to the kitchen to eat. But he'd make Mommy lock Margo in her room first. Margo smiled at this. Doors never stopped her. Once Daddy told Mommy, "I sacrificed her eyes for power and glory, but there isn't any. Hell, woman, we're still poor. Margo's gonna have it all."

Then, late one night, Margo was taken to a Black Sabbath Mass by ladies from the church, despite Mommy's protests. Nathan was in charge that night, and Nathan called for a human sacrifice. He told the members that one of them would be avenged; one of them, who harbored a hatred, would use the powers of darkness and the pets of the beast to exact revenge. Then he added, "And a child will lead them."

And Margo knew that Daddy wouldn't make it through the night. Nathan was talking about her. *She* was the child who would use her powers to turn the beast loose on Daddy.

So, when she came home from the Black Sabbath Mass, she went straight to Daddy's room and tried the door to see if it was locked. Daddy had been rocking in his chair by the window. When he heard Margo brush against the door and saw the knob turn, he started to laugh, not a normal laugh, not like anything

Margo had ever heard before. It wasn't an amused thing, rather it was a loud, dreadful, cackling noise laced with fear.

Then Mommy came up behind Margo and put her hand on Margo's shoulder and asked her about the mass. Margo couldn't see Mommy's face or her expression, but the dullness in her voice said it all. "Don't do this," she pleaded. "Find it in your heart to forgive."

Margo turned away from the door and explained how, thanks to Daddy, she had these dead eyes. Then Margo listened as Mommy explained about the Bible, and how there was this verse that read, "Vengeance is Mine, sayeth the Lord."

Only Margo didn't know which lord she was talking about. Was it the Lord of the Christians? Or was it her lord, Satan? If it was her lord, then he—the master beast himself—was having his vengeance tonight, and Margo would help.

Margo then turned back to Daddy, still locked in his room and still laughing, and heard him gleefully explain how Margo had lost. He was in there safe and sound, while Margo was outside.

Margo raised her tiny arms and begged the master beast to help her avenge the pain she'd suffered at the hands of Daddy, and she stood back and listened while the walls of the house rumbled and shook on their foundation. She listened when the wind outside whipped up to hurricane force, carrying the enraged voices of a thousand beasts inside to assault her senses.

She listened again when Daddy stopped

laughing and screamed and screamed and screamed.

Mommy didn't go in there when the screaming stopped. Mommy put Margo to bed, then Mommy sat up for a long time and read her Bible until she found the courage to use her key to unlock the door.

Daddy's body coated the walls—his blood, his hair, bits of his flesh.

There was no skin left on his torso.

Mommy found a mass of raw flesh and knew he'd been skinned first, before his head exploded and left his shoulders and coated the walls.

An older and wiser Margo stirred the dying embers and thought of Nathan and how Nathan helped her obtain her revenge. Now Nathan lived here, up in her chapel. Nathan was an honored guest, dead though he was, and Margo hoped he was enjoying his stay.

"Should I add another log to the fire?" Jared asked. He'd come in while she was lost in her dreams.

"Yes, dear, please. I'm chilly." But then this was nothing new, this chill that racked her body and made her flesh crawl. Margo had experienced this many times in the past. It usually happened whenever she was thinking about Daddy and Nathan, and how she'd taken her revenge on both of them.

Margo was upstairs, in the private chapel she'd had built especially for her own use, starting her morning prayer, when Jared's words came back to her. It wasn't anything outlandish, yet there had been an underlying threat in his tone, and Margo didn't like it one bit.

Of course the threat wasn't directed her way, so she wasn't worried over the possibility of Jared harming her. No, the threat was directed at Valerie's children, at Jonathan and Joelle and Eve.

Pausing to genuflect in front of the altar, she approached it and lit the black candles on either side of the white bowl. Once done, she removed a canister containing sacred oils and sprinkled them around the room, praying to the four corners of the universe, praying to the four crown princes of hell—to Belial from the north, to Satan from the south, to Lucifer from the east, and Leviathan from the west.

Then she added an extra dose of sacred oils to the air, sprinkling it over Nathan's head as she did and—heard him growl? But that was impossible! Nathan was dead! In fact, Nathan had been dead for years now. He simply wasn't buried.

Studying Nathan closely, she thought there was something different about his posture. He was leaning to one side, at a more relaxed angle, and his hands had been moved. Instead of being one over the other the way Margo had placed them years ago, they were now spread apart and covering his knees. The corpse of Nathan was sitting in almost the same, exact position he often enjoyed when he was alive.

Her mouth trembled slightly when, she swore, he turned a bit and stared at her, the empty sockets in his skull burning into her with their anger. Then she stiffened her back and told herself about the dead, how once you were dead it was all over. There was no moving around, no noises coming through your lips, and certainly no turning of the head.

Moving back to her place in front of the altar, Margo tried to proceed with her rituals, but her mind was partly on Nathan and partly on Jared and his threats.

"If those three bastards get too nosy, I'm getting rid of them," he'd said. "And if they try to harm you, they're history!"

While it was true he had a right to be angry about their snooping, the same as she'd been, he still had no right in assuming they'd ever try to harm her. After all, they were Valerie's children, blood of her blood and flesh of her flesh. Therefore Jared was wrong when he threatened to make them leave.

She wondered if it came down to it—if push came to shove—would she allow Jared to run them out? Or would she ask Jared to leave instead?

No, she could never ask Jared to leave. Jared was her life, her breath, her reason for existing. She had but one road open to her; she had to keep an eye on Valerie's children and make sure they did nothing further to anger Jared. That way she could hang onto all of them.

She finished her thought while cold spasms of

fear racked her body. Nathan had made a
promise before taking his last breath to come
back for revenge, if ever he found the secret of
crossing the river called Limbo, separating the
living from the dead.

Hell, Nathan must have found a boat, she
thought, because Nathan was kneeling next to
her now in front of the altar, his lips moving in
prayer. His eyes—or rather the empty sockets
where they should have been—were open and
wide and focused on Margo's face.

But Margo never even saw him move, never
saw him rise and then fall down beside her!

Rising to her feet, Margo genuflected again
and left the room, bolting the door behind her as
she did. Then she made up her mind not to come
here to pray again. She'd have to find some
other place for her daily devotions, some place
where it was safe to kneel and close your eyes in
prayer.

But then one thought stayed with her, and she
knew she'd have to find a way of sending
Nathan back instead of finding another place to
pray. Locked and bolted doors never stopped
Margo, and they certainly would never stop
Nathan.

"Do you want me to get rid of him?" Jared
asked, suddenly coming up behind her.

"Yes, Jared, I'd like you to," she said, her
lips quivering with fear. "And by that—getting
rid of him—I don't mean that you should simply
chase him away. I want you to send him back
where he came from."

"No problem," Jared answered. "I understand. This is why your husband sent me here to begin with—to get rid of life's little pests."

Chapter Eight

DENNIS WINDSAPPLE HAD to see Margo at once. Dennis had been managing her money for the past ten years, and Margo was so wealthy that she lived on the interest from her investments and never touched the principal. And there was the problem—the principal.

Margo didn't have a will. This is where Dennis felt he'd failed her, and why he was so desperate to see her now. What if she had a heart attack and suddenly died? Then New York would be a very wealthy state, and Margo's relatives would spend the next 20 years in court fighting over their share.

Why he'd only thought of it this morning was beyond him. Usually when he came across an extremely wealthy client, the subject of a will became the most important factor in their discussion. To be fair about it, Dennis had been so beguiled by Margo's beauty when he first laid eyes on her that every sensible idea he'd ever had flew away in the face of love.

In fact, he could still see her now as she was then because she looked the same way now as she did then, so it wasn't hard to remember. Margo had been sitting in her den in front of a roaring fire, waiting for him to arrive. Bank business wasn't usually conducted this way, but when a client was as wealthy as Margo Windsor, and she wanted to keep her money local, making a house call had been a wise move on his part.

He remembered now that she'd told him to let himself in, that the front door would be unlocked. This surprised him because he expected her to have at least one servant, but she was a recluse and wanted nobody within arms reach. So he let himself in and went straight to the den and could barely speak when he first laid eyes on her. Margo was so beautiful. God, she took his breath away.

"Miss Windsor?" he'd said, his voice trembling with shock. She was in her late 50s then, old enough to be his mother, but she didn't look a day over 30. "Yes, I'm Margo Windsor," she'd answered. Then she rose to greet him with such grace and dignity that he choked on his own saliva, and when he took her hand, his stomach fluttered like a boy's on his first date.

Her hand was soft, her smile sensuous and alluring. Of course she'd been wearing her usual old maid's outfit—a black, long-sleeved dress that came down past her ankles. Her hair had been pulled back in a severe bun, but it didn't work. She couldn't hide her beauty.

Dennis stared at her and felt something savage in him stir. He wanted to rip the bun out of her hair and set it free. He wanted to take her clothing and burn it. He wanted her to look the part she was playing with little or no effort—the part of an extremely desirable woman.

And she never changed. Ten years had gone by, and she still dressed the same, still looked as young, and still made his heart flutter whenever he gazed upon her countenance.

Standing outside of her door, Dennis had already knocked several times and had received no answer. That was certainly strange since Margo never left the house. He suddenly wondered if he was too late with his suggestion of a will. What if she'd died today? Was it possible that his remembering the will and thinking of Margo at the same time had been a part of some horrible premonition?

No, she could't be dead! Margo Windsor was invincible.

But then why didn't she answer the door?

Why didn't he just go on in? Why stand out here and try to ignore those awful, blue flowers growing everywhere, growing in such an abundance that the town bore their name—Monkshood.

Perhaps it was their punishment for burning 13 possibly innocent victims at the stake, their punishment for committing crimes of extreme cruelty against their neighbor in the name of religion.

Oh God, looking at those flowers was more than he could take. He was tired of looking and remembering and waiting for the possibly dead Margo Windsor to open the door. Grabbing the knob with a trembling hand, he let himself in and stood in the oversized foyer wondering what to do next, when suddenly she was beside him.

He wanted to grab her and release her hair from its imprisonment in that horrible bun. He wanted to lift her chin and taste the sweet nectar of her sensuous mouth. He wanted to remove her clothing and make wild, abandoned love to her. But he didn't, and he wouldn't. "Hello, Margo. I'm sorry for breaking in like this, but when you didn't answer the door, I became alarmed."

"And so," she was saying to Dennis Windsapple, "you think it's a good idea to make out a will, do you?"

"Yes, Margo, it would be a good idea."

"Why? Do I look like I'm dying?"

He peered into the dark lenses covering her eyes and, seeing his own reflection, wondered what she thought when she looked back, what she thought of the middle-aged banker with the thin mustache, until he remembered that she was blind. "No. In fact, you're the healthiest creature I've ever seen."

"Thank you," she said and smiled. He loved

to see her smile, to see her mouth turn up at the corners, revealing white, perfectly even teeth, but then everything about Margo Windsor was perfect. "Will you contact a lawyer for me?" she wanted to know.

"It'll be my pleasure."

"Dennis, he'll come here by appointment only. I don't want strangers snooping around unexpectedly."

"Of course. It'll be done as you wish." He rose to leave, wishing he had a valid reason for staying longer, and watched her moving towards him, her body swaying with the rhythm of her hips. She was more beautiful now than he'd ever remembered seeing her before.

He loved her so much, and it wasn't fair that she didn't love him back. It wasn't fair that she couldn't feel his love. Maybe if she did . . . but that was absurd. Margo Windsor loved no man and needed no one. If she did, she wouldn't be living here alone in this house like a hermit, shut away from the world and everyone in it.

She would have had a man or a boyfriend or someone, even a servant. She was blind and helpless. How many times had he laid awake in bed at night and wondered about her roaming this house alone? What if a prowler broke in? Margo wouldn't be able to defend herself. What if a fire broke out? Margo would burn to death. He shuddered and followed her lead to the door, knowing that she'd rather face every danger imaginable than succumb to his love.

It was just so unfair.

"You'll be leaving your estate to the three youngsters I brought here, no doubt," he said to prolong the agony of saying good-bye.

"Yes. And a share to their father. And Dennis, there'll be something for you, too."

"That's not necessary," he said, keeping his voice steady to hide his surprise.

"Yes, it is. You've been more than a financial adviser. You've also been a dear friend, and I appreciate your efforts."

"I'd better be going. I've taken up too much of your time as it is," he said, looking directly at her, his stomach knotting from wanting her so badly and knowing it was never to be.

"It was my pleasure," she said, closing the door behind him, closing him out of her life now as she had so many times in the past.

He stood outside for a moment, his hands hugging the insides of his pockets in a gesture of defeat, and stared straight ahead, trying to think of Margo Windsor and not those terrible, blue flowers smothering her lawn. Love was painful, especially one-sided love. That was the worst kind of all.

Even if he'd loved her and lost, he would have felt some kind of satisfaction at this point. He started down the steps but stopped when he saw the three young adults coming around the side of the house. He smiled and spoke to them but got no response. They were out of breath and pale, as if they'd just gone through the worst experience of their lives.

"Something wrong?" he asked. Though they

didn't answer, he knew they were troubled just by the way they kept looking at each other and then at the ground. "Anything I can do?"

"Not really," Jonathan said tensely, and Dennis decided to drop the matter. Whatever their problem was, it was something they wanted to work out among themselves.

"Well, if you ever need me . . . and, Jonathan . . ."

"Yes, Mr. Windsapple?"

"About that incident in town. You wanted to ask me why those men hated your aunt, and I told you to wait and I'd tell you why."

"Yes, I remember."

"I just couldn't explain their hatred until you had a chance to meet your aunt. You hadn't seen her for ten years or more, and I felt it was better to see her first in order to form your own opinion of her. Then you'd see how stupid some of those people in town are."

"Why do they hate her?" he asked dryly, ignoring what Dennis had just said.

"They think she's responsible for the disappearance of several people here in town. As you can see, they're wrong. She's alone and blind and helpless. That's why I wanted you to wait."

"In other words," Joelle said, "you were afraid we'd form an opinion of her ahead of time if you told us she was a murderess."

"She's not a murderess! Those are just unfounded rumors with no basis in fact. Margo Windsor is a warm and kind person, only most people don't know her as I do because she keeps to herself. Everytime some drunk or some mental case leaves town, they try to blame her. They say she killed them.''

"You were right in waiting," Jonathan said quickly to keep Joelle from squaring off with Dennis Windsapple. "After spending two days with my aunt, I know she's not a murderess."

Dennis smiled. He was satisfied; he'd accomplished his purpose. "Well, I'll say good-bye, and if you need anything . . ."

"You'll be the first person we'll call," Joelle said, her eyes narrowed into slits. There was a cold nastiness about her, and Dennis couldn't deal with it just now.

He continued on down the steps to his car, his body flinching visibly when he heard the front door close behind him. It was as if she was shutting him out again, as if Margo had closed the door on him twice in one day. He couldn't take that, not while the Monkshood plants were still in full bloom, while everything else was dead, reminding him of burned Carl Ruttenberg and his baby daughter burning next to him.

He opened the door to his car and started to climb in, but turned first to glance back at the house, hoping for one last look at Margo Windsor, hoping to see her standing by the window. Someone *was* at the window, but it wasn't Margo Windsor.

While he couldn't see a face, he knew he should leave quickly, because there was hatred directed at him. It was strong enough to carry through the air and slam into him right where he was standing. To think he'd been inside of that house up until a minute or so ago—with this phantom who wanted him dead.

The person behind the drapes was tall and broad-shouldered. It wasn't one of the three young adults staying there. And if not, then who was it, and how long had he been living there without Dennis noticing?

Margo returned to the den and wondered why Dennis Windsapple had come here. There was more to his visit than just the subject of a will, only Dennis hadn't put it into words. He could have sent her a letter and said the same thing. Dennis was a very important man. Why did he leave his desk at the bank and make a special trip here just to talk about a stupid will?

And why, she asked herself, once she was alone and sitting in her favorite chair by the fireplace, why didn't you ask him about the incident in town? Her fists were rolled into tight little balls by this time because of those bastards at the train station. To think they'd started a fight with Valerie's children, her two nieces and her nephew.

Margo knew she should have gone to pick them up herself. She should have rented a car and had Jared drive her there. Jared would have fixed them if they'd started with those kids in front of him. But then Jared wasn't . . .

No! He was as human as . . . ?

But he had short fingers and he was getting rid of Nathan!

Rising to stand by the window and wait for

the three youngsters to come home, she saw them talking to Dennis and wondered what it was all about. Were they discussing the incident at the train station, the one Jonathan had mentioned this morning?

What could Margo do about it now? How could she make sure it wouldn't happen again before the two weeks were up and they were gone? This wasn't something she could ignore or forget. Those bastards had started with members of her family. Her pride was at stake here.

So Margo returned to her chair to dwell on what course her revenge would take.

Jared watched Dennis Windsapple for the longest time. In fact, he waited until Dennis' car had passed through the front gates and was out of sight before he thought about his newest chore—getting rid of Nathan.

Nathan was a problem now, because Nathan had found a way to come back—and Margo wasn't the least happy to see him. Margo sounded frightened, as if seeing Nathan kneeling there beside her had scared her badly when all she had to do was use her powers to send him back herself.

She could do it. She was strong enough to call up the beast to make Nathan go back to Acheron.

Yet Nathan wasn't happy in Acheron, his new home. Nathan had been put on the same level as Margo's father, who was the world's biggest whiner. "Why am I being tortured?" he constantly asked of Nathan. While Nathan tried telling him it was because the pets of the beast had nothing else to do, the man just wouldn't shut up.

So Nathan eventually became angry at Margo because Margo had sent her father there as well as Nathan. Margo had made sure they were teamed up in the same area, so it was no wonder Nathan was furious.

Jared smiled and waited until those bastard relatives of Margo's were in the den with her before he went after Nathan. It wasn't that he was afraid of Jonathan and Joelle and Eve seeing him as he was now, in his human state. Even with the shortened fingers, he wasn't too bad-looking. In fact, going by human standards, Margo thought he was handsome.

But he knew he couldn't take Nathan on as a human. He had to go through a transition and return to normal, and that would have scared anyone who gazed upon his countenance.

Bowing his head to pray to his master for strength, Jared felt his body changing and knew he was no longer human. He gazed down at his hands, at the long claws the humans called fingers, and at the bulbous tumors on them, and knew he was back to being himself again. And, Satan, he wanted this to last. He wanted to stay this way so he wouldn't have to worry about being handsome enough to join Margo Windsor in bed.

He wanted to stay like this because it was

more comfortable to him than playing the role of human, and it didn't physically hurt like the painful process of standing upright and walking on two legs when he preferred four. Of course, he'd have to stand tall in order to take on Nathan, just as he had when he'd gotten rid of Aubrey Soames and his son, Tom, along with the others he'd killed.

But that was only a temporary thing, so he could bear the pain for the ten minutes or so that it took to rip a body to shreds. He could bear ten minutes, whereas he'd been standing upright for 50 years now as Margo's lover. That was a long time to suffer, although Margo was worth it.

Going up the stairs on all fours, he realized he was dribbling saliva on the carpet. His teeth were just too large for his mouth, and he hoped Margo would stay in the den until his trail of slime dried. Otherwise she'd notice it and be inclined to investigate. She'd follow the trail to its source.

Jared didn't need those problems at this point. He had to keep his real identity a secret until her husband came back, or until her husband sent for her, which ever came first. Otherwise Margo wouldn't want him anymore, and Margo had to want him. Margo had to be kept satisfied.

Then Jared wondered what would go wrong this time. After Nathan was taken care of, he had to make the transition back to human form. Would it be short fingers again or something more noticeable this time?

* * *

"We took a lot of pictures," Jonathan was saying, trying to sound cheerful, but there was something in his voice that told Margo he was upset. She didn't ask though, figuring it was better to wait and let him tell her himself.

"Yeah," Eve said. "We took pictures in the stable—"

"The stable? Why there? The horses are gone."

"But you can still hear them," Eve said wistfully.

"By that she means her imagination is running wild," Jonathan said. "She only thought she heard them."

"Did not," Eve said, pouting.

"And we took pictures in the woods," Joelle said, speaking for the first time since entering the den.

Margo gazed at the three of them and smiled, while trying to make it appear as if she was just looking in their general direction, drawn by their voices. They were so beautiful, so innocent, and suddenly, so grown up. "We'll have to develop those pictures right after lunch. I can't wait to . . ."

The last of her words trailed off. She was about to say, "I can't wait to *see* them," but that would have been a giveaway. They would have known she wasn't truly blind. How stupid, she thought, vowing to be more careful in the future.

"Aunt Margo," Eve said, plopping down on

the footstool at Margo's feet. "We saw Matthew Soames in the woods—"

"No, Eve, don't!" Joelle cut in, but only after it was too late. Margo had heard what Eve said, and Margo was curious about Matthew Soames.

"Tell me about it. Where did you meet him? And what did he have to say?" Margo knew they'd spoken to him. Otherwise, how would they know his name? She was curious, too, because Matthew Soames was related to Aubrey and Tom, the two men Jared had run off her property days ago.

Eve spoke then, telling her story. When she finished, Margo had nothing to say. She sat and stared down at Eve, her face a mask of rage. Now the bastards in this town were coming right onto her property to warn the children about how dangerous she was. Margo knew she had to find a way to stop this.

"Why is he afraid of you, Aunt Margo?" Eve asked. "And why is he warning us about you?"

"Eve, you're being rude again," Joelle said tensely.

"Let her speak," Margo commanded. "She has a right to an answer." Then Margo felt her face soften a bit as she turned her attention on Eve. "Because," Margo began, her voice as tense as Joelle's, "he'd feel better if I moved."

"But why?" Eve asked again, resting a small, frail hand on Margo's knees.

"I don't really know why," Margo answered with a heavy sigh. "Maybe it's because I keep to myself and don't bother with anyone. Maybe if I told them all of my business . . ."

"Mr. Windsapple said the same thing," Eve said. "He said the people around here were just nosy and curious."

"Well, Mr. Windsapple's right. And another thing, Eve . . . sometimes people dislike us because we're different."

"You mean like the kids at school who make fun of me 'cause I'm not smart, Aunt Margo?"

Margo didn't answer right away. She'd never considered how much Eve was suffering due to her damaged brain, and now that she knew, she wanted to grab Eve to her breast and protect her. "Is that what happens?" she asked Eve, her voice full of emotion.

"Yes, Aunt Margo. Those kids laugh at me, but I don't care. Daddy and Jonathan and Joelle say I'm better than them 'cause I don't laugh back at them."

"And you are, my love, you surely are. Not only are you better than them, but you're special as well because you're so beautiful."

Eve smiled and broke Margo's heart with her beauty and innocence. She was so very much like Valerie. Then a funny sort of expression crossed Eve's face, and Margo thought about what she'd said—that Eve was beautiful. Now Eve would ask her how she knew if she were blind. "And Eve," Margo said quickly, "I don't know what you look like physically, but inner warmth and caring makes a person beautiful."

From the expression on her face now, Eve

seemed satisfied with Margo's answer.

"Well, now," Margo said, turning to the twins, "shall we have lunch?"

"But I wanna ask you something else first," Eve whined.

"Eve!" Joelle hissed.

"I hafta. Aunt Margo, these people in this town remind me of those people back home with the axes."

Jonathan and Joelle moaned aloud then, letting Eve know she should never have mentioned what happened back home. It was a sore spot with their father and most likely bothered Aunt Margo, too, but Margo paid them no mind. Deep inside she felt it was time the children knew the truth. After all, those men with the axes had killed their mother, Valerie.

"Sit down," Margo said to Jonathan and Joelle and waited until they did before going on. "I told Eve a few minutes ago that people sometimes dislike you when you're different, and that applies to everything in life, not just your appearance or your personality. It covers a whole, wide range of things.

"Our church was different. We didn't worship the God of the Christians. We worshipped our lord, Satan, and our church wasn't a conventional type of church building. It was different as well. So the people in our hometown hated and feared us, as though we were a threat to them directly because we did our own thing and didn't follow the crowd, so to speak.

"Anyway, out of their fear and prejudices, they decided to get rid of us, to run us out of town, but before they did, they wanted to gather enough evidence against us and our church to be able to use in court if possible. So they infiltrated our church—"

"They what?" Eve asked, her eyes wide with curiosity.

"It means they sent one of their members in to spy on us," Jonathan answered.

"Yes, Jonathan, that's true. They sent one of their members, a man, to join our group and spy on us. It wasn't fair. Why didn't they just leave us alone? We weren't bothering them or harming them in any way. And this man, this bastard, became really close to Nathan, so it wasn't hard to learn our secrets."

"And you didn't know about him?" Eve asked.

"No, dear, we didn't. Not at first. It wasn't until the night those good, God-fearing Christians stormed our church with axes that we knew he was a fraud. He led them, you see. He came into the church first and led the way. And do you know why those Christians decided to go after us with axes, why they tried to kill us and not run us out of town?"

Margo waited for one of the three to answer, but they were as puzzled now as they were over the entire incident, so she answered the question herself. "This man, the spy, found out about the prophecy and decided it was just too dangerous to let us live. So he went back and told the others, his friends in church, about the prophecy, and they came and tried to kill us.''

She stopped speaking then as the memory of that incident came back to haunt her. She could see it now as clearly as when it happened. One of those axe-wielding bastards tried to storm the nursery to kill the child of the prophecy. Valerie's children were in that nursery. Margo covered her eyes with her hands and tried not to see it again—Valerie's head leaving her shoulders and the blade of the axe covered with her blood.

''Mommy had a heart attack and died,'' Eve said in her usual wistful manner. ''And we had to leave town. But why?''

''Because,'' Margo said slowly, not hiding the pain in her voice, ''the prophecy involves one of you. It was important to protect the child of the prophecy because after those bastards destroyed our church and killed half of our members, we had nothing else left.''

''Is that why there's been an imposed silence between our families for the past ten years?'' Joelle asked. ''Why there's been no letters, no visits, no phone calls?''

''Yes,'' Margo said. ''If those men with the axes were to find any of us—say it was me for instance—there would be nothing around to let them know where you children were.''

''But . . .'' Jonathan began, then hesitated. ''Isn't the prophecy a myth? I mean, could it really be fulfilled?''

''I don't know, Jonathan. I have no answers

to those questions. In fact, I don't even know why I've told you about what happened in church ten years ago. I promised myself I wouldn't, and I also promised myself that if you brought it up, I'd swear it never happened. But maybe you're old enough to know the truth. Anyway, the three of you were involved in this.''

After Margo finished, they sat for a long time without saying a word, and the silence between them was heavy and threatened to consume them. But Margo didn't care, not at first. She was too taken with the memory of Valerie's death to be concerned with the shock of what she'd told Valerie's children.

Yet she'd made Valerie a promise, when the children were first born. She'd promised to look after them and to protect them if Valerie should die. While the elder Jonathan Blake had done a splendid job up until now, Margo was failing them by allowing their depression to hang in the air like a great beast and threaten their sanity.

"Well," she said suddenly, forcing herself to sound cheerful and carefree, "let's go have lunch. I'm starved! And after lunch we'll develop Jonathan's pictures. Okay?"

"Okay, Aunt Margo," they answered in unison and followed her down the hall to the dining room, their bodies bent and old from the truth of what Margo had just told them. Deep down inside, all three of them knew that their mother didn't just die of a heart attack as they'd been led to believe. No, one of those men with the axes must have gotten her while she was protecting her children, while she was protecting the child of the prophecy, and that was just too horrible for them to bear at the moment.

"How do we know for sure how Mommy really died?" Joelle asked Jonathan, hesitating outside of the dining room until he answered. "How do we know she was killed with an axe?"

"Beats the hell outta me," he said quietly. "But for a moment there, I almost *saw* it happening through Aunt Margo's eyes."

Chapter Nine

DENNIS WINDSAPPLE WAS back behind his desk at the bank when Matthew Soames happened by, almost unnoticed by Dennis.

After all, Dennis had a lot on his mind. Dennis Windsapple was a man scorned—scorned by Margo Windsor, the bitch!

Here he'd been pitying her for ten years because she was alone and helpless and blind. Now he discovered that she had a man in her house, and one who hated Dennis with everything in him.

Not fair, he told himself. Not one bit fair!

What could he do about it? Nothing! She had a man and sure as hell didn't need him. How come she never told Dennis about her boyfriend? Dennis was only her banker, true, but they were friends. In fact, right here in this damned and forsaken town—this town that was guilty of burning 13 innocent victims at the stake, 12 adults and one baby—he was about the only friend she had.

Now that was destroyed. Friends didn't keep secrets. Friends were open and honest with one another. Therefore, he concluded, Margo Windsor was no friend of his, not anymore at least. She'd treated him like an outsider, and an outsider he was. There'd be no more special favors like picking up relatives at the train station, no more house calls. Let her hike her ass to the bank like everyone else. Let her boyfriend drive her.

Dennis came out of his reverie when he felt a draft on his legs; the door to his office was open. He turned to find Matthew Soames, ugly and dirty as ever, plopped down in a chair in front of him. While he was tempted to tell Soames to get his smelly carcass out of his office, he was curious as to how long Soames had been there, watching him mentally vent his anger at Margo.

"Something you want?" he asked Soames. "Or is this a social visit?"

"It ain't no social visit. I came to talk to you about that Windsor woman. 'Course I didn't wanna jump right in and bother you seein' as how your mind was somewheres else."

Dennis looked at Soames and wondered where the hell this scum found the nerve to let Margo's name cross his lips. Dennis was mad at Margo, but she still had more grace and dignity than anyone walking or crawling the streets of Monkshood. "She owe you some money?"

"No, I ain't never done no work for that woman. What'dya think I am, nuts?"

"Then get to the point!"

"Well, mister banker man, since you handle her money, maybe you got influence with her, whereas the rest of us don't."

"And?"

"I wanna know what she done with my kin."

Here we go again, Dennis thought to himself. Everytime some drunk or nut either gets himself lost or leaves town, right away Margo's to blame. "Who's missing?" he asked, trying to sound as if he cared.

"My pa, Aubrey—"

"Aubrey's a drunk. He's probably out on a binge somewhere."

"He had Tom with him, and Tom don't drink."

Dennis reached under his suit jacket and released the buttons on his vest. There was a slight protrusion in the area of his abdomen now, better known as a pot belly or middle-aged spread, and it was just too uncomfortable to be "mister banker man" when it wasn't necessary with the likes of Matthew Soames. He sucked in his breath and let it out again, scratching the ridges in his flesh where the vest had dug in above the belt.

"Listen, Matthew, Aubrey's probably out on a binge like I said before. As far as Tom goes, Tom might have found himself a woman." After it was said, Dennis didn't know whether to puke or laugh. The thought of any woman, in this town or any other, bedding down with one of these dirty, scruffy Soameses was unbelievable.

Matthew Soames was quiet then, his face drawn up tight as though he was trying to swallow the excuses Dennis had given concerning his father and his brother. Then he rubbed his face with a dirt-caked finger and narrowed his eyes and Dennis knew he'd lost. Soames didn't believe him. "What about the others?" he wanted to know. "The twenty-one people who disappeared since that Windsor woman's come to town? What about them? Are they on a binge? Did they find women to sleep with?"

Dennis sucked in his breath and dug his nails into the palms of his hands. It was the same old bullshit all over again. Here we go, boys, let's lay it on Margo Windsor. There's no one else to blame, and she's so goddamn secretive and uppity. Don't stand in town and gossip with the other women. Don't screw the men. Oh yeah, she's a prime suspect, all right.

"What are you trying to say?" he asked Soames, as if he didn't already know.

"That woman is somehow responsible. She has somethin' to do with their—"

"Oh, balls!"

"She has," Soames insisted. "Every time someone gets too close to her—"

"Yeah, yeah. They disappear. The next question is—what would she be doing with Aubrey and Tom? Why would she even let them get next to her?'' She may be blind, he thought, but she still had a sense of smell.

"They hadda pass her place to get home. Maybe they stopped to . . ."

"To what? Stopped to what? Take a leak on her property? To peek in her windows? Stopped to what, Matthew? Tell me what reason they could possibly have to come in contact with Margo Windsor." And be careful, you bastard, he wanted to add, because I may be mad at her now, but I still love her.

"I don't know," Soames answered quietly. "All's I do know is that she had somethin' to do with them not comin' home a few nights ago. I ain't seen them since."

"And you wanna run her out of town."

"I didn't say that."

"No, you didn't, at least not in front of me, but you've been saying it all over town. And I'm damn sick of it. I don't wanna hear it any more."

"Are you threatenin' me?" Soames asked, his eyes narrowing even more. "What're you gonna do if I say it again, in front of you this time?"

Dennis figured he'd had enough. He wanted to kick the slime bucket in the balls and watch him squirm, but he didn't, because he was still a cut above these tooth-sucking bastards in this town. Why go down to their level now? Rising to his feet, he motioned towards the door and told Soames to leave, but not before promising to ask Margo—as ridiculous as the idea was—if she'd seen his kin.

Once Soames was gone, Dennis settled back

into his chair and thought of Margo Windsor
and her boyfriend and wondered how he'd
handle the loneliness. Dennis was a bachelor,
and while it never bothered him before, it started
to gnaw at his guts when he met Margo Windsor
and fell in love for the first time in his life.

In fact, he dreamed of one day proposing
marriage to the elusive Margo Windsor and
making her his own, because he was tired of
going home nights to an empty house and an
empty bed. Only he never quite found the
courage. Margo was ten rungs up the ladder of
success above him, so he felt he wasn't good
enough for her. Though the loneliness got worse
as the years went by, loneliness is a funny thing.
As long as there's a chance of it coming to an
end, as Dennis always hoped it would, he felt he
had something to look forward to and learned to
deal with it. Now, however, there was nothing to
look forward to. Margo had someone else. So
the loneliness that had begun with her was now
about to get worse because of her.

Oh, God, it was so unfair!

The prophecy. Men with axes. His mother's
head wheeling from her shoulders. An axe
covered with blood—his mother's blood. All of
these things preyed heavily on Jonathan's mind
now that Aunt Margo had finally told him the
truth. Oh yes, he'd seen it through Aunt
Margo's eyes, the whole bloody scene.

It now caused him to wonder if perhaps he,
Jonathan, was the fabled child of the prophecy,

but only because he'd seen the past through the eyes of another, a talent the child of the prophecy would surely possess!

No! It was too awful to even contemplate.

But then what could he think? He'd looked at Aunt Margo, and the massacre of the Satanists by the Christians came zooming into his head like pictures on a television screen. That was something only the child of the prophecy could have done. No, he told himself. Get your mind on something else, like Joelle, for instance, and how he'd keep the truth of their mother's death from her.

Joelle had been listening to Aunt Margo's story with such intensity, she didn't bother to read into Jonathan's mind. He could have kept what he saw to himself, but did he? Noooo! He had to go and tell Joelle that he almost saw their mother's murder through Aunt Margo's eyes, and wished later that his tongue had fallen out before he'd spoken those words.

Yet there was a plus side to this. Joelle never believed anything he said. Not once in the past did she ever accept his word as gospel, so why should she believe him now? Therefore, if he kept his tongue glued to the roof of his mouth, maybe, just maybe, time would erase the memory of what he had so very foolishly told her, and she'd go back to believing what she had in the past—that their mother had died of a heart attack.

Only it wasn't so simple for Jonathan. He now knew the truth and had to live with it for the rest of his life, along with this new vengeful feeling that was so foreign to him. Yes, he wanted revenge. He wanted to find the man with his mother's blood on his axe. He wanted to see his face as Aunt Margo surely must have, despite her alleged blindness.

And when he did, he'd kill the son-of-a-bitch, and it wouldn't be quick. Jonathan had visions of mutilating the bastard first with an axe, little by little, starting with the toes and working his way up to the top of his skull.

"You know," Joelle said, interrupting his thoughts. "We missed our big chance tonight."

"Big chance?" Jonathan knew that up until now Joelle had been as involved in her own thoughts as he was in his. Since he hadn't bothered to scan her brain, he had no idea what she was talking about. "Big chance?" he repeated.

"Yes . . . but hold on a minute. I wanna check something out."

Jonathan sat on the edge of his bed and watched as Joelle walked to the door and listened, then opened it to check the hall outside. When she was sure they weren't being monitored, she went on with her explanation. "Aunt Margo was in a rare mood tonight. She was being more honest with us than anyone has in a long time."

"So?"

"Well, we missed our big chance."

"You already said that, Joelle. What are you talking about?"

"While Aunt Margo was baring her soul, we

should have asked her how Nathan died and how the horses died, as well.''

Jonathan couldn't believe he was hearing this. ''She was telling us a very painful account of why we've been in hiding for ten years—and you expected more? What the hell's wrong with you?''

''Nothing!'' she answered defensively. ''It's just that she might not be so quick to tell us anything ever again. Maybe we'll leave here never knowing the full truth.''

''And maybe that would be a good idea. Maybe she'd be doing us a favor. I mean, I don't know about you, sweetie, but I've had enough! Violence . . . bloodshed . . . dead bodies. Joelle, let it be!''

''I can't, Jonathan, I just can't.'' Her eyes were on his now, his torment mirrored in her vision. ''We know about Mommy. I want to know about Nathan, too.''

''We don't really know about Mommy,'' he lied, ''so just drop it.''

Jonathan heard a knock then and was grateful for the diversion. It drove a wedge between her questions and his answers. Maybe, just maybe, it was enough to break her train of thought, and she'd let it go. ''What's that noise?'' he asked.

''It's someone knocking on the door. It's Eve.''

''How'dya know?'' he asked, wondering if Joelle could see things, too, the same way he'd seen his mother's death through Aunt Margo's eyes. If that were true, then he was no closer now to guessing the identity of the child of the prophecy than he was before. It could be Joelle, too. "Are you sure it's Eve?"

"Yes," Joelle answered tensely. "She's right next door. That's where the knocking's coming from. Why does everything between us forever turn into a battle of . . . what?"

"Wits," he answered, and rose to let Eve in.

Jonathan and Joelle saw Eve and remembered something crucial at the same exact moment, something concerning Eve. While either one might have picked up the thought from the other, they decided not to argue over who'd thought of it first. After all, it was important to stand together and not quarrel in front of Eve. Eve was developing a mind of her own and would be easier to handle if they showed a united front.

"Eve," Joelle began, as self-appointed spokesperson for Jonathan and herself. "This afternoon you mentioned staying in your room and not letting anyone in. Who have you been letting into your room, Eve?"

"That's what I came to tell you," Eve said, her eyes aglow with excitement. "He's in my room now, and he wants to see you. He's the man who followed us here from Philadelphia."

"Are we going into that again?" Joelle said, rolling her eyes in exasperation. Then she pointed to Jonathan, silently telling him to take over.

"This man's in your room, you say? And he wants to speak to us?" Jonathan asked softly.

He was as annoyed as Joelle, yet Jonathan had the ability to curse under his breath with a smile on his face, something Joelle hadn't learned so far.

"Yes, he's in my room. Come on!" Eve said, leading the way. "He's dying to meet the two of you."

Joelle walked in behind Jonathan and saw a huge, muscular man—with a short arm and no ears? Oh, lord Satan, she wanted to run. He had no damned ears! He wasn't human!

But he did have a nice smile and a beautiful set of teeth. What the hell! As long as he was smiling, how dangerous could he be?

"Joelle," he said, extending his hand in a gesture of friendship.

She was reluctant to shake hands with him until it came to her that Jonathan had just done that very same thing, and Jonathan was still alive. Before touching him, she stared into his eyes and tried to read his emotions. Surprisingly enough, his eyes, and the message written there, told her she was safe.

In fact, she found it hard to divert her gaze from his once it was locked in. Joelle had never stared this hard at a man in her life, and Joelle had never had anything to do with a man or a boy her own age, not even a date. Now she felt she'd missed out, because this man was sending messages to her with his eyes, and what she heard was stirring up emotions in her that she'd never given much thought to until now.

Not taking her eyes from his, she laid a palm against his and felt goose bumps lumping her skin. His hand had been soft and warm and—what? Sexy?

Shit, she thought, how can a hand be sexy? But it was! When her flesh touched his, something passed between them.

"I'm pleased, I'm sure," she said. Then she cursed herself for sounding so young and immature. She could have tried to make the words come out lower, more seductive.

But he didn't seem to notice. His gaze was still riveted to hers, then he scanned her face and lit up at what he saw. "I'm Garth," he said.

And I'm in love, she wanted to shout back.

"Garth?" Jonathan said, interrupting her thoughts. "What the hell kinda name is that?"

"A very old one," Garth answered, never taking his eyes off of Joelle. "It's as old as time itself. Actually, it's a shortened version of my real name, which you'd never be able to pronounce anyway."

"Garth," Eve said, a strange hint of annoyance in her tone, "tell them how you followed us here from Philadelphia. The twins don't believe me."

"I did," he said, turning to face Jonathan and Eve, but still standing close to Joelle. "And I followed you for a special reason—to protect you."

"To protect us? From what?" Jonathan wanted to know.

Garth sighed heavily and stared at the floor

for a moment. Then he looked up at them again, his muscled arms tightened into knots. He was tense, and they wondered why. "Do you know about the men with the axes?"

"Yes," they answered in unison.

"Good. Then I don't have much to explain. I'm protecting the three of you from them—in case one of them decides to try and find the child of the prophecy and kill the child before the prophecy is fulfilled."

"Which one of us is it?" Jonathan asked tensely.

Garth straightened himself up to full height before answering. He was a head taller than Jonathan, Joelle noticed, and nearly two heads taller than herself. And he was gorgeous, even without ears and hair. His skin was tan, his eyes honey brown. "I'm not allowed to reveal the identity of the child of the prophecy," he said, then held up a hand to silence their protests. "And before you ask why, it's another form of protection."

"Protection? That's bullshit! I bet you don't even know—"

"Oh, yes, I do, Jonathan. Yes, I do!"

"Then why—"

"To keep the other two from letting jealousy take over."

"Jealousy?" Joelle half-shouted. "This whole prophecy thing is a nightmare. None of us wants to be the one. What would we have to be jealous about?"

Garth smiled down at her and melted her

anger. "With the prophecy goes a great deal of power, and while you may not want it now . . . well, it's like anything else. You may not want it, but once you have it, once you try it out, you'll never want to live without it."

"And this power," Joelle said softly, "will suddenly appear on the night of Dagu's Nacht?"

"Not exactly."

"I don't understand." Her voice cracked when she spoke, and she hated the sound of it. Her passion for this man was building, and it showed. "Would you please explain it to us?" she asked.

"The chosen one was born with the power to do anything, to possess anything, to command the master beast and his pets to do his bidding." He stopped speaking then and stared at Jonathan, who was busy examining his hands, first the backs, then the palms. "You can't see the power, but it's there," he said and laughed.

"So you feel that the two of us who aren't the chosen one will be so jealous we'll try and kill the child of the prophecy. Is that it?" Joelle wanted to know.

"Yes," Garth answered softly, "I do. Family or no family, blood relation or no blood relation, jealousy is a strange creature. It can make you do almost anything."

"And the chosen one has the power now?" Jonathan asked, as if he still couldn't believe it.

"Yes. But the child is unaware because the child has never tried it out."

"So what's the purpose behind waiting for the

eve of Dagu's Nacht? I mean, why is the prophecy supposed to be fulfilled then?''

''Because on that night, the master himself will appear to confirm the fulfillment, to cement the powers of the chosen one, along with the appearance of the full moon to lend an extra measure of strength. You know how it goes. Everything has to stand on ceremony. In the meanwhile, all of you can try your individual powers to see which of you it is, but I caution you to be careful when you do. Make sure your commands don't backfire, or you'll wind up either hurting yourself or being at the mercy of the master's pets!''

Joelle gasped and felt her knees buckle. This was all too much for her to absorb. Garth, who was still standing nearby, reached out and lifted her into his arms, then he laid her across Eve's bed.

''Why don'cha carry me like that?'' Eve demanded, with the same hint of antagonism in her voice as before. ''You never pick me up!''

''Do you see what I mean about jealousy?'' Garth whispered to Joelle who nodded silently.

''Is she all right?'' Jonathan asked, pushing Garth away from Joelle. ''I can handle it from here. We usually take care of each other. We don't need an outsider.''

''But that's what I'm here for—to protect.''

''Oh yeah?'' Jonathan said, rising to face Garth squarely. ''Where the hell were you this afternoon when that Soames guy grabbed Eve? He scared us half to death. How come you weren't protecting us then?''

"I couldn't come and help you because I dared not enter those woods. You see, you were walking on hallowed ground. The thirteen Monkshood witches and warlocks are buried there, and the ground is blessed by the church to keep them in their graves, to keep them from walking the Earth, seeking revenge.''

"The thirteen who?'' Joelle asked.

"Monkshood witches and warlocks.''

"And the ground was blessed, you say?''

"Yes, as it often is to keep the dead from seeking revenge. Of course, this is usually done only when the dead have been victimized in life or killed without just cause. Then a holy man from the Christian church comes and prays to their Lord and buries crucifixes under the soil covering the graves, so that the dead will rest in peace.''

"Who killed them without cause?'' Joelle asked, fascinated by his knowledge of the history of Monkshood.

"I'll explain it to you some other time. Meanwhile, I want the three of you to relax, and remember that I'm here if you need me.''

Then he disappeared in a whirlwind of smoke that startled them and kept them silent for a moment or two. Eve, however, recovered faster than Jonathan and Joelle, because Eve was used to seeing Garth, used to seeing him disappear as fast as he appeared. When were they going to develop the pictures they took, Eve wanted to know, while Jonathan's mind raced down a wild path and zeroed in on the blue mist covering his lens.

Hallowed ground indeed, he thought to himself. Joelle had said that blue was the color of evil, and if that were true, then the blue mist didn't belong in those woods where there was hallowed ground. So where did it come from?

Why was it just sort of hanging around them when Garth dared not walk there? Why was it hanging around them when those cursed, blue flowers didn't grow there? Hallowed ground, indeed!

Garth had never given much thought to the prophecy or the meaning behind its fulfillment up until now.

But then Garth had been an obedient servant up until now, and nothing more. He was sent there by the master to protect, and protect he did. He'd spent the last ten years of his life playing bodyguard without asking questions. However, at the moment he was disturbed.

He was disturbed because this was an awful lot of power to be giving a child. True, they were teenagers and almost grown-up, but they still had childish, immature minds, hardly what one would consider wise enough to more or less take over such an important role.

Jonathan, for instance, was young and impetuous. Joelle was young and hot-headed —hot-blooded as well. He would have his fill of her before this was over. And Eve . . . Eve was young and stupid. Garth knew which of them it was, which of the three was the chosen one, and he shuddered with the knowledge of that particular one wielding so much responsibility.

It would be more than just being the gatherer of souls, more than just replacing Death. There were two parts of the prophecy, and the second part frightened him twice as much as the first.

Not only would the child of the prophecy claim the dead for their master, Satan, before they died, thus insuring a continuance of the line of evil, but the child would also have control over them after death. The child would have the power to call them up to use for revenge.

It was quite a bit different from controlling the pets of the beast, for the pets didn't always listen or do as they were told. No, the pets had minds of their own, strong ones, and often they rebelled and turned on the person giving the orders. The dead had no minds, nothing to think or reason with. The dead lacked the evil slyness of the master's pets and did as they were commanded without asking why.

Garth shuddered again as he imagined one of the three young Blakes calling up the gruesome, decayed corpses of hundreds, maybe even thousands, of dead ones to settle a dispute with some classmates or perhaps teach a lesson to someone who'd offended them.

Not one of their victims would see it coming. They'd be beaten and torn to pieces by invisible entities, controlled by a ranging child hellbent on getting even. The dead walk by night, in the dark, or else they hover in the shadows and wait. They strike when your eyes are closed, when your breath is low, and even in sleep, when you least expect it.

The child of the prophecy would also control the Six Archdemons of Hades, along with their 66 legions of demons each. If the child decided not to avenge a slight by using the silent, invisible dead ones, he could employ the ravaging forces of warrior demons who were nothing more than killing machines, who thrived on maiming and torture.

"Why, master?" Garth asked aloud, his voice small and still, carried on the crest of the night's winds storming Margo Windsor's mansion. "Why give the gift of Death to a child with a child's mind and a child's emotions? For what if this child turns his powers against you?"

Garth's own words echoed in his ears but went no further. They were lost, drowned out, beaten down in a torrent of howling wind. It wasn't just an ordinary wind, not when it shook the trees around him and bent them almost to the ground, not when it made Margo's mansion shake and rumble on its foundation.

Rather, it was the master's voice, and the master's answer to Garth's questions, telling Garth not to be concerned. He, the master beast, had complete control of the child of the prophecy. His word was the last anyone would ever hear. His word and his wishes were final!

Chapter Ten

JONATHAN WAS STILL upset about the blue mist when he developed the film, and he wasn't surprised when something showed up on it.

It was not something you could point to and say it made any sense, hell no. The only thing gratifying was that it confirmed his suspicions about the blue mist.

As he and Joelle stood and stared at the photos—Eve hadn't wanted to help and had gone to bed—he thanked Satan for having given him the sense to talk Aunt Margo out of helping them. Aunt Margo had been all set to lend a hand, but Jonathan was afraid of what they'd find in the pictures. He told her that it would be awfully crowded in the bathroom, what with three people in there moving around, and although Aunt Margo agreed, she wasn't happy about being left out. She was blind but not useless, she'd said, then she left. At the moment, Jonathan was relieved. Hell, she was old and helpless and lived alone, if you didn't count those occasional visits by her boyfriend. Why scare her with these pictures? She had to go on living here after they left.

"Who are these people standing around us?" Joelle asked.

"Beats the hell outta me," he answered.

"They sure look strange, staring at us with their eyes wide open as if they're in a trance."

"Or dead!" Jonathan blurted out.

"Do you really think so?" she asked. "Do you think they're dead?"

Jonathan snapped on the overhead light and caught a glimpse of Joelle's pale face contrasted against her black hair. Jonathan wished that he'd kept his opinions to himself. "Maybe it's just a double exposure," he said quickly to stem her fears, but it was no use. Joelle wasn't stupid like Eve, who'd believe anything he told her.

"But a double exposure is one picture on top of another. If you'd taken pictures of these people, then us, I could believe it. But there was no one around, at least not anyone we could see."

"Joelle," he said quietly, "you're being hysterical. There's a reasonable explanation for this. I just have to find it, that's all."

"Well, while you're looking for it, have a gander at this." Joelle had taken her eyes off him for one second to stare down at the endless photos lying on the counter in front of her. One particular photo caught her attention and made her face turn even paler than before. "Explain it," she said, handing the photo to him.

Reluctantly, Jonathan glanced down at the photo. It was a picture of Eve in the stable, standing in front of a horse's stall. He read the name "Chrysaor" and saw a horse behind Eve—not an apparition, but a real, flesh and blood horse! The poor devil's eyes were sloped way back, slanted upwards in fear and terror, while its mouth was pulled hideously tight over its teeth, as if the horse were screaming with pain!

"We have to talk to Aunt Margo," Joelle said. Jonathan heard her, only her voice must have been coming from the depths of a bottomless chasm because he had trouble understanding her words.

In fact, the only thing he understood at the moment was that death was all around them, all around Aunt Margo and all around this house. If they didn't get the hell out of there, if they didn't leave this house before the two weeks were up, then this creature called Death was sure to consume them the same as it had consumed Nathan and the horses and the victims in the photos, as well.

"Jonathan, two of the men in the photos—see, the ones standing behind me—they resemble Matthew Soames. One looks older than Matthew, so it must be his father, Aubrey. The other one standing on my left is about the same age. It must be Tom. We have to tell

Matthew that they're dead."

"We can't! Because then we have to tell him how they died—*if* they're dead, that is."

"Oh, they're dead all right."

She'd said it so matter-of-factly and with such conviction that Jonathan wanted to kick her know-it-all ass. "Why are you so sure?"

"Because they look funny . . ."

"Maybe my film was damaged."

"No, Jonathan, it wasn't. You seem to be losing sight of the most important thing of all. These people were nowhere around when these pictures were taken. We didn't see them. Here, look at this." She grabbed another batch of photos and held them up. "See those men and women in the background? Look at the old-fashioned clothing they're wearing. They've been dead for a long time, Jonathan, at least a hundred years or more."

Jonathan took the photos from Joelle and was tempted to torch them; he'd had enough. But that would only send Joelle into one of her famous rampages. So he looked and saw what Joelle had pointed out. Then he counted and wanted to scream.

There were 13 people in the background. There were 13 counting the baby being held by one heavy-set gentleman. If that were so, then the 13 Monkshood witches and warlocks were actually 12 adults and one baby.

"No!" he screamed. "No, they couldn't have killed a baby, executed it as a witch. No!" Then he stopped as suddenly as he'd started. After all, why was he shocked about what happened 100 years ago when his coven had done the same thing only ten years ago?

Hell, the brutality of the coven members was even worse than the brutal acts of the good citizens of Monkshood. Not only did the coven kill babies, but they ate them as well!

Jared had been on the other side of the bathroom, bathed in a veil of invisibility, listening to what the twins were saying about the dead ones in the woods. When he heard Joelle suggest they tell Aunt Margo, he panicked.

Margo Windsor had to be protected from the truth at all costs. At least she had to be protected from a truth that would drive a wedge between Jared and herself. Margo had her own version of just what "getting rid of" someone meant, and surely her version didn't include murder, as Jared's version did.

Jared struggled for an answer. He had to keep these two quiet, yet he couldn't do anything to risk losing Margo. Killing them was out, even though it was the most wonderful way of silencing a loose tongue.

And if murder was out, then what?

He scratched his chin and considered beating them until they were brain-damaged and suffering from amnesia. No, that wouldn't do. Margo would only use her powers to restore their memories.

The only other alternative, as far as he could see, was to go back to his original plan of beating Jonathan and Joelle so badly he'd scare them into silence without causing any real damage. As far as Jared was concerned, he was one step ahead because they were already scared, scared of what they'd discovered in the few short days since they'd arrived.

In fact, Jonathan was so frightened he kept trying to forget what was going on around him. He was forever telling Joelle to keep quiet and forget what she saw, as he was doing this very minute.

Joelle wanted to go running to Aunt Margo with the photos and ask her what she knew about them. Jonathan, however, didn't think it was such a good idea. "Why get Aunt Margo all worked up?" he was asking Joelle. But did Joelle listen? No! She was stubborn and unruly and had to be punished in order to teach her a lesson.

And Jared had a pretty good idea of just who he'd use to give them both a lesson. While his power wasn't strong enough to use the Walk of the Dead, he was strong enough to use the pets of the beast. Once called up, Jared was the only one who could control the pets, for the caller was the controller. He alone would decide when enough was enough.

Raising his hands high overhead, he called first to the master beast. Then he saluted the four corners of the universe and the four gods governing each. He hailed Satan several times, then asked his master to send up the jackals and the trolls, the strongest and vilest creatures that

Jared could think of on such short notice.

These would be his lesson teachers, and with beasts like these doing his bidding, once is all it would take.

Joelle wasn't sure just exactly what was happening when the first blow was struck. All she knew was that someone had just punched her in the abdomen, causing her knees to buckle. She fell to the floor in front of Jonathan and stared up at his startled face.

"Joelle, what's wrong . . ." he began, before the wind was knocked out of him, and he joined her on the floor.

Then something hard and awful came across Joelle's face, striking one cheek and the side of her nose. She felt tears welling up as her mind shot back to what Garth had told them about the Walk of the Dead and how they beat you while masked by invisibility.

This was something that only the child of the prophecy or someone equally as strong could conjure up, and since she was there with Jonathan, that left Eve! What a horrible thought—that Eve was the chosen one!

Joelle winced and cried out when the sensation of a foot connecting with the small of her back caused her body to jump involuntarily. Jonathan reached out for her and screamed as well when an invisible entity pummeled his groin. He placed his hands over the area to protect himself and watched as Joelle rolled past him, slamming into the base of the toilet bowl.

Someone had obviously kicked her again with such fury she was like a rag doll in their hands.

Jonathan realized then that he was bleeding from the mouth and nose. He also realized that they needed help, someone to stop these invisible entities who were beating them like raving maniacs, but he couldn't scream. His throat was constricted with fear. Joelle was screaming though. "Aunt Margo!" she called. "Oh, lord Satan, help us!"

But calling for Aunt Margo and Satan did little good. It was useless. Time and again she and Jonathan were either punched or kicked, and Jonathan's head was being banged and slammed against the tile floor, his head rolling back and forth on his shoulders as though it belonged to a stuffed toy and had no substance.

Someone was trying to kill them . . . Eve! Was it Eve?

Joelle was pushed over onto her back then and her face was slapped so many times it felt as if her skin was raw, as if her flesh had swollen to the point where she feared it would burst. Her vision was blurry, and her brain was being overtaken by a strange kind of blackness. She was being killed. She was sure of it. Both she and Jonathan were going to die and neither of them could do anything to help themselves or stop the invisible, senseless assault.

Jared stayed on the other side of the door and listened and was pleased with the noises coming from within. The twins were being beaten as he'd commanded. Maybe, just maybe, it would be enough to teach them to keep their bastard snooping to themselves.

"Call it off!"

Jared heard the voice but thought he'd imagined it. He was still inside of his veil of invisibility and couldn't be seen by anyone human, other than Margo, but the voice belonged to a man. Garth! He suddenly remembered Garth and turned to find his bald adversary with the short arm standing behind him, also clothed in invisibility.

"Call it off!" Garth said again, in a low, controlled, emotionless voice that grated on Jared's nerves.

"And what if I don't?" Jared asked and smiled. "What do you intend to do about it?"

"Do you really want to know?" Garth asked. "We're equal in strength. Do you wish to take me on?"

As Jared thought about the meaning behind Garth's words, he listened to the screams coming from inside of the bathroom, the screams that were growing fainter now. He quickly calculated his chances in a hand to hand battle with Garth—and decided to call it off.

Raising his hands over his head, he commanded the pets back to Acheron. All was still and silent inside of the bathroom once again, except for the agonized sound of two teenagers who were crying hysterically.

"Try it again and you'll regret it," Garth said, before leaving Jared's side to walk through the bathroom door to help Jonathan and Joelle.

"Maybe," Jared said. "We'll see." Then he stepped back even further into the shadows when Margo entered the room, her long, black dress whipping up around her ankles as she ran. She was out of breath and ready to faint from the excitement of hearing the twins screaming.

Hugging the wall, he dared not make a move until she was inside of the bathroom. While it was true that he was still invisible, Margo had powers. Margo could see when she wanted to, and Margo might have seen Jared standing there, hiding in the shadows. If she saw Jared, she might have been able to guess that Jared was responsible for the beating the twins had just taken.

Then she wouldn't love him anymore, and Margo had to love him, had to want him. Jared, in return, had to do everything in his power to keep her happy. After all, isn't that what her husband wanted when he ordered Jared to "go and take care of my wife!"

Margo was still shaking when she climbed into bed next to Jared. He was asleep but she could have easily awakened him. Still, there were no passions in her now, if one didn't count the raging anger that continued to make her tremble long after it was over.

She'd found Jonathan and Joelle in Jonathan's bathroom, bloody and wounded. She thought she'd faint at the sight of them—so much blood—but she didn't. No, she was Margo

Windsor! She was strong, the one to be leaned on.

Covering her mouth to stifle the sounds of her crying, she stared at the moon outside of her window and thanked her god for keeping her steady when she was needed the most. The twins had to be helped. Their wounds had to be cleaned and healed. Then they had to be sedated and put to bed. They'd mentioned these invisible entities who had allegedly beaten them.

Margo didn't believe them, not at first, not until she sensed someone standing close by, watching her every move. She heard someone breathing and knew it wasn't one of the twins. Was this one of the creatures they'd spoken of? She waited for it to strike her, but it never did. Whatever it was, it stayed in its invisible world of darkness.

Crying aloud then despite her attempts not to, she cursed the darkness and the world she'd willingly entered where darkness was worshipped above all else. Turning away from Jared, she tried to make sense of everything that had happened since Valerie's children had entered the picture. For the life of her, she couldn't.

"They'd been taught to worship the powers of darkness," she moaned, "and the darkness and the creatures hiding therein turned on them. Why? It doesn't make sense."

How could the twins have been beaten and physically abused by creatures they knew well by name? They'd spent their lives studying about

these creatures and how to control them. The
twins learned it all in church. They read the
coven bibles, attended worship services and
youth group meetings.

So how did this happen? Why did those
bastards, those entities of the dark world of
Acheron, attack her family? And why did they
imagine they'd get away with it when Margo had
the power to make them regret their actions?

Margo would make them suffer, there was no
doubt about that. The only thing troubling her
now was finding the method of torture she'd
demand in retaliation. It had to be good, and it
had to be painful. It had to be lasting, enough to
teach those bastards never to harm her family
again.

"But they had to have been called up," she said
aloud, and shot up in bed as though she'd been
struck by lightning. "They wouldn't just take it
upon themselves. They never do! Someone
ordered it!"

Eve? Could it have been Eve? After all, she
wasn't there when it happened. She was in her
bed, conveniently sound asleep, unless she was
pretending to be asleep when Margo went in to
check on her. And Eve wasn't touched! Not one
hair on her head had been harmed.

Why on Earth would those creatures attack
the twins and spare Eve? If they had it in for
Jonathan and Joelle, then they surely would
have beaten Eve as well. Eve was one of
Valerie's children, and yet, Eve was spared,
causing Margo to again wonder if she was the
one who'd summoned the pets.

Then, as quickly as the suspicions about Eve came to her, they vanished. Eve would never do anything to harm her own sister and brother, her own flesh and blood. Besides, she wasn't smart enough to cast a spell, to conjure up a few demon beasts for revenge.

If it wasn't Eve and it surely wasn't the twins themselves, then the only other person left was Jared!

No, Jared wouldn't harm them and chance bringing Margo's wrath down upon his head. So it wasn't Jared . . . but there was no one left to blame for this. Rising from her bed to stand at the window, she felt her mind racing for answers, and yet there were none. Someone had called forth the master's pets, someone who was in this house at this very moment, and she couldn't figure out who it was.

This part of it was as important as punishing the master's pets, for the person who'd used them had to be punished as well.

If she could only clear her head enough to be able to use her powers to scan the minds of the inhabitants of this house, then she'd find the answer. But she was too upset, too overwrought from the violence she'd witnessed this evening.

She thought of going to her chapel to meditate, but Nathan was there. Nathan! Maybe Nathan sent the beasts. While it was true that Jared had sent Nathan back earlier in the day, Nathan had the power to obtain revenge from the other side, across the River of Limbo.

What better way to fix Margo, to have his

revenge against her, than to beat those poor, dear, sweet children and watch her suffer at the sight of it. If that were so, if Nathan was the one, then Margo would fix him now as she had so many years before.

How would she do it? It had to be good so that Nathan would never forget her, and it had to be good so that Nathan would think twice before messing with anyone she loved ever again.

"Darling."

Margo heard Jared's voice and turned to find him sitting up in bed, his eyes aglow with passion. There was no mistaking why he'd called to her. "Did I wake you up?" she asked.

"No. The need for you did."

"I don't know if I can. I'm so upset." She'd never refused him before, but then nothing like this had ever happened before. Jared remained silent for a moment, then rose and joined her at the window, his body naked and alluring and perfect.

He was perfect in every sense of the word. Even his fingers were perfect. They were all the same length now from what she could see of him in the light of the moon, wedging in through the window behind her. Oh, yes, he was perfect . . . almost . . . except for one thing. Two toes were missing from his left foot! He had a big toe, a middle toe and a pinky toe; the two in between were gone.

He wasn't wobbling or walking funny like someone without a few toes normally would, so she really wouldn't have noticed that they weren't there if she hadn't been looking for a deformity. Now that she'd found one, the truth came to her with the force of a slap in the face. Jared wasn't human, nor had he ever been, not now, not ever.

Margo tried to keep her body from shaking as her lover, the man who'd been sent by her husband, the man she'd shared her life with—No, not the *man,* you idiot, she told herself, *the demon!* Jared was a demon!

This wasn't fair. Everyone else in her life had been a sort of disappointment so far, and now Jared was as well. Her life was over, because she'd rather die than go on without Jared's love and support.

"Darling," he repeated, unaware of her inner turmoil. "Come to bed."

But she couldn't—not with a demon! And yet, he was nibbling at her ear. Then his lips found their way to the back of her neck, while his hands worked their magic on her body. Oh, how she wanted him! Demon or no demon, he could still stir up this lustful hunger inside of her.

Besides, he *looked* human.

When Jared moaned heavily and lifted her into his arms and walked back towards the bed, she didn't resist. Jared thought so much of her that he had been pretending to be human for the past 50 years, and, as the old saying goes, two can play the same game. Now it was her turn to go along with it.

After all, she had nothing else. Jared was it.

Matthew Soames heard dead silence when he pried open the front door to Margo's mansion and listened to see if anyone had heard him. Matthew was looking for his kin—for Aubrey, his father, and Tom, his brother.

Not that he expected to find them here, inside of her house, not alive anyway, but at least he might be able to uncover a clue as to what happened to them. Then he could go to the authorities and have this bitch put in jail where she belonged or have her run out of town. Either one sounded good to Matthew.

He knew he was taking a chance being in this house called the lair of the damned by most of the folks in town. At the moment, he would have preferred to be anywhere but here, but Matthew figured he had no choice. Nobody wanted to help. Folks listened to him about how this Windsor woman musta done in his kin, and yet they were all too scared of her to help him investigate.

In fact, the only one who wasn't afraid of her was Dennis Windsapple. That was why Matthew had gone to see him earlier in the day, only Dennis didn't believe what Matthew told him.

For Matthew, that was his last chance at seeking help. Now he had to do it himself. Frightened though he was, he had to investigate and find the truth. Closing the door behind him, he stood in the foyer and scanned the interior of the house. Then he put a hand to his mouth to stifle the urge to whistle.

This woman had money! He saw the tapestries on the walls, the crystal chandeliers, the heavy carpeting, and felt instant envy. Matthew had never seen anything so elaborate in real life, not even in the movies. She was loaded, all right, and he wished to hell he'd brought a bag or a sack with him.

She had all kinds of silver ornaments lying around, stuff he could have easily carried away and hocked or sold. The shit was real silver from the looks of it, some even encrusted with gold! One load of this and he'd be set for life.

For one minute he was almost tempted to forget about Aubrey and Tom and run home to fetch a sack. Then he sighed heavily and thought about it some more. Aubrey and Tom were kin. He had to take care of his original business first. Besides, he could always come back later and help himself. He'd gotten into the house very easily this time, and if he could do it once, he could do it again.

Stepping forward into the main part of the house, he shot a look into the den and decided he'd go there last. The upper part of the house was probably where the evidence was hidden, or where she was keeping his dead kin if she hadn't buried them yet. He'd start upstairs and kinda work his way down.

He'd kinda ignore the movement in the shadows around him. This was a big house, and big houses were fairly spooky. Naturally he'd see things. He knew this before he walked in, and he had to remember it now. The moving shadows were just that—moving shadows and nothing else. They were empty corners filled with illusions.

Matthew was in front of the staircase by this time and decided to just go on up and search for his evidence. Once found, he'd take the evidence and leave, but he wouldn't go to the police, not right away at least. If he did, then there'd be cops swarming all over the place. They'd come here and arrest that Windsor bitch and seal the house, and Matthew would never have a chance to come back and fill his sack with goodies.

Taking it carefully and quietly, he climbed up one flight, then another. He wanted to start at the very top and work his way down. He was doing a good job of it, moving right along and making no noise. Also he was ignoring the feeling that he was being watched, at least he felt there was someone watching him.

'Course it could have been another illusion like the moving shadows on the ground floor below. Big houses were full of illusions, he told himself, only this one was almost real. It was so real, in fact, that Matthew was afraid to stop and turn around. He was afraid there'd be someone standing behind him.

Matthew had been standing very still, just listening and waiting for his knees to stop quaking, when he noticed two things. Noises were coming from the other side of the door in front of him, and a light was streaking under a door down the hall.

Sneaking up to the first door, he put his ear to

the keyhole and heard a woman moaning with passion. Then he smiled because it sounded as though Margo Windsor was getting it and liking it, too. Well, he thought, that oughta keep her busy for the next ten minutes or so, just long enough to give him a chance to have a look inside that room down the hall.

The light under the door made him curious. Lights meant that someone was in there. Since Margo Windsor lived alone, except for this man screwing her, maybe this was where she was keeping his kin. If so, all he had to do was to take them and leave—if they were still alive.

Approaching the door at the end of the hall, Matthew stopped outside, listened and heard nothing. There was dead silence coming from within, and this bothered him more than anything. The lights were on, but why wasn't there any noise? Unless she had Aubrey and Tom in there tied and gagged, and if they were gagged, they couldn't talk.

Without thinking about it twice, Matthew turned the knob, opened the door and felt the fear in his heart explode, sending fragments of horror to his brain. This was a church, at least it looked like the inside of a church. There was an altar, but there was a bowl on it, with a dagger lying across the top and a whip wound around its base. There were black candles on either side of the bowl.

Oh, God, there was a skeleton dressed like a monk in white robes, sittin' in a chair next to the altar, and the skeleton was smiling at him!

Matthew choked on a mouthful of accumulated saliva at that point and came out of his shock. The first thing he thought about was running. He had to get the hell out of there and fast. He had to leave this house, and he had to forget about his kin and about his sack of goodies as well. This was a demon's lair, a house of pure evil. Margo Windsor was pure evil, and she was dangerous.

If she'd killed his kin, then so be it. His investigating days were over. He didn't want to die, not here. All he wanted at the moment was to get out of the Windsor Mansion. "Do you hear me, God?" he prayed inside. "Get me outta here, and I'll never come back. I'll leave things be, and I won't tell anyone what I've seen." Anyway, who'd believe him?

"You never know, Matthew. You just never know."

Matthew heard the voice coming from behind him and froze, his heart skipping several beats before it started up again. Someone had just made a remark about what he'd said in his head. "Not possible!" he told himself.

"Really?"

Oh, shit, they was doing it again. Then he thought about the voice he'd heard and how it didn't sound like an old woman's voice, so it wasn't Margo Windsor. It was a young person, only he couldn't make out if the voice belonged to a male or a female. Hell, she had those kin visiting her, the boy and the two girls. It could have been one of them.

If so, kids were generally pushovers. Maybe he could lie his way outta this. He could tell this kid he was drunk and didn't know what he was doing here. However, the incident in the woods shot back into his head, and he knew it wouldn't work. Matthew had told those three kids that he was looking for his kin. Then he had shot his mouth off about their Aunt Margo because he figured they were different, not crazy killers like her.

Now what, he wondered, turning slowly to face his fears head on. He almost fainted when he saw the black monk's robe, the cowl pulled over the face. "Who are you?" he asked.

"Why is my identity so important?"

"Because I wanna know who's gonna be doing the killing before I die. Shit, I'm entitled to that much."

"You're entitled to nothing!" the voice answered. "You're an intruder and have no rights. Besides, what makes you think I'm about to kill you?"

"Well, ain't you?" he asked, taking notice of the hint of antagonism in his own voice. His fears were making him angry, a foolish thing to happen now when his life was on the line. He should have been pleading, he thought. "Aren't you gonna kill me?" he asked in a different way this time, keeping his voice timid and respectful.

"No."

"Oh, God, thank you," Matthew said and fell back against the frame of the door as a wave of relief passed over him. But it was short-lived, as he soon realized when the robed and hooded figure continued to speak.

"I'm not about to kill you, but you will die."

"Please! Please don't kill me! I'm sorry for what I done, breakin' in here and all. Please let me go, and I'll never come back again. I promise!"

"It's too late for promises, Matthew."

Again Matthew listened to the young person in front of him and tried to recognize the voice through his fears. He'd spoken to all three of them in the woods today and should have known the voice. Yet it was still neither male nor female. Somehow it seemed a crazy combination of both. "I'm gonna scream and let your aunt know what you're doing!" he shouted as the idea came to him. Maybe the kid was afraid of the aunt. Maybe the aunt was stronger.

"Go ahead and scream. You're going to die whether you do or not."

Matthew opened his mouth but nothing came out. His vocal cords were frozen. He couldn't scream, couldn't speak, couldn't make a sound of any kind, and he knew that he couldn't because this kid had done something to him, something to stop him before he started. This kid had powers, strange ones, the kind Matthew had heard about when the men in town got together in front of the general store and told horror stories.

Matthew's body was trembling visibly by this time. Though his voice was gone, he still had legs and could run. He tried, only his legs wouldn't cooperate. They wouldn't listen to the command from his brain telling them to move.

This was the end, all of his options having been exhausted. He had no choice now but to stand where he was, in frozen, horrified silence, and think about his coming death. He had no choice but to listen to the kid laugh and explain how he'd die—and it was just too awful for words.

"You've come here searching for your kin, and the effort was a good one. Therefore you've earned the right to see them once more before you die."

As Matthew watched helplessly, the robed and hooded figure in front of him bowed its head, crossed its hands over its heart and prayed in some crazy, foreign-sounding language. Then he heard the front door downstairs open and close, and two sets of footsteps began climbing the stairs to the third floor.

They weren't ordinary footsteps. He wasn't listening to the lively gaits of Aubrey and Tom. No! From the sound of it, he was listening to a couple of old, tired people, dragging their feet and shuffling up the stairs.

Either that, or it was two dead men coming his way.

No, that was impossible!

Then it happened, and Matthew became aware of the powers of the young one in front of him, the powers to call up the dead. He looked at Aubrey and Tom, at their half-decayed bodies and faces, walking slowly, shuffling down the hall towards him—and knew they were not of this world. The young one had summoned them here!

As Matthew watched them approaching him, he felt tears of angry indignation welling up inside. These bastards in this house had killed his kin, and now they wouldn't even let the poor devils rest. They had them walking around, probably for their own entertainment.

"Not entertainment, Matthew. No. I had something else in mind," the young one said, waiting until the two corpses were beside him. Then the young one spoke again, two words this time. Two words were all that was said, but for Matthew, it was the end. "Kill him," was the command to Aubrey and Tom.

While Matthew waited for the two to close in, he stared at the murderous rage in their eyes and wondered why they didn't know him and stop. Then he thought about what the young one had said in the beginning, and he smiled. At least the kid hadn't lied to him. The kid said he wouldn't kill Matthew, but that Matthew would die. At least the kid had spoken the truth.

Chapter Eleven

MARGO HAD SHOWERED and gone back to bed with Jared, but she still couldn't sleep. Her nerves were dancing under the skin with rage. Jonathan and Joelle had taken a terrible beating. Of course she'd used some of her powers to make them heal faster, but it was the beatings themselves that had her so upset.

Overwhelming desire for revenge against Nathan had her upset, too. Nathan was about to learn the true meaning of pain, just as Margo had shown him that same meaning years before.

After turning from side to side a few times and knowing she couldn't sleep, Margo rose to go downstairs for a snifter of brandy to help her relax. Grabbing her robe and slippers, she put on her dark glasses and started down when she noticed the door to her chapel was open. Someone was lying on the floor in front of it, lying in what looked like a pool of blood!

Bowing her head, she prayed silently to her lord, Satan. She couldn't make out who the body was, and her only wish was that it wasn't one of Valerie's children.

And it wasn't, she noticed, once she was standing over the corpse, staring down at the body of a man who'd suffered terribly before he died. In fact, he'd been torn and slashed with such fury she might have mistaken him for Jonathan if it weren't for the clothing he was wearing. Jonathan wouldn't have been caught—dead?—in the black, dirt-caked trousers and shirt worn by the dead man.

As she stood there, trying to deal with the shock of finding a dead stranger in her home, she thought about the incident in the bathroom with the twins. Was this poor creature a victim of the pets of the beast, too? Had they torn him apart after they'd finished with Jonathan and Joelle?

Then she wondered what he was doing there. How had he gotten into the house? Deep inside she knew her questions would never be answered, not by this man at least.

"Margo?"

Turning slowly to face Jared, craving the strength from his body to take for her own, she couldn't answer. She just stood and stared, as though she expected him to tell her what this was about, but how would Jared know when he'd spent the last hour making love to her?

"Margo?" he repeated softly, his gaze now focused on the body at her feet. "Are you all right, dear?"

"Yes. I'm fine, only he's not," she answered, pointing at the body.

Walking to her side, Jared took her into his arms and cradled her for a moment. "What happened?" he asked.

"I don't know. I was going downstairs for some brandy, and I found him lying here. The door to the chapel was open."

"You should have woken me up," he scolded. "I'd have gotten the brandy. Then you wouldn't have seen this." When she didn't answer, he pulled away from her and brushed his lips against the side of her face gently, as though he were handling a child. "Now listen to me. I want you to go on downstairs as if nothing happened. You hear me, Margo?" She nodded silently. "And while you're gone, I'll get rid of the body. Then I'll meet you in the den. Okay?"

"Okay." Forcing a half-smile, she left his side and never turned to look back. There were so many mysterious things going on around her without finding a brutally murdered man in her hallway. She didn't want to think about this any further until Jared was by her side and could help her find the answer.

Margo put some logs into the fireplace, lit them, and had her brandy in her hands by the time Jared joined her in the den. While she was waiting for him, she thought back to the wonderful way he'd calmed her down, how he wrapped her in his arms and kissed her and suggested she get her own brandy while he disposed of the body. He was trying to spare her.

Demon or no demon, he was the best thing that ever happened to her. He took such good care of her; her happiness and tranquility were important to Jared. Odd that a demon could show that kind of emotion, especially when he displayed so little at finding the body.

Margo had gone into shock when she saw the corpse, but Jared stayed calm and cool, saying he'd dispose of the body as though it were something he did everyday. The poor, dead creature she'd discovered had died so brutally that he didn't even have a face left. Some of his limbs had been separated from their joints, and his throat was cut.

And there was Jared, calm and cool and collected. How come, when he showed so much affection for her? He was capable of sympathy, so his lack of emotion couldn't have had anything to do with his genetic makeup—with his being a demon.

"I don't give a damn about anyone but you, Margo," he said, coming into the den so suddenly she didn't realize he was even there. "And I'm sorry you found out about me."

"If you didn't read my mind when you shouldn't, then it would have remained my secret." She rose and poured a brandy for Jared, waiting on him for a change.

"Where does this leave us?" he asked, his tone full of uncertainty.

"I knew the truth before you made love to me

tonight. Does that answer your question?'' Margo asked, standing in front of him with the brandy in both hands. Nothing was said between them for a moment. Margo was staring at him, taking a hard look at the man she'd spent so many years with. Jared was, in turn, staring back, waiting and wanting her to say more.

"I don't know what to think about what's gone on here tonight,'' she said, handing him the brandy. "The children were beaten up, and that man was killed.''

"Then maybe you shouldn't think about those things. Maybe you should concentrate on something else.''

"Like what, Jared? Do you want me to concentrate on us? Are you looking for my approval?'' Asking such a question was senseless. From the expression on his face, she already knew what he wanted. "I love you, Jared.''

"Margo!'' he said, suddenly unaware of the brandy she'd handed him. He dropped it and grabbed her. "You never said it before. I always wondered.''

"Well, wonder no more. I love you now as I've always loved you.'' His body was tense against hers. His hands trembled when he caressed her. She found herself waiting for him to say the same, to say he loved her, but he didn't. Then she remembered that demons were incapable of love. The majority of them could only experience hatred. The fact that Jared felt anything for her at all was a small miracle.

"Come, let's have our brandy," he suggested. "I'll pour myself another."

Returning to her favorite chair in front of the fireplace, she watched him moving about the room. He was wearing a bathrobe over his pajamas and slippers, and she now found it odd to see him dressed like a man. In fact, he always dressed like a man. For the first time since discovering the truth, she wondered what he looked like when he wasn't human.

But something distracted her thoughts, and the picture she'd begun to build in her mind was gone. There was blood on his robe, blood from the body he'd disposed of. The sight of it made her wonder what he'd done with the body, only she couldn't ask and didn't really have to. Jared read her mind again and answered without thinking. What he said drove a wedge between he and Margo that signaled the beginning of the end of 50 years of love and passion.

"I threw it in the woods behind the house along with the others. I can't enter those woods because they're on hallowed ground, so I just flung it as far as I could."

Margo listened to him, listened to nearly every word, but her brain stopped making sense of it when the phrase, "along with the others," was spoken. What others? While she tried to ask, again there was no need. Jared had ceased talking long enough to think about what he'd said. He was silently staring at her now, his face draped in shock.

He'd exposed her to the truth. There was nothing more to say, nothing he could say to mend the crack in their relationship. It was over, 50 years lost in the five seconds it had taken him to utter a thoughtless statement.

Margo threw her brandy at his feet and started to leave but couldn't. Jared crossed the room with such swiftness it made her head reel. He grabbed her and refused to let go. "We have to discuss this," he kept saying over and over while she tried to cover her ears and not listen. "Margo, please!" he pleaded.

She didn't want any explanations, not from him. Her world had just gone crashing to the depths of hell, and she wanted to be alone to wallow in her misery. She tried to push him away as his words echoed in her brain, threatening her sanity. On top of the other things that had taken place tonight, she couldn't take any more. "Jared, stop!"

"Not until you listen!"

She knew she'd have to, whether she liked it or not. Jared was strong; Jared had super demonic powers. He could hold her there for an eternity if he wanted to. "I'll listen, but it won't change how I feel."

Leading her back to her chair in front of the fireplace, he made her sit. Then he paced back and forth and said nothing at first. She could see from the workings of his jaw that he was trying to choose the proper words. There was a lot at stake here. Finally he stopped and stood near her, blocking her path to the door, she noticed, and began to speak—and Margo wished he hadn't.

"When your husband sent me here, it was to

keep you safe at all costs. If that meant killing
people to insure your safety and happiness, then
kill them I did. And before you comment, let me
finish! You know the people in this town and
how they think. You're an oddity because you
live alone and don't bother with them.
Sometimes oddities are curious things; people
love to stare at oddities. They love to get close to
them. So when they got too close, when they
threatened your privacy, I killed them—"

"Just to keep them from staring at me? You
killed them to stem their curiosity? That doesn't
explain much, Jared." Her voice was cold, her
words biting, her heart torn to pieces.

"Margo, it wasn't just to keep them from
staring. It was to silence them, to keep them
from saying ugly things when they got too close
to you. And I had to kill. Frightening them
wasn't enough, don't you see? The people who
came here . . . if they did it once, they'd do it
again. They'd never stop. You'd be driven crazy
by their constant badgering."

"So you killed them whenever I said to get rid
of them?"

"Yes, but I did it for—"

"How many, Jared?"

"By last count twenty-three, including
Aubrey and Tom Soames."

She listened to his answer and felt tears
stinging her eyes. There were 23 people flung
into those woods out back, 23 dead people,
killed to keep them from staring at her. "Eve
asked me earlier this evening if I knew why the

residents of Monkshood hated and feared me, and I had no answer. Now I do. They think I'm responsible.''

"The hell with what they think!"

"And the hell with you too, Jared, the hell with you, and when you go, when you leave . . . oh, no, you couldn't have! Jared, the horses! Eve told me she heard wailing noises coming from the stables. I had no idea what those noises were, but now . . . Jared, you killed people when I told you to get rid of them. . . .'' She stopped speaking and put her hands to her mouth as a wave of nausea made her gag.

"Are you all right?" he asked, his voice full of concern.

Margo didn't answer right away. She couldn't. Her thoughts, if true, were just too awful for words, but she knew she couldn't stop. She needed the whole truth, no matter how painful. She took a deep breath and asked a terrible question, one she wasn't sure she wanted the answer to.

"After Ben Anderson, the blacksmith, crippled my Arabian, I was so depressed I told you to get rid of him, to get him out of my sight, and the other horses as well. I didn't want to look at the others. I didn't want any reminders of Chrysaor. Jared, did you . . . ?"

"Yes."

"*All* of them?"

"With a machete!"

Margo tried not to scream then, but she did.

Throwing her head back, she screamed and howled her outrage and wanted to kill Jared, to get rid of him as he'd gotten rid of the others. Those wailing noises Eve heard in the stable were the tortured wailings of her horses, wailings that had hung in the air and lingered long after they were dead.

Jared came to her then and tried to comfort her, but she pushed him away. Jared was an untouchable thing to her now—a demon, a dead animal, a representative of the evil men do in the name of love. She vowed to keep him away from her for the rest of her life.

But Jared wouldn't have it her way. He couldn't. "Your husband sent me, and he wants me to keep you happy," was all he kept repeating over her protests.

"Damn my husband to hell! The only person I ever wanted killed was my father for giving me to the coven so that Nathan could blind me. I didn't need my husband to send you here to slaughter every human being I ever came in contact with. I didn't need you here to take responsibility for the senseless killings of my horses. Where did you get off doing those things? Who the hell do you think you are? And as far as my husband goes—"

"Would you like to see your husband?" Jared asked. He was calm now, but not in a normal way. "Do you want to see him?" he repeated.

"Why? Is he here?" she asked. "Did the bastard finally decide to put in an appearance after fifty years?"

"No, he's not here, but I can show him to you anyway. He doesn't have to be present for that." There was something about Jared now. He was angry and resentful; he seemed to want revenge. The stranger she'd slept with for the last half century wanted revenge against her. Margo should have stopped him, but she was curious. And, like the townspeople, she paid for her curiosity.

"Close your eyes, Margo, and see him through me."

Doing as she was told, Margo closed her eyes and was suddenly transported back in time to her wedding day. . . .

Valerie was nervous, more so than Margo, even though Margo was the bride. Giggling and speaking fast and making no sense at all, Valerie centered the pearl tiara on Margo's head, then adjusted the veil. "Oh, you're beautiful," Valerie said.

Margo wished to rush through this part of the past—Valerie was dead now, and her death was still so painful—but Jared would do this his way; Jared would take his time.

Valerie was making sense now, her words spoken out of a deep sense of sympathy for Margo's blindness. "I wish you could see, then you'd know how stunning you are." Only Margo's gift of sight hadn't come to her yet. It wasn't until her wedding night in Jared's arms that she had been given the gift—from her husband, Jared had said.

Yet, right now, at this very moment, she was able to see the past and the things she'd missed, by viewing them through Jared. For the first time ever, Margo saw two young girls—one 18, the other in her early teens, both dark and beautiful, both with long, black, wavy hair.

The younger one was leading the mature, 18-year-old bride to the back of the chapel to wait for the organist to play the wedding march. While they waited, Margo took this opportunity to scan the faces of the guests who were standing around. These were important people, she'd been told. These were senators and judges and congressmen, all come to her wedding.

But why? This was something she'd never given a thought to when it first happened. Only now the question was a burning one. Why had so many important people come to see Margo Windsor, a blind girl of no significance, get married?

Scanning the front of the chapel, Margo wanted to throw her head back and scream again when the answer came to her with the force of a thunderclap. Margo was now able to see the groom and his bodyguards, for the first time in her life—and she wanted to die.

He was a tall man, dressed in a white tuxedo. His hair, she noticed, was as dark as hers and as wavy as well. If she were to be perfectly honest about it, he was extremely handsome when compared to most men. There was nothing to be frightened of so far.

Then she made the mistake of looking into his

eyes, when she shouldn't have! She made the mistake of looking and of seeing his blood-red pupils and the tiny horns protruding through the top of his skull. As he looked to the rear of the chapel to stare back at her, as their eyes locked in unison, Margo was able to see the power he possessed, able to see the thousands of years of ageless, timeless power—power to control the evil that men do in the name of greed.

She felt her legs go limp and knew that if she hadn't been sitting in her favorite chair at the moment, she would have fallen to the ground. This was her husband in the flesh! But no, things like this didn't happen in real life.

Some called him "master," while others called him, "father." Margo preferred, "lord, god, Satan!" And her lord he had been until she now finally saw him in the flesh for the first time in her life, and reality slapped her in the face. He wasn't her savior, her guide, her strength. He was pure, raging evil, someone to be frightened of rather than someone to worship.

"He gave you the gift of sight for marrying him," Jared said then, speaking for the first time since showing Margo her husband.

"But why? Why did he marry me?"

"To have children, to bear him a son, because he felt you had the potential to be worthy enough when you ordered your father's death at the age of five and a half."

"And yet he never showed up on our wedding night. How were we supposed to have children?" She was being sarcastic because it was so hard to accept the truth. Surely these visions, as shown to her by Jared, were fraudulent. Jared was making this up to hurt her, to get even for wanting him to leave. "Anyone ever tell him the facts of life?" she asked.

"The idea was to wait until you grew older and wiser and matured a bit. Yet it didn't work out the way we planned. Instead of being obedient and serving our cause, you turned out to be a rebellious bitch, headstrong and aggressive, always wanting your own way. The master then changed his mind about you. He deemed you unworthy to bear his children and had Nathan make your womb barren."

"Oh, this is bullshit!"

"But it's the truth, Margo. It happened. Accept it." Jared's voice had lost its edge of revenge. It was almost back to normal now. But then he'd had his revenge—he'd shown Margo who her husband was. Knowing Margo as well as he did, he knew she'd never find peace with this knowledge.

"And I suppose the bodyguard next to him, that hideous-looking demon—"

"It's me. But I'm not hideous, not by my standards. By yours, maybe."

Margo remained silent for a long time after that, just staring at the image of her husband and his bodyguard. Two horrors! Two horrors that were too terrible to be true, and yet she had become involved with both of them. How?

By joining a church? By having the courage to do her own thing and not follow the God of the Christians?

"You make it sound like punishment, Margo. It wasn't. It was an honor bestowed upon you."

"An honor? Marrying him was an honor?"

"Yes. If you were really one of us, it was."

"And killing? Learning that people were killed to protect me, is that an honor as well?"

"Yes."

"Okay, Jared, I've seen as much as I want to." After she'd spoken, the scenes vanished in her mind's eye, and she was back in the den with Jared. There was one final question that needed answering, and once asked, Margo would be able to put the rest of the puzzle together by herself, the mysteries filling her life of late. "Did you order the pets to beat Jonathan and Joelle?"

"Why do you ask?"

"Because I want the truth. I don't care to punish the wrong person. I thought it was Nathan, but now I'm not so sure." Margo stopped speaking long enough to listen to Jared's laughter. "What's so funny?" she wanted to know, her voice even colder now. For surely there was no humor in this, nothing funny at all.

Yet Jared didn't agree. "You think you can punish me? Do you realize who you're talking to? I'm not just a demon, Margo. I'm a marquis—"

"Big deal!"

"And my powers are a hundred times greater than yours. Since you want the answer—yes, I ordered the pets. And now, what do you intend to do about it? How will you punish me?"

Jared broke into laughter again as Margo's entire body went limp. She felt as though there was nothing left inside of her. Too much truth had been spoken this past hour, and it was too much for her to deal with all at once. "I want you to get out! I want you to leave this house!"

Jared stopped laughing long enough to remind Margo that he'd been sent there by her husband. Jared took orders from him and him alone. "I'm sick of your nonsense, Margo. You wanted to play with the big boys, and we let you. We allowed you to join our church after giving you more inner power than most people possess, and you've loved it enough to go along with it all these years. But now, it's different. Now you realize this isn't fun and games. This is serious business. So now you want me to get out! Sorry, my dear, it's gone on too long to stop now. You're involved, and you'd better stop your nonsense and straighten out—or else!"

"Or else what?"

"Death is the only way to break the ties that bind someone of your stature with the master."

"I'm breaking those ties. I'm renouncing the evil in my life. And your killing days are over, Jared. That man upstairs, the one outside of my chapel, is the last one you'll ever kill in my name!"

"You're talking like a fool, so I'm leaving,

but not forever. I'm going upstairs to our
bedroom to wait for you. But before I go, let me
say this. I didn't kill this one, this Matthew
Soames. I was entertaining you, remember? I
suggest you think back on the prophecy
concerning Valerie's children, because the
chosen one is the one who did the killing, and
not with its own hands. It used the Walk of the
Dead to do it!''

Margo watched him leave and knew he was
telling the truth. Jared was with her when it
happened. True, he could have summoned up
the pets again to kill for him, but he couldn't
perform a ceremony and make love to her at the
same time. No, Jared didn't kill Matthew
Soames who evidently came here searching for
Aubrey and Tom.

Oh, would the pain of it ever stop? Jared had
killed Matthew Soames' relatives, and so he
came here searching for them, only to be killed
by the dead ones summoned by the child of the
prophecy. This was the second part of the
prophecy, being able to call up the dead for your
own use, and this was the part that frightened
her the most. This was power on the highest
level, more than one so young should possess.

Therefore, she had to discover which of
Valerie's children was the chosen one, and she
had to stop the chosen one from fulfilling the
prophecy, even if it cost her dearly, even if she
were killed in the process. Anyway, from what
Jared said, she was just as good as dead at the
moment. Death was the only way to renounce

the evil in her life, and renounce it she must. Margo couldn't live with the truth that had just been made known to her.

Chapter Twelve

MARGO SAT ALONE for a long time and listened to the wind howling against the eaves of the house, howling as it did the night her father was killed. She started to think back on his death and then went back even further, recalling the night she was blinded by Nathan.

She tried to relive the fear she felt then, to measure it against the fear she felt now. Was it as strong, or was it stronger? It was hard to tell, considering she'd only felt fear twice in her life—the night she was blinded and now.

Only the fear she felt now had nothing to do with the unexpected, as it had years ago. It didn't even have anything to do with an expectancy of physical pain as it had when she saw Nathan wielding his dagger. Also, this fear wasn't for herself. It was for a child, one of the three upstairs, that she had unwittingly led down the road to the prophecy's end.

"You wanted to play with the big boys,"
Jared had said, "and we let you."

Yes, they had let her, only it didn't start out
that way. When Margo joined the coven, it was
with the idea of doing something different, of
not conforming to the usual Christian beliefs.

Lying bitch! she told herself. You've been
lying to yourself for years. You killed your
father with the powers given to you by the
coven. Didn't you learn from that?

But no, she hadn't. She was young and naive
and saw the power to kill as something to be
used only once. When her father was dead and
the rage in her put to rest, she could get on with
her life without the evil of killing. Yes, it was
something to use on a limited basis, a power
supplied rather sparingly by the coven and by
the master of darkness as well.

The master of darkness was now better known
to her as her husband! He wasn't even human.
He was a savage animal, a beast. She couldn't
and wouldn't think about her marriage partner
for too long a time. It was a subject guaranteed
to drive her insane if she did. So Margo forced
her mind to return to her original line of
thought—why she joined the coven and what a
fool she'd been all these years.

Reliving it again, going back over the ideals
she'd cherished, she could see the fool in her at
work. To begin with, joining the coven had
meant having a place to go when she was lonely,
having others her own age to play with, having
someone to talk to. The coven had a nursery

where the children gathered, even the babies that were sacrificed on the altar. The babies were there, too.

Margo never thought much about those babies after she learned what their fate was, mainly because she tried to ignore the things she couldn't change. She had to wait until she was older and had influence. By that time she planned on having the power and backing of the other members to rid the coven of its human sacrifices, its cannibalism, and its self-mutilations as well. She had intentions of turning the clock back, of returning the coven to its original way of thinking.

In the beginning, as she understood it, Satan was thought of as a different person. He wasn't a powerful, hate-wielding, revenge-mongering, war lord. The power to kill your fellow human being wasn't something to be handed out like leaflets at a rally, and there were no such things as pets of the beast to be called upon to do your evil bidding.

Rather, the coven was started as a sort of rebellion against the inner, political workings of the Christian church. Parishioners were dissatisfied with the constant bickering and criticism between the different facets of formal religion: Catholics versus Protestants, Jews versus Christians, etc. They were tired of one level of Christianity always claiming to be the one, true religion, while finding fault with another.

People became sick of being told how evil they

were, how breaking just one of the Ten
Commandments was enough to banish you to
hell for an eternity to come. They were tired of
being labeled sinners, tired of trying to be good
and yet always managing to fail in the eyes of the
church.

So the members of her coven found an
answer, a way of doing their own thing, with no
criticism from others and no constant
comparisons. They founded a church that was
different, a church where they could worship
and sometimes have the freedom to display their
basic, lustful instincts without being banished to
hell for merely being human.

They founded a church without a supreme
being to answer to. They founded a church
where Satan was but one in a line of gods, and
these gods that they worshiped were nothing
more than fun loving, mystical creatures
borrowed from the pages of mythology such as
Pan and Diana.

In fact, up until this evening when Jared
revealed the truth to her, Margo saw Satan as
being very similar in character to Pan, a devilish
creature with horns and a flute who loved to
indulge his fantasies, an innocent who was
nearly destroyed by a world of reality. He was
her father, her creator.

But somewhere along the line things went
haywire, and the coven members began to stray
in their beliefs. Margo figured it must have been
around the time that Nathan was chosen as
their High Priest. Nathan was aggressive and

forceful. Nathan had charisma. Nathan turned an otherwise innocent ideal into something dreadful and disgusting. Nathan raised their lord, Satan, to the highest order and eventually made him the supreme ruler, the one being to be worshiped above all others!

How he got away with it, how he turned the members to the world of darkness and brainwashed them into worshiping the seven deadly sins, Margo would never know. But nobody challenged him, not even Margo's strong-willed father. He, too, let Nathan do as he pleased, while he sat home nights and talked about how awful things were getting and how frightening some of Nathan's ideas were.

There came a time when Margo's father stopped criticizing Nathan in the silence of his home and began to look forward to going to church. This was around the time when Nathan's constant badgering and brainwashing was starting to show results.

Nathan was in charge. He, with all of his lunatic ideas, was their leader, their guide in life. Nathan arranged her marriage, and nobody tried to stop him—not even Margo!

She sighed heavily and added another log to the fire, wishing it would supply enough heat to remove the chill of shock. But there wasn't enough wood in all of the world to burn away the horrors of revelation from her soul. She'd played with the big boys, hoping to somehow make a difference, to somehow change things and turn them around. Now she found that nothing had changed, that she'd spent the past half-century blinded to reality. She'd refused to believe that people were getting hurt.

"Are you forgetting about my mother? She got hurt, and she died. So how can you say you've been living in a dream world?"

Margo heard the voice but didn't recognize it. The voice, although it belonged to one of Valerie's children, was neither male nor female, but a combination of both. Margo stopped stirring the logs in the fireplace long enough to turn, with the poker still in her hand, and face the child of the prophecy.

"Did you kill that man upstairs?" she asked. This was a nephew or a niece, a child she'd loved and cherished as her own, but it wasn't a child she was facing now. It was an evil, all-powerful creature with no conscience, wearing a coven robe with a cowl pulled over its head to protect its identity. It was the closest to being demonic that a human being could ever become and still look human.

"Did you kill him?" she repeated.

"Yes."

"Why? Why did you do it? We didn't raise you to—"

"That's true, but Nathan did. Nathan taught us about our lord, Satan, and now I only live to serve him. Besides, isn't that my job? I'm replacing Father Death as the gatherer of souls, remember?"

"Yes! But only when they're ready to die, not when they're still in their prime."

"Oh, well, that's unfortunate."

"Bastard!" she spat and turned away. This was one of her children, the children that, although not born to her, were the same as her own. Now the child had killed without mercy. "Who are you?" she asked with her back still turned. She had to know which of the three it was.

"Can't you tell, Aunt Margo?"

No, she couldn't. The voice had no gender. Though the girls were small and Jonathan larger, it was hard to compare size under the flowing robe. "Which of you is it?" she asked, and waited a long time for an answer.

Standing where she was, stirring the logs again, the wait became maddening. Straight answers were uncommon among evil entities, and she knew that the child would never reveal its identity on its own. The only choice open to her now was to rip away the robe and see for herself.

Turning back to face the chosen one, she was startled to find herself alone again. The chosen one had left as quietly as it had come in. Dropping the poker, she thought about chasing it to its room, but it already could be upstairs in bed at this very moment, looking as innocent and helpless in sleep as Valerie's other two children. Margo would never be able to tell which of the three it was.

The only choice she had now was to wait and bide her time and speak to the children. Perhaps she could appeal to the humanity of the evil one once it was stripped of the facade behind its title. Then and only then would she stand a halfway decent chance. Now it was a waiting game, and while waiting, she hoped the child would kill no more.

"Aunt Margo's making hot cocoa for us after we build the snowman," Jonathan told the girls. Margo could hear him now as she'd listened to those same words so many years before.

Climbing the stairs like the old woman that she was, her lively gait had vanished with the appearance of the chosen one. She wanted to be anywhere other than where she was at the moment. This was a house of horror, a house of murderers it seemed, for Jared had confessed to 23 killings, not counting the one committed by Valerie's child.

She was alone. Climbing the stairs, walking the hall to her door, knowing Jared was waiting for her, she remained alone and had never experienced such complete depression since Valerie had been killed.

There was no one to turn to, nowhere to hide, no way to stop the senseless slaughter.

"Aunt Margo, can we have gingerbread cookies with the cocoa?"

"Yes, dear, I just made a fresh batch."

After she answered Jonathan, she stood quite still in the semi-darkness of the hall and wondered why he'd been so real. His had been merely a voice from the past, a memory, and yet he'd been real enough that she could almost reach out and touch him.

Was her mind slipping? Was she losing control? Or were the illusions of the past an escape to prevent the insanity she felt creeping up on her? If so, then she needed those memories now.

"Aunt Margo, if you wanna take a ride from the top, you can use my sleigh."

"Thank you, Joelle. I used to love doing this as a kid. I wonder if I can still do it."

"You never know till you try, Margo."

"Yes, Valerie, you're absolutely right. I will try it, but only after you do." Then she laughed as the vision of Valerie, her legs hanging over the side of a child's sleigh, went zooming down the hill in front of her.

"Now it's your turn, Margo," Valerie said, dragging the sleigh up the hill, her breath heavy and labored. "Boy, if I don't stop smoking . . ."

"Best idea you've had yet, Valerie. To stop smoking, that is."

And Valerie did stop smoking—cold turkey. As Margo now recalled, standing in the hall with the knob of the door in her hand, Valerie made her, Margo, responsible for keeping her off of the weeds, as Valerie called them. Margo remembered the calls during the day and late at night. "Help! I'm about to have a cigarette."

This was Margo's signal to play psychiatrist to her baby sister, and play it she did. She kept Valerie off of cigarettes and healthy because Valerie was over 40, and, as Margo saw it, close to the heart attack age. Hell, Margo was saving her life.

"Margo!!!"

Another memory from the past, but an ugly one this time. Valerie was calling her name—or rather, it was Valerie's head, leaving her shoulders, that was calling her name, its mouth open in a wail of agony. "Margo!" it called, as if by doing so Margo could save it from death as she'd saved it from cigarettes. Only Margo was helpless this time.

"But the children," the head said. Or did it? Margo heard those words and didn't know to this day if the severed head of Valerie had reached out to snap Margo out of her shock, or if it had been a case of an overactive imagination.

Whatever it was, the words were enough to make Margo raise her hands over her head and summon the pets of the beast to stop an axe-wielding bastard from killing the children. Yes, she saved the children—and Nathan, too, if the truth were known. Nathan was attacked and close to death when the pets stopped his attacker.

"Oh, Aunt Margo, we were so scared," Jonathan said, his tiny body quaking while he tried valiantly to cover his sisters' bodies with his own. "I tried to save Joelle and Eve from those terrible men. I tried so hard, Aunt Margo."

Oh yes, Jonathan, you did well. You helped save your sisters, and I helped too. Only now I regret my powers. Now I regret being able to summon monsters from the bowels of the Earth to save the lives of . . . to save the life of a murderer!

Perhaps it would have been better if I'd let you die, all three of you! Better for your future victims at least.

Joelle woke up and felt no pain. If it weren't for the slight, fading bruises on her flesh, she would have sworn last night never happened, and that she and Jonathan hadn't been beaten by invisible entities.

Thinking back, she could recall every punch, every slap and every kick with great accuracy, and it seemed to her now that the bruises should have been larger, deeper in color.

Rising gingerly, she grabbed her robe and slippers and knocked on Jonathan's door. She wanted to see him, to see if he'd healed as mysteriously and miraculously as she had.

Jonathan answered right away, but it took him a while to open the door and let her in. His face, she noticed, was full of barely visible bruises, but his eyes told a different story. He was still in pain, still feeling something.

"It seems we should look worse," he said. "I hurt all over, but not badly. You know, the kind of beating we took, we shouldn't be able to move for a week."

"I know," she said. "I don't understand it either, except I sort of remember Aunt Margo—"

"Chanting over us," he broke in. "Maybe she healed us with her prayers."

"Yeah. Well, Jonathan, what happened last night?"

Jonathan looked at her as though he felt her

mind was slipping. "You were there. We got our asses kicked!"

"Sure. But who did it?"

"Beats the hell outta me."

"Damnit," she said, clenching her teeth, "that's all you ever say—'beats the hell outta me.' It seems to be your answer for everything lately."

"Yeah, that's true, at least since we came here."

She watched him get up and turn on the bathroom light. He went inside for a moment without closing the door, then came back with some photos in his hand.

"Jonathan, burn that shit! That's why we were beaten in the first place."

"Because of a few photos?" he asked, as if he found it hard to believe.

"Yes. Because of those photos and what we saw in them—those dead people and the horses."

"But why?"

"Beats the hell outta me."

"Joelle! That's my line."

"Jonathan!" Eve suddenly blurted as she opened the door and came rushing in. "Where are the pictures? Did you do them?"

Jonathan stared at her in horror and shock. The last thing he wanted to do was to show those photos to Eve and watch her get attacked by someone she couldn't see. He shoved them down deep into the pocket of his robe, but Eve spotted them and made a grab for the photos. "No," he said, pulling away from her. "You can't see them."

"But why?" she asked, pouting, her lower lip stuck out just far enough to show that she was ready to cry. "I wanna see them. Why can't I see them?" Then, realizing she was getting nowhere with Jonathan, she tried appealing to Joelle. "Why can't I see them?" she asked Joelle.

"Beats the hell outta me," Joelle said and shrugged, although she knew better. Those pictures were shocking, and Eve couldn't take as much as they could, not mentally, emotionally or otherwise.

"Joelle," Jonathan shouted, "you're no help at all." Then he shoved the pictures down deeper inside his pocket and told Eve they were ruined. "They're full of white spots, and you can't even make out who's who."

"Ohhhh, boy!" Eve said and shrugged, accepting Jonathan at his word. "Maybe we can go out this afternoon and take more. Maybe this time they'll turn out good. Anyway, I wonder if Aunt Margo's made breakfast. I had a bad nightmare last night, and it made me awfully hungry."

"You had a nightmare and it made you hungry?" Joelle asked, repeating her words. Putting her arm over Eve's shoulder, she took Eve to the foot of Jonathan's bed and made her sit. "What kind of a nightmare?"

"I don't know. It was just awful, that's all." Eve's thin, fragile face looked bewildered. Her eyes looked larger than they were as she thought about the question, then she turned back to Joelle. "Why'dya wanna know?"

"Well," Joelle began softly, "I had a nightmare, too, and I figured we'd compare them."

"Why?"

"Because nightmares come back if you don't talk about them. Eve, do you want the same nightmare tonight?"

"Who told you that bullshit?" Jonathan asked, plopping himself down on the bed next to Eve.

"Mommy did," Joelle answered in all seriousness. "Mommy said it to me a couple of times. She used to sit me down after I had a bad dream and feed me hot chocolate and we'd talk about it. And she was right. Whenever I didn't tell her about my nightmares, they came back."

"Okay," Jonathan said, "I can buy it. Mommy was pretty smart. So, Eve, tell us about your nightmare."

"Why doesn't Joelle go first?"

"Because you mentioned it first," Joelle protested.

Jonathan saw a good fight starting and tried to stop it before it got out of hand. "Girls, I had a nightmare, too. Let me tell mine first. Then Eve goes, then Joelle. Agreed?" After they shook their heads, he noticed that Joelle seemed upset. He almost never had nightmares, and Joelle knew it. Now she was probably wondering if he was making it up.

"It's true, Joelle, I did—and it was bad!"

Stretching himself into a position where he could see both girls' faces and thereby measure their reactions to his nightmare, he began.

"I was out in the hall when the dream began, and it seemed as though I was hiding in the shadows waiting for this guy who'd broken into the house to come upstairs—"

"So you could kill him," Eve blurted out, while Jonathan went into shock because her answer had been right.

"How do you know?" he asked when he was finally able to speak.

"Because my dream was like yours. I was wearing a pretty, black robe—"

"With the hood pulled over your head," Joelle said quietly. Joelle had been silent up until now, but her silence had more to do with shock than anything else, such as politely listening to Jonathan. "The hood was over my head, and I followed this man—"

"Upstairs to Aunt Margo's chapel," Jonathan cut in. "Once I had him cornered—"

"I called up his dead father and brother to kill him," Eve said, her voice soft and subdued like the twins.

"I was the child of the prophecy, and he was Matthew Soames," Joelle said, putting the finishing touches to the story.

After it was over, the three of them sat silently and wondered why and how they'd all managed to have the same, exact dream. This was absurd. Just because Jonathan and Joelle were twins and came from the same egg didn't mean they had to have similar dreams. Besides, if it did, then how come Eve also had this dream?

"I don't wanna even try and think of an answer," Joelle said, getting to her feet. "I just wanna get dressed and go downstairs for breakfast."

"Right," Jonathan agreed. "We'll all do the same and forget the dream. I mean, really forget it. And Eve, don't slip and mention this to Aunt Margo, okay?"

"Okay," she said brightly and rose to get dressed. "Anyway, I feel better. At least by telling you the dream, I won't have the same one tonight." She was halfway through the door when something made her stop and turn, something she'd only just remembered. She had to tell Jonathan and Joelle right away because it was important.

"Jonathan, you said not to mention the dream to Aunt Margo, but what if she asks me about it? What do I say then?"

"Why would she bring it up? We had the dream, Eve, all three of us. Aunt Margo's not aware of it."

"But you don't understand," Eve said, pausing to bite her lower lip as though she'd just committed the ultimate crime. "In my dream, after I killed that man, I went downstairs and spoke to Aunt Margo in the den."

Jonathan sighed heavily because his dream had ended the same way—speaking to Aunt Margo in the den while still wearing the robe with the cowl pulled over his head. Judging from the expression on Joelle's face, hers had ended the same way, too. Jonathan slowly explained to Eve why they had to keep this to themselves.

"You see, Eve, like I said before, this was *our* dream—yours and mine and Joelle's. Since it was only a dream it's not real. It never happened, so there's no reason for Aunt Margo to know about the murder or the incident in the den. Understand?" He waited while Eve nodded silently. "So we'll keep it to ourselves, okay?"

"Okay," she said and was gone, leaving Jonathan and Joelle alone and scared and feeling sick inside.

Chapter Thirteen

MARGO HAD MADE scrambled eggs and bacon for breakfast, and now, here she was, ready to face Valerie's children, while Jared sat in the den and drank whiskey. Jared had flatly refused to cook for "those three bastards," so Margo had struggled in the kitchen alone, something she hadn't done in at least ten years or more.

Now, taking her place at the head of the table, she was about to sit when they came through the door, two of them bruised due to Jared, and she wanted to die. She let out a cry and motioned for them to come into her arms, and come they did.

They still remembered, she thought to herself, while tears of angry anguish stained her face. They remembered their Aunt Margo as she was years ago, how she'd mothered and babied them to no end. Now they were seeking comfort in the warmth of her arms to keep from shaking, to keep from being scared.

"We love you," Eve said, and that was all Margo needed to let the wall she'd built around her these past ten years completely collapse. As they stood and held her, she cried as she'd never cried before.

She cried for her blindness—not in terms of lost eyesight, but for the passions in her heart that kept her blinded to the truth all these years. And she cried for the unmerciful killing of her father, and for Valerie's death, and for the three, helpless, young adults in her arms.

It seemed to her as though the three teenagers in her arms were softly crying too, their bodies ridden with sobbing, and it felt good, this release they were doing through silent agreement.

When it was over, when Margo's grief had run its course, she forced them to stand at arms length so she could look at them, really look at them for the first time since they'd arrived here days ago—Jonathan, tall and lanky; Joelle, small and pretty; Eve, even smaller than Joelle, and simple-minded.

While she looked at their puzzled faces, she found herself going back over the night before, wondering which of the three was the child of the prophecy—or rather, which of the twins. Eve was no contender.

"Are you all right, Aunt Margo?" Jonathan asked, wiping his tears with the palms of his hands.

"Yes. For the first time in my life, I'm all right, as you say."

"Then why are you crying? Why are *we*

crying?'' Eve asked, her face marred with wetness.

"Because,'' Joelle began softly, not allowing Margo to answer, ''we're all sad, Eve. We haven't seen Aunt Margo for a long time, and now we realize the years between us didn't matter. We still feel the same way about each other, only we acted so stupid when we first came here. We treated Aunt Margo like a stranger.''

Margo listened to her words and wanted to cry some more, but instead, she gave a sigh and pointed to the buffet table, hoping to lighten the mood. "There isn't much to eat. Jared usually prepares the food, but Jared's angry at us so he didn't cook this morning. I had to . . . I'm sorry,'' she said, her voice breaking into nervous laughter.

"Oh, that's okay, Aunt Margo,'' Eve said, breaking away to lift the tops from the warmers. After she did, she took a plate and began scooping food onto it.

Jonathan and Joelle, meanwhile, stayed near their Aunt Margo, their hunger for the truth outweighing their physical hunger. "Then there is someone else staying here?'' Jonathan asked.

"Yes,'' Margo said, sitting down because the answers she had to give them were already making her feel old and tired. "He's been living with me for almost fifty years now,'' she said, and stopped talking when Joelle gasped.

At that point, Margo considered saying no more, but she'd gone this far and mentioned

Jared. Now she was compelled to tell the rest. "I want you to eat something. Then we'll bare our souls as much as we can."

Starting with the night she was blinded, and her initiation into the coven as a result, Margo told the twins how she'd ordered her father's death. Eve wasn't paying attention, but was rearranging some pretty blue flowers she'd picked the day before. They were in a vase on the buffet table, and Eve seemed more concerned with the flowers than with hearing Aunt Margo recall the past. But then Eve didn't have the mental capacity to focus her attention on anything for too long a time, and so they forgave her.

"You mean your father, our grandfather, gave you to the coven, knowing they'd take your eyesight away? And he did it for money and power? But you were his child! How could he?" Joelle was dumbfounded. "I never knew what happened—"

"We thought you were born blind," Jonathan said, cutting in, his face a mask of anger. "Was he crazy?"

"Yes," Margo answered, "he was crazy—mad for power. Only . . . now as I sit here and think back, I realize he wasn't to blame. It was the coven. They turned his head around and made him the way he was. It was Nathan and the others, promising him more than he had in life. He was poor, so they promised him great wealth. He was pathetic, a mouse of a creature, so they promised him power. Then they gave him nothing and convinced me to kill him—"

"He was screwed!" Jonathan spat.

"We all were," Margo said scornfully. "You, me, your parents, my parents. All screwed. Hell, I played right into their hands. They promised me power, too, and great wealth. All I had to do was order my father's death—the death of an innocent man, who was brainwashed into sacrificing his only child's sight for the glory of their lord. First they used him to get to me, then they used me to kill him. But I was only five, not old enough to think for myself."

"But, Aunt Margo, they did come through for you. They kept their promises," Joelle reminded her.

"Yes, they did. They came through for me. I have supernatural powers, and I'm wealthy—but at what price?"

"I don't understand."

"Let me explain it, but first let me tell you a bit about our lord, Satan. Then all the rest will fit in—"

"Can I go out and play?" Eve wanted to know. "This is boring."

"I don't care if it's boring!" Jonathan shouted. "You're gonna stay and listen." Joelle touched his arm then to calm him down. Their roles had suddenly been reversed, Margo noted.

"Sit down, Eve," Joelle said softly. "It'll only take a while, then we'll all go for a walk."

"You promise?"

"Yes." Joelle said, pulling the chair next to

her away from the table for Eve to sit in.

Once they were settled, Margo began her story. "Sometimes we make ourselves blind to the truth by refusing to accept it for what it is. I never really believed in the existence of good and evil, at least not in terms of actual physical bengs that represented both ideas. Rather, good and evil, at least not in terms of actual physical beings God of the Christians representing purity, and there sure as hell was no Satan standing for the defilement of all that is good.

"Keeping this in mind, I refused to take sides with either the good or the evil, or to recognize them for what they were—the ideals of living entities. Do you follow me so far?"

"I think so," Jonathan said, while Joelle nodded silently.

"I attended a Christian church a few times when I was real young—"

"You're kidding?" the twins said in unison.

"No, I'm not. It's true. I used to attend Sunday School in a Baptist Church near my home, and sometimes I still wonder if I drew the attention of those axe-wielding Baptists myself, but I can't make the connection for sure. Anyway, the minister there was forever expounding on the subject of good versus evil, and how evil people faced a life of damnation and fire and brimstone. Being only five, I figured it was one helluva good fairy tale.

"Good people died and went to heaven, whereas evil people went down below. Then he'd go on and tell us what being good meant and how to live up to the ideals of the church, but I was so young I didn't understand. So I disregarded most of what he told me and refused to believe in good and evil as entities. I believed these things were only ideas that lived in people's minds.

"Then I was introduced to my father's church, rather harshly, I must say. Still, even though they hurt me, they were kind to me—a lot kinder than those Bible-quoting Christians. The coven members listened to my stories about what the minister of the Baptist Church told me and laughed. They said he was only trying to scare me and didn't want me to have any fun.

"So I started to think about religion—really think about it. In one church I was a born sinner and had to work hard to make the grade. I had to sacrifice everything that made growing up fun—dancing, jewelry, makeup. Whereas in another church, I could do as I pleased and not feel guilty. After all, religion was only a state of mind.

"But then, after it was too late and I'd already sold my soul into bondage, I discovered the truth. There really is a lord, Satan. He lives!''

Closing her eyes because this was all so painful to her, Margo told them the story from beginning to end. When she was finished, she hoped they'd just get up and take the walk they promised Eve, without commenting.

She wished the three would just leave and not force her to dig deeper into a story she'd just merely skimmed over lightly, but Margo knew differently. Putting herself in their place, she knew she'd never be able to face the past and then drop it as though it didn't happen. Margo, herself, would have asked questions and demanded answers, as the twins were getting ready to do now.

"Then my mother didn't die of a heart attack," Jonathan said quietly. "She had her head—"

"Please don't say it. I can see it. Please don't put it into words," Joelle asked, a pleading quality to her voice.

"What you see is the truth," Margo said.

"Let's go back to the beginning," Jonathan said. He was speaking to her, but his head was bowed and his hands locked in anger. Margo stared at the white rings around his knuckles and listened as he continued. "You ordered your father's death, and now you regret it. Why? He blinded you."

"If you ask me that question, then you haven't been paying attention."

"But I have!"

"Then you didn't understand what I was saying. My father turned me over to the coven *after* he was brainwashed by Nathan and the rest. It wasn't his fault. They had him convinced he was doing the proper thing, that he would gain from it."

"From what you've told us, Nathan sounds like a real bastard."

Margo heard Joelle's words and sighed heavily. Joelle had seen the true Nathan through

Margo's eyes. "He was," she said in agreement, "but he paid for it—dearly!"

"Nathan's body is still here—upstairs. Did you kill him, too?" Jonathan wanted to know.

Margo looked away from him. Up until now she'd wondered if they'd seen Nathan the night she'd caught them spying through the keyhole in the door to her chapel. Now she knew they had. "I didn't kill Nathan. In fact, I saved his life. Nathan was wounded badly by those axe-wielding bastards who killed your mother. I stopped them from killing him, and when I fled here to Monkshood, I brought him with me to recuperate."

"Then how did he die?" Joelle asked.

"Of old age. Nathan was in his late twenties when he blinded me. That was sixty-three years ago. He was an old man when I brought him here."

"But, Aunt Margo," Eve said, speaking up for the first time, "you said you got even with him. How?"

To their amazement, Eve had been paying attention.

"When Nathan died, he wanted me to bury his body in the woods out back—"

"On hallowed ground."

"How do you know about the woods, Jonathan?"

"It's a long story. We all know about those woods, but I can't tell you now because there's so much more to discuss . . . like how you got even with Nathan, for instance."

"Nathan found Christianity before he died, or at least he said he did. He told me he'd had lots of time to think after he was wounded, and how the more he thought about his life, the more he came to realize he'd followed a false prophet."

"A what?" Eve asked, her head nestled down on top of her folded arm.

"Sit up straight, honey," Joelle told her.

"Leave her be. It doesn't matter. She's paying attention. Now, Eve, a false prophet is one who creates his own gospel, but who lies while doing it. Nathan followed the gospel of our . . . of Satan, and later came to realize it was a pack of lies. So, before he died, he wanted me to bury him on hallowed ground so that Satan wouldn't be able to get to him when he came for his soul."

"Being on hallowed ground would do that?"

"Yes. Satan and his followers cannot walk on hallowed ground, so Nathan would have been safe there."

"But why?" Joelle asked, her face marred by confusion. "Why was he afraid? Wouldn't Satan take care of a great leader like Nathan? Wouldn't he give him an honored place in his kingdom?"

"Not really. What Nathan had preached was what Nathan had been led to believe by the representatives of the kingdom of evil, but none of it was true. It was all bullshit, meant to entice us to follow a false prophet. Not only did Nathan come to realize this when it was too late—when his soul already belonged to the prince of darkness—but Nathan also renounced his ties with the prince's church.''

"He was gonna burn, right, Aunt Margo?"

"Yes, Eve. He asked me to bury him on hallowed ground, but I didn't. So when Satan sent for him, he was easy to get to. Just before it was Nathan's time to die, a courier came with two great hounds and killed him. I heard Nathan pleading and screaming as the hounds attacked. Then his soul was carried back to Acheron, while I prayed that Nathan would spend an eternity on the same level of darkness as my father so that he could listen to my father's bitching for all time to come. I thought it a fitting punishment for someone who was responsible for destroying so many lives in the name of his god!''

"I kind of like it, Aunt Margo. You did good."

"Joelle, what's wrong with you? Didn't you listen to her?" Jonathan asked, his face livid with rage. "None of it is right!"

"No, it isn't," Joelle answered calmly, "but at least the one person who started everything didn't get away with it. His ass is burning now, and I'm glad. Good for you, Aunt Margo!"

Margo smiled then for the first time in days. She hadn't thought that facing the truth would turn out as good as it had. Valerie's children had understood and, so far, had managed to forgive her.

"There's only one thing I don't get," Joelle

said, after they had been speaking for what seemed like hours. "When I was real young, around six or seven, I remember you having a fight with Nathan—something about you wanting to become a priest of the church. If you were unhappy with a lot that was happening in the church, why did you try and put yourself at the head of it?"

"To be in a position to stop the human sacrifices and control most of the evil. A priest wields a great deal of power. I would have been able to take Nathan on, perhaps change a lot of things he started, and return the church to its original ideals. These are changes I wasn't able to enforce as a church member, so I figured if I became a priest—"

"What original ideals?" Jonathan asked. He was nasty now, but Margo understood and sympathized with him. Everything he'd ever believed in had just now been exposed for what it was. "It doesn't sound like our church ever had any ideals."

"The members did in the beginning, before Nathan and his human sacrifices and his cannibalism and his self-mutilations." Pausing to gather her thoughts, Margo went on to explain the members' dissatisfaction with formal religion and what was the basis behind the formation of the church. She was about halfway through it when Jonathan interrupted her again.

"And you think they were right? You think it was okay to form a church where people could satisfy their basic lusts? Where they could have sex and do anything they wanted to? Where they could live out their sexual fantasies? Men chaining women up and beating them with whips to get their jollies. Women climbing on top of men in coffins and screwing because this was their fantasy. You think it was right?''

"Why are you asking me this now? You went to our church. You've seen these things."

"Yeah, we went to church all right—after you talked my mother into bringing us there!"

Margo felt another crack in her heart. Jonathan was right. Valerie hadn't been much of a churchgoer until Margo talked her into it. Valerie preferred to stay home and play housewife to her husband, and Margo, thinking it was a sin not to attend church, made Valerie realize she'd never find happiness in this world without her god!

"So you brought my mother back. And then my mother brought us after we were born."

"I thought I was doing the right thing," Margo said with her head bowed, not facing him.

"Well, you weren't," Jonathan said, resuming his attack. "And you had something to compare that church with. You went to an outside church, so you knew what they were doing was wrong. But us . . . hell, we had nothing to compare it with—nothing, that is, until now. I mean, you're telling us what's what, and it's a little late, isn't it?"

"Jonathan, I'm sorry. I was so confused. All these years I really believed I was doing right by

you. I really believed I could make a difference
and change things.''

"Oh yeah, you changed things all right. You
got my mother killed. If she hadn't listened to
you, she wouldn't have been in church when
those maniacs broke in with the axes. Maybe,
just maybe, it would have been your head they
chopped off instead of hers!''

"Jonathan, stop this!'' Joelle demanded, but
Jonathan was too angry to listen.

"And what about the child of the prophecy
prediction? If you hadn't made our mother
bring us to Nathan's church, we wouldn't be
involved in that. Was that doing the right thing,
too?''

"Let up,'' Joelle pleaded. "Everyone makes
mistakes.''

"Sure, but it doesn't always mess up lives the
way her mistakes did.''

"He's right, Joelle. I deserve his
wrath. . . . And now the child has killed.''

"No!'' Jonathan bellowed, getting to his feet.

Margo listened to the dull thudding noise his
chair made when it fell over and hit the carpet
and wanted to die. She'd just told one of the
loves of her life that either he, or one of his
sisters, was a murderer, and the knowledge of
blood on their hands threatened to destroy all
three of them.

"It was a dream,'' he insisted, his eyes wild
with shock. "Nothing more . . . a stinking
dream! It didn't happen!''

Margo lifted her head, tried to regain her

composure and stared at Jonathan. He was
anger and rage personified. "The child has
killed," she'd told him, wishing her tongue had
fallen from her mouth before she had done so.

"I think you're lying," Jonathan said, his
voice as cold as if he were speaking to a stranger.
"After all, aren't you Mrs. Satan? Didn't you
marry the 'lord of lies' as you yourself called
him? How can we believe anything you say when
your old man is—"

"Because I never knew about my marriage
until last night when Jared showed it to me!"
Margo screamed with more passion than she
knew she possessed. "I'm not like him. My
words don't revolve around falsehoods!"

"And his Jared showed it to you—your
marriage? How do you know you can trust
him?"

"Because Jonathan, dear, we've been living
together for so long now, I'd know if he was
lying or not," Margo answered tensely,
struggling to control her anger. Jonathan had
beaten her down so low, that now she was
fighting to get out from under his wrath. She felt
like a trapped animal. "Jared never lied to me
before—"

"But you said he was a demon. If the old
master beast is the lord of lies, than how can one
of his henchmen tell the truth? Besides, Jared
lied to you about being human, didn't he?"

"No, Jonathan, he didn't. A lie is the false-
hood you tell when confronted with the truth.
Jared never lied about his identity

because . . . well, I never noticed his physical abnormalities until you arrived here and called them to my attention. Once I knew what he really was, Jared confessed. So, as you can see, there was no lie involved here.''

"Okay," Jonathan said, pacing the length of the dining room. He was calmer now, his anger somewhat vented by screaming at Margo. "How do you know the child killed?"

"Before I answer, let me ask you a question," Margo said, getting to her feet with her coffee cup in hand.

"I'll get ya coffee, Aunt Margo," Eve said brightly. "You just sit back down and talk to Jonathan so we can go for a walk."

"Thank you," Margo said and half-smiled at Eve. "Now, Jonathan, a few minutes ago you mentioned having dreamed about the murder I mentioned. Tell me about that dream."

While Margo listened, Jonathan reluctantly told her about the dream shared by all three of them. When he reached the part about the child visiting her in the den, Margo went white.

"From what I know, everything you've told me is accurate. I was visited by the child of the prophecy in the den last night."

"But how?" Joelle wanted to know. "Aunt Margo, this is bizarre! We dreamed about what really happened? Things like this don't ha—"

"Yes, they do!" Margo said curtly. "Things like this do happen in real life. Once upon a time I used to tell myself a different story, but through the years I've found that stranger things happen in real life than in any book I've ever read."

"Aunt Margo," Jonathan said suddenly, falling to his knees in front of her. She looked straight into his eyes and saw the raw torment raging inside of him and wished with all of her heart that she could go back and relive the past 60 years, if only for his sake alone. "Look," he began, "I'm sorry about the things I've said."

"Don't be. Your life has been a hell on Earth, and I'm largely responsible."

"I shouldn't have faulted you for doing the things you did because your intentions were good. Like Joelle said, everyone makes mistakes—and I love you, Aunt Margo."

Taking him into her arms, Margo rubbed the back of his head and listened to him crying softly against the nape of her neck. He wanted to know which of them was the child. Who did she see? And, please, Aunt Margo, don't say it was me!

"I don't know who it was," she explained, still holding him. Then she went on to describe what she'd seen and heard when the child came into the den, and how it had been a combination of both male and female.

"Are you sure?" he asked, pulling away to look at her face.

"Yes, I'm sure," she said, removing her glasses so that Jonathan and Joelle and Eve could see her eyes. "My husband gave me the gift of strong insight, which is the same as actually seeing with your eyes."

"Then I was right about you!" Joelle shouted, exhilarated rather than angry. "Jonathan, she can see!"

"I heard her," Jonathan said, never taking his gaze from Margo's face. "So it wasn't a question of being blind. You didn't recognize the child of the prophecy because it was a combination of male and female?"

"Yes."

"Okay," he said, sighing heavily and getting to his feet. "We saw the murder in our dreams. Did you see it? I mean, were you in the hall when it happened?"

"No. Jared told me about the murder. And before you ask, Jared, as a demon, knows all." She felt herself flush because she'd bent the truth.

Jared only knew about the child of the prophecy committing murder because he was with Margo at the time. If she told him how Jared knew about the killing and who committed it, then she'd have to confess that Jared was the one who'd called up the pets of the beast to beat them. She just couldn't tell them that her boyfriend wanted them dead, not when they were starting to love her again.

"I can't figure this out," Jonathan said at last. "If all three of us dreamed about something that really happened, then somehow all three of us are directly involved—and yet, only one of us is the child."

"Are we going out yet?" Eve wanted to

know, her voice full of exasperation. "Or is this gonna take all day?"

"You're going out," Margo said, "and right now. We all need time away from this, time to give our brains a rest. Then perhaps we can come up with the answer to our biggest mystery yet—the identity of the chosen one."

"Yes," Joelle agreed. "Sometimes when you think too hard about something it never makes any sense. Come on, Jonathan, let's go out and walk and maybe it'll clear our heads a bit. We can always talk again later."

"Okay. Only I hope that when we do reach a conclusion it doesn't lead back to me. As far as I'm concerned, there's no glory in being the chosen one."

Chapter Fourteen

HANK WALLACE, THE old station master, had never closed the Monkshood train station this early in the day in over 40 years of service, but this was different. Hank was about to embark on a mission, the importance of which could be measured in terms of human lives—missing ones.

Hank poured himself a fast whiskey, one for the road, and laid his station master's cap on the counter near the ticket window. He and a group of the boys were goin' over to that Margo Windsor's place and demand that she either leave town or give them a reasonable explanation as to her innocence.

Aubrey Soames and his two sons, Matthew and Tom, were among the missing now, bringing the total number of missing persons, at last count, to 24.

Two dozen!

And that was just about 20 more than was allowed in a small town over a ten-year period. Hank and his buddies could have accepted four, could've taken it for granted. Four people were unhappy with the way things were going in Monkshood and had simply up and left.

But now 24 was a bit hard to swallow. And what with the Soames men disappearing within such a short space of time, well, that made Hank and his buddies more than a little suspicious, especially since Matthew had been all over town telling folks how Margo Windsor had somethin' to do with his kinfolk bein' among the missin'.

Now Matthew was missin' himself. That only served to fire Hank's imagination, because he was sure that wherever Aubrey and Tom were—wherever Margo Windsor had sent them—Matthew was there, too, bringing the total number of missing persons in this town to an alarming, all-time high.

Since the disappearances had started around the time the Windsor woman first showed up in town and bought herself a mansion, that made her a prime suspect in Hank's eyes!

Now he intended to do something about it. He intended to go over there, with five or six men at his side, and ask that woman just what the hell she did with his friends. And he didn't want no shit! She had better damn well tell the truth or, female or no female, she'd be tarred and feathered and run outta town damn fast!

Downing his drink as quickly as he could, so

as not to hold up the boys, he locked the front door to his office, then stepped around to the side of the building to wait for Bart Anderson to come and pick him up. Bart's father, Ben, was once the town smithy—until he crippled Margo Windsor's Arabian by shoeing it wrong. Ben died one awful death after that.

So naturally, Bart, his son, wanted in on this. Bart was sure his Pa's death was no accident like the Medical Examiner claimed it was. Shitty old M.E. couldn't find a way of explaining how it happened, that's all, and when some old doc can't find an answer, then it has to be an accident.

"Stupid bastard!" Hank said and spat a mouthful of brown saliva back between the tracks. Then he shifted his chewin' tobacco to the other side of his mouth and checked his watch to be sure it was still early and that the boys hadn't chickened out on their word to face that Windsor woman.

But he saw that he had ten minutes to go, ten minutes of waiting and thinking before taking the long ride to Margo Windsor's mansion. He shuddered then and pulled the collar of his jacket up higher around his neck. There sure was a bad nip in the air this morning, or he was more scared than he wanted to admit. It was his own fear making him shiver, not the cold winds blowing out there by the side of the station.

Checking his watch again, he realized a full minute had gone by, and he now had nine more to wait, nine minutes of standing there in the ass freezing cold, nine minutes of waiting and hoping.

Actually he was hoping not to be seen by Dennis Windsapple over at the bank. Dennis could see the station from his private office window, and if Dennis happened to look out and see a lock across the front door of the station, Dennis was sure to come over here to check on Hank, seein' as how Hank had never closed this early before.

Dennis was sure to try and stop Hank and the others from going over to Margo Windsor's, because Dennis was in love with her, and everyone in town knew it. They didn't hold it against Dennis, not a bit. In fact, everyone who knew Dennis pitied him more than anything. Margo Windsor had him bewitched.

Yes sir, that woman had sure as anythin' cast a spell years ago and made Dennis fall in love with her. Now Dennis was still under the same spell. 'Course, there might have been another reason for Dennis' uncontrollable love for Margo Windsor.

Hank had heard one time—from a man who'd seen her and lived to tell about it—that Margo Windsor was one good-looking woman—tall and buxom, head held high, stately as they came. She was a real, aristocratic beauty.

So maybe folks was wrong. Maybe Hank was wrong. She might not have cast a spell. Dennis may have fallen in love with her because she was more woman than he was used to seeing. Whatever the case, Hank prayed for the locked door to go unnoticed by Dennis.

Dennis or no Dennis, Margo Windsor had to be stopped, even if they had to kill her and them three relatives of hers, too. After all, those three teenagers, the ones he'd seen step off the train days ago, reminded him of Margo Windsor. Bold and sassy they was, except for the little one, as he now thought about the violent shouting match in front of the train station. The little one had sort of stayed off by herself and maybe not just to avoid trouble. She did seem a bit daft. Maybe they'd leave her out of it, but them other two, them twins, sure as hell had the Windsor attitude.

And to Hank, that meant only one thing. Them two were as spooky as their aunt and probably had the same power as well—the power to turn men's heads and twist their thinking around. Yeah, them two had to be watched, and them two had to be questioned. In Hank's opinion, they knew about as much of their aunt's business as old Margo Windsor herself!

"Aunt Margo's Mrs. Santa?" Eve asked, once they were outside.

Jonathan heard her and smiled despite his anger. Then he looked at Joelle in her woolen cap, her face framed by her long, black hair and wondered if she'd heard it, too. "No, Eve, she's not Mrs. Santa."

"But that's what you called her, Jonathan."

"I was making a joke, Eve. It was meant to be funny," he lied.

"And it was," Eve said and giggled. "Any-

way, her hair's white enough to make her look
like the Mrs. Santa I seen in pic—''

"What are you talking about?" Joelle asked.
"Her hair's black, just like ours."

They were nearing the main gate to Margo's
mansion by this time. Eve had wanted to go
walking in the woods again to play with the
squirrels, but Jonathan and Joelle knew that
walking through those woods meant consorting
with the restless dead, the ghosts of tortured
victims of days past.

Eve didn't know about this, since she hadn't
been allowed to see the photos after Jonathan
and Joelle had developed them. Keeping Eve's
ignorance of the situation in mind, Jonathan
lightly suggested they go elsewhere and find new
territory to explore. Eve agreed, without a fight
this time.

"Eve, did you hear me?" Joelle asked,
because Eve hadn't responded to Joelle's
comments about Aunt Margo's hair. "It's
black!"

Eve stopped walking and faced Joelle.
"What's wrong with me? I look at Aunt Margo,
like you and Jonathan do, and all I see is an old
woman—old and wrinkled with snow-white
hair."

Joelle shot a fast sideways glance at Jonathan,
but kept her voice steady even when she
answered Eve. "Maybe it's your eyes. You
might need glasses. We'll tell Daddy to have
them checked when we get back home."

"Okay," Eve said brightly, satisfied with
Joelle's explanation. Walking on ahead, she

opened the gates and stepped out onto the shoulder of the road while Jonathan and Joelle lagged behind.

"What do you think?" Joelle asked Jonathan.

"I don't think anything. There's too much happening, and I don't wanna think about that house or Aunt Margo or anything else until I walk back through that front door. For now, let's just give our heads a rest." Turning away from Joelle, he called on ahead to Eve. "Go left, towards town."

"Oh, are we gonna go there and stop in some stores and look around?" Eve called back.

"No. Aunt Margo said to stay away from there. We're just gonna walk on the road for a while. Then we'll turn around and head in the opposite direction."

"I wanna go see some stores," Eve wailed in protest. "Walking's boring."

"I don't care," Jonathan shouted, losing his temper again. "You'll do as you're told! No town, no stores. That's that!"

Jonathan had barely gotten the words out of his mouth when an old, beat-up car stopped on the road in front of them, and five men got out with bats in their hands. "There they are," one shouted. "Them relatives of hers. Let's get 'em!"

After hearing those words, Jonathan, Joelle and Eve turned to run, to get back to the mansion and the safety of Aunt Margo's arms, but they were too late.

"Stop!" Eve screamed. She'd been walking

ʌ the twins, as usual, and was the first
ʟaught.

Jonathan stopped running and wheeled in his
tracks, determined to go back and help her, but
he couldn't move because by this time some
guy had a vise-like grip on one of his arms.
Unfortunately Joelle was seized at almost the
same, exact moment.

They were helpless. They couldn't help Eve.
All they could do was stand where they were and
stare in horror at the scene unfolding before
them. Eve was on her knees, her head bowed
with fear, while a huge man stood over her and
raised his bat, bringing it down towards Eve's
bowed head with all of the raging fury that was
in him.

With the bat seconds away from her head, Eve
looked up and let out a muffled cry. She was as
good as dead. This man was about to finish the
job started years ago by a lack of oxygen.

Jared waited until those three bastards had
left the house before going after Margo.

Margo was in the dining room, drinking
coffee, when he found her. She looked upset.
"Can I get you anything?" he wanted to know.

"Sure. You can get out," she answered
quietly, while he grinned. "But since you're not
about to leave on your own, and since I can't
force a so-called marquis to do anything he
doesn't want to—leaving me alone is enough!"

"Impossible!" he said, sitting at the table
near her. "I will not leave you alone. Your
husband sent—"

"Fuck my husband!"

"Don't you wish you could?"

"Funny, Jared, real funny."

Her face, he noticed, was still twisted with rage, only slightly marring her beauty, but then again her beauty was an illusion created by Jared, to keep her young and desirable for all time, so he could go to bed with her and not remember how old she really was.

Yes, he kept her looking the same now as she was in her mid-twenties. At least she appeared this way to Jared and to others as well, except for Eve. Eve saw Margo as she really was.

"It's hard to fool an idiot," he said aloud and wished he hadn't. If Margo asked him to explain his remark, he'd have to lie in order to avoid a bigger argument than the one they'd already had. Margo worshiped those kids, especially Eve.

Margo never let on that she'd heard him, probably because she was doing her best to ignore him and shut him out of her life. He couldn't really blame her for feeling this way. Margo had seen him as he was, minus the illusion of being human, and while he was considered attractive to females in his demon state, Margo, unfortunately, wasn't a demon female.

"Did you sleep well last night?" he asked, hoping to break the ice.

"I slept in a chair by the window."

"Your choice."

"How do you think I slept?"

"You could have come to bed with me."

"Sure, and have you jab me all night long

with those claws of yours. Tell me, Jared, are you housebroken?"

"That's not funny!" he said. He wanted to leave, but he still craved her. He'd spent so many years satisfying her appetite, that now he'd developed one of his own. "You've never spoken to me this way before."

"Oh, hell," she said and smiled, her lips a cold line of anger. "Of course I haven't, but then I've never seen you in your natural state before. What are you? Half-wolf, half-dragon?"

"I'm a marquis, and that's all you have to know. You've been happy with me up until now, until those bastards came here and spoiled things."

"No. Correction, Jared. You spoiled it yourself by trying to control my life."

"I did it for your own good," he shouted, and rose to pace the length of the dining room. "I had to protect you."

"At what cost?" she shouted back. Valerie's children had left the house, so she was free to vent her anger without fear of them hearing her. "You had no right to keep me in the dark. You should have told me the truth about yourself, and the things you've done, years ago."

"Sure, and maybe we wouldn't have lasted fifty years. You would have rejected me sooner."

"You never gave yourself a chance to find out, did you, Jared?"

"What's that supposed to mean?" he asked, striking the table in front of her.

Margo jumped slightly when his open palm connected with the table, but then she composed herself and cursed beneath her breath. "I could have shown you how to handle things other than going by your own basic instincts. I could have shown you how to get rid of people other than by killing them. There are other methods to use."

"Such as?"

"Well . . . I don't know. I can't think straight when we're fighting, but there has to be a better way. You can't just go around killing."

"Show me, Margo," he said, dropping to his knees by the side of her chair. "Show me how."

Jonathan had done the same thing moments before, and Margo, in turn, had responded by wrapping her arms around him and demonstrating her love. But this was different. She couldn't show her love to a . . . beast.

"Margo, please," he said.

He'd never begged before, but then begging was a human instinct. "You had those kids beaten. I can't forget that. You killed my horses, and I can't forget that."

"It won't happen again . . . ever, not if you show me a different way to handle things. You must remember that we come from two opposite worlds. Yours is governed by love and compromise. Mine is beset by hatred and destruction. I swear I'll enter yours if you show me how."

Margo looked into his eyes, heard the pleading quality in his voice, and felt herself weaken despite herself. Whatever had gone on between them these past few days, he was still Jared, her lover, her companion for almost half a century. And Jared was asking . . . no! Jared was begging for another chance, and she owed it to him considering all they'd been through together.

"Will you try things my way?" she asked. She didn't fight when he stood up and lifted her into his arms.

"Yes," he said, carefully omitting the words "I promise" from his pledge. By speaking those words, he would have been compelled to follow through and do things her way, but Jared had no intention of changing at this stage of the game.

After all, he'd kept his actions a secret from her for so long a time, and he never would have been caught if those three bastards hadn't come to visit. They'd be gone in less than two weeks, so, if he went back to his old ways, Margo would never know the difference.

Who'd be around to tell her?

"Yes," he repeated, carrying her up the stairs to their bedroom, kissing her lips and her neck. "We'll do it your way, Margo." *Like hell!*

Bart Anderson stood still and stared at the bone protruding from the lower part of his leg. It kind of stuck out between the ridges in a flap of skin and hurt like hell, but it was only a bone, so why did it hurt? Yet, since it was his bone he was staring at, maybe it hurt because he was aware that it wasn't back where it belonged, tucked neatly inside of his leg.

Dropping the bat from his hand, because the damned thing was layered with his skin and his blood, he thought about climbing back into his car and going to the hospital, only he couldn't drive, not like this.

The other men were in worse shape than him. One had two broken arms, and another wasn't as lucky as the rest—his spine was crushed, or so it seemed from just looking at him lying on the ground all stiff and not daring to move.

He said he couldn't move, not his legs or his arms, and it hurt to try and sit up. Taking this into consideration, Bart started thinking as how he and a few others had been lucky, even if he did break his own leg. Hell, a leg could be fixed, but a crushed spine . . . never!

Looking around for someone to help them, Bart noticed that them three bastards were gone. Then he wondered if they'd ever really been there to begin with. He scratched his head and stuck his leg straight out to retrieve his discarded bat, lying on the ground at his feet.

Dropping the bat had been a foolish move on his part. Bats had lots of uses. A bat could be used for a crutch, in case he wanted to hike his ass back to town for help. Naw! It was too far.

A bat could be used to splint a leg, and if he did that, then he could drive back to town for help. But if he tried to set his own leg, it would hurt like hell, and Bart wasn't into pain. Hell no! He wasn't one of them masochistic bastards who enjoyed pain, who liked to be whipped by their women and have pins stuck under their fingernails, and all that bullshit. No, he wasn't no friggin' sadist!

So what do I do now? Do I stand here and pray, and hope that if I wait long enough the bone will go back inside by itself? Or do I holler for help and call attention to myself?

After all, the only folks within hearing distance were those inside of the Windsor mansion. Maybe they'll hear me and finish the job them three teenagers started.

As he evaluated the situation, he realized them three kids didn't do a thing except scream when he and his buddies came to a screeching halt on the road in front of them and got out with their bats. Them kids saw five, angry, raging men coming at them and froze in their tracks. Then the three of them turned and ran towards the mansion like the devil himself was after them.

The devil?

For one fleeting instant, Bart felt many, different sensations—all at the same time and none of them pleasant. He felt his body quake with a fearsome cold, he felt his nerves jab at his skin like tiny razors, and he felt bile rise in his throat. The devil, he'd thought, the devil.

The word had come to mind as naturally as anything else, but only because he used it every-day, in so many different ways. He never gave it a second thought until now, when there was a very real possibility that the devil was real.

Laughing a bit to himself because he was scared, he told himself it couldn't be true. Things like this didn't happen in real life, so he must have dreamed it up. He must have hallucinated, or, to put it another way, he must have had visions, right there in broad daylight.

He remembered approaching them three kids with his bat, throwing that little one to the ground, and screaming at her to come clean about her aunt. ''Tell us what she did with them twenty-four people!'' he'd screamed at her bowed head.

While she knelt on the ground in front of him, her crying and wailing just about driving him nuts, he had a sudden urge to bring his bat down across the top of her head. He had an urge to see her skull split wide open and her brains spill out, coating her hair with membranes.

He'd thought at the time that while she might not have been directly responsible for the disappearances of 24 people or the death of his father, she was kin to that Margo Windsor! He saw this as the perfect opportunity to turn things around, to let Margo Windsor know how it was to lose a loved one.

So, he raised the bat and brought it down towards her head with all of the hate and fury of the past ten years working his hands.

He saw her fly off the ground, right there in front of him, as if someone, or something, invisible had lifted her from harm's way. Then he saw the bat headed towards his own leg, only he couldn't stop it. Once it was in motion, carrying his full weight and all of the hatred he could muster up, he couldn't stop the bat from shattering his own leg, couldn't stop the bone from flying out.

"Oh, God, please make it stop hurting," he pleaded aloud.

"Now you're praying to your God? You're pathetic!"

Bart heard the voice coming from behind him and wet his pants. The devil!

"Not quite!" the voice said.

It was a strange voice he was listening to, for it was neither male nor female, neither alive nor dead, neither good nor evil. It was just a voice. The devil!

"The hell you say! I'm no devil. I'm stronger than any devil you'll ever meet!"

Using his bat to lean on, Bart turned and saw a creature wearing a monk's black robe with a hood pulled over its face. He thought about those rumors concerning Margo Windsor, and how she was related to Satan himself, and wondered why he'd been foolish enough to come here . . .

"You came to find your missing friends, true? Or did you forget?"

"You readin' my mind?" Bart asked in a small, squeaky voice. " 'Cause I didn't say nothing you could hear. I only spoke in my head . . . and you're hearing what I'm thinking?"

"Of course. And before you say, or think, another word, come and I'll show you where your friends are. They're waiting for you."

Bart thought about what it said and felt he'd rather not go anywhere just now, except to a hospital. And he was sure his buddies, those lying on the ground all crushed and battered, felt the same. No, he wasn't going anywhere.

"The hell you say!" the voice repeated, using the same expression it did when it told him it wasn't a devil. The expression wasn't said in a nasty way, rather it sounded more in line with friendly kidding, as if this creature was trying to be one of the boys.

"But my leg," Bart said, pointing out the obvious. "I can't walk."

"Yes, you can. And so can the others."

As Bart watched, the creature raised its black, robed hands high overhead and sort of sang some words he couldn't understand.

"Follow me," the voice said.

And miraculously, Bart did, without using the bat. His leg, he noticed, was still broken, and the bone still stuck out, but it didn't hurt to walk. "What about my buddies?" he wanted to know. He sure wasn't doing this alone, not without a backup of some sort.

"They're coming, too," the voice said.

And they did—Henry with his broken arms, and Hank with his crushed spine. They all walked behind Bart, all blindly and involuntarily following the robed creature to find their friends.

"What happened to you?" Bart asked Hank.

"I was about to kick that boy, to stomp his ass into the ground," Hank answered. "Only it was me who was kicked and stomped, right in my spine."

"I had that twin girl by the arms," Henry

added, "and I was gonna twist them arms behind her back until they snapped like twigs. Only it happened to me."

"Bad day," Bart said, sounding depressed. "For all of us."

"But it'll get better," the creature said. "You'll see. It'll be better once you're back in the company of your friends."

"Where are they?" Bart asked. "Where are we goin'?"

The creature said nothing at first as it led the way down the side of the road, away from Margo Windsor's mansion. It suddenly stepped onto a path leading into the woods, and for the life of him, Bart never remembered seeing that path before.

"Only because you've been too busy living your life to notice much of anything," the creature said, answering the questions in his mind. "Now, this path leads to a woody area behind the mansion. That's where your friends are, and that's where they're waiting for you."

The child of the prophecy came back alone, fully intending to drive Bart's car into the woods somewhere so it wouldn't be found, before returning to Aunt Margo's house.

The child was alone because Bart and his buddies had seen their friends, and those friends had killed them. Of course, killing these men had been harder on the dead ones than killing Matthew Soames was, because Matthew—although horrified by the sight of two, rotting corpses approaching him—was trapped.

Matthew had been standing up against the door to Aunt Margo's chapel, and the child was better able to control his movements until he was dead. But this was different. The child had given these men the ability to walk and run, after their bodies had been crushed and broken by the pets of the beast, at the child's command.

So there they were—five men, all running in different directions.

But their friends got them.

And so they were dead, and the child was satisfied.

Oh yes, the child was catching up to Jared real fast!

Chapter Fifteen

MARGO WENT TO her chapel after dinner, even knowing Nathan was there, but Nathan was harmless. Jared had sent him back to his home in Acheron, so the figure in her chapel was nothing more than an empty, skeletal shell, nothing more than a ghost of his former self.

Margo felt her lips form into a smile—a ghost of his former self. Well, hell, she hoped not. She hoped that Nathan would just kind of sit in his chair and be good and not act like a ghost normally did.

After lighting her black candles and praying to the four gods of the universe, she fell to her knees and could think of nothing further to say. She'd already exposed the truth of her religion to herself, as well as to Valerie's children, so what the hell was she doing here praying to a force she no longer believed in or respected?

Then again, old habits were hard to break, and this habit—honoring her lord, Satan, in prayer—had gone on for the past 60 years or more. And without this time to herself—time to free her head—Margo was lost.

This was therapy, better than a psychiatrist's couch and hard to give up.

Just because she was here in her own private chapel, that didn't mean she *had* to pay homage to the beast. She could just rest and not dwell on how Valerie's children were almost killed by those bastards from town.

She need not think about the child of the prophecy, and how, according to what Jonathan had told her, the child had called up the pets of the beast to save them.

Perhaps she even could forget the hours she'd spent this morning explaining the true meaning of their religion and how they had to give it up.

Her words ultimately had been wasted. The child of the prophecy hadn't been listening, didn't hear one thing she said.

For the child had used its powers again—but in self-defense this time.

Then was it so wrong what the child did?

Yes, she shouted inwardly. Yes, it was wrong. For surely the child, the one born of evil, hadn't stopped at beating those men. Margo would be willing to bet that the woods behind her house had five new tenants, thanks to the child.

A while back, Margo had been lying in Jared's arms discussing the prophecy while Valerie's children were being terrified by those men. Oh, could she ever forgive herself? She wasn't there when they needed her. She was in bed, instead, enjoying the raw pleasures of Jared's flesh.

Start over, she told herself. Don't let your conscience beat you to death for being human!

A while back, she had been lying in Jared's arms, discussing the child of the prophecy. She was disturbed because it had killed at least once that she knew of. Hell, the child was hardly a child in the true sense of the word, as she'd pointed out. The child was in its teens. So the very phrase, "child of the prophecy," was ridiculous, to say the least.

"I mean, Jared," she'd said, "what is your conception of a child?"

Before allowing herself to dwell on his answer, Margo was forced to open her eyes. Something had moved in the shadows around her. There had been a rustling of skirts—or robes! The sound of light footsteps had screamed for her attention and driven her from her reverie.

Nathan's footsteps would have been light, she thought, wondering if the chair beside the altar was empty. Nathan was nothing more than a ghost of his former self, so his footsteps would have been light.

She thought of just turning her head a bit to the side to see if Nathan had stayed in his chair—his body at least, for his soul was back in Acheron. At least she hoped it was. But she didn't have the courage to look at Nathan.

So she tried something else. Cocking her head to one side to determine where the footsteps were coming from, she was assaulted by dead silence. Nothing!

That meant Margo must have imagined the footsteps and the rustling of robes. Now, get your head together, she told herself, and stop being so damned jittery. This is your chapel, your private place. Don't start letting your imagination run wild or you'll never want to come here again. Think of something, anything, to stop listening. Think of Jared, and what he'd said about the phrase, "child of the prophecy."

Jared had told her that the terminology used in the phrase had been correct. "Considering," he'd said, "the age of the being chosen to replace Father Death, it's correct. You see, Death is ageless, having performed its duty for millions of more years than we care to count. Therefore, in comparison, a teenager is but a mere child, a baby, because that child is destined to exist for as long as Death has—millions of years."

Horrible, she'd thought at the time. To think of one of Valerie's children roaming without end and gathering bodies for the master beast. They were only children, young adults, innocent and naive.

When the noises reached her again, the noises she'd already charged up to imagination, she became alert—but for what? Who was making those noises? Who was in her chapel besides the corpse of Nathan?

Why was she so afraid when she had powers of her own, powers given to her by Satan? The answer was obvious. She was strong, but the child of the prophecy was stronger!

Listening to the rustle of a robe coming from behind her, she counted the footsteps, as someone approached her, and wondered how many it took to reach the altar. She'd never considered counting them until now. In all her visits to the chapel, she very stupidly had never given thought of counting the steps.

Of course, to give herself credit, she'd never had to. This was her chapel, her very own private place. No one came here, except Jared on occasion. So why be concerned with length and distance?

Yet it was important to her now. She needed time to compose herself, time to gather her courage to stand up and face the child—if it was the child. But why are you afraid of the child? It's one of Valerie's. You helped to raise it. Why be afraid now?

Because, she said to herself, I spoke against its lord, Satan. I tried to show it the error of its ways. I said that killing was wrong. The child must now silence me before I tell others, before I tell the world.

Therefore, Margo had to be prepared to do battle with one of her own. But what if the intruder behind her wasn't the chosen one, the child of the prophecy? It could be one of the dead ones the child had killed, or one of the dead ones Jared had killed.

That would mean sending the dead one back, but that was no problem! Let's see, she thought to herself, how does the chant go? *Cius, Acarius, Volanum!* No, you idiot. That's for calling up, not sending back.

One footstep, then another . . .

She listened and thought about how the chapel was longer than she'd known it was. The footsteps were taking so long to reach her side. Good! She had time. Now, what was that chant? *Satanus, lord of the four corners of the universe!* Satanus? How dramatic can you get? She laughed then, but it was an effort.

One footstep, then another . . .

For the life of her she couldn't remember how the chant went. That's because you've allowed Jared to take over and do your dirty work for you. It was always, "Jared, get rid of this one," or, "Jared, get rid of that one," as if she were the Queen of Sheba, speaking to a slave. And Jared did it.

Of course, he didn't get rid of people as you wanted him to, Margo dear, she scolded herself. If you weren't so lazy, you'd know the chant as well as you know your own name!

One footstep, then another . . .

Closer still . . .

Whoever it was, they must be old, she surmised, or they'd have reached her side by this time. While she was old as well, she could still beat the shit out of anyone her own age.

One footstep, then another . . .

This was getting boring. After all, this was her house, and whoever was walking behind her was an intruder. Hell, girl, she told herself, get up and throw them out. Then she laughed again, but it didn't sound funny.

A hand was on her shoulder . . .

A small one . . .

The kind that would belong to a teenager . . .

The child . . .

"Aunt Margo."

Jared lay in bed and listened to the footsteps approaching the chapel. Then he listened to them grow dull and start to fade once they stepped inside. He knew he should have gone to investigate. Margo was in there alone, but she wasn't helpless. Margo had powers of her own.

Keeping this in mind, he rolled onto his side and ignored the situation. It was probably one of those three bastards, whining and complaining.

As he thought about it now, those kids had never entered her chapel before. Never! They couldn't! Nathan was there, and Nathan was dead. They were afraid of him, so they stayed out.

One of those three bastards!

The child maybe?

Then so be it, he thought, and pulled the covers higher over his shoulder. So be it. If it was the child, and the child wanted to kill, wanted blood . . .

But you're here to guard Margo's life, with your own if necessary! Isn't that what her husband said when he sent you here?

Yes! And if that were the case, then her

husband should have given me more power than
the child. For the child is stronger and would
beat me in any battle we'd engage in. Keeping
this in mind, Jared closed his eyes and tried to
sleep.

But it was impossible. He couldn't sleep. He
couldn't relax, knowing that Margo might be in
danger. After all, this was *his* Margo!
His . . . he'd almost ended the thought with the
word "love," but he wasn't capable of love.
Still, he did feel something after all these years.

Grumbling, he threw off the covers and
rushed to the chapel door, hoping he wasn't too
late, hoping Margo was still alive. After all,
Jared had more powers than Margo, even
against the chosen one.

There was someone hovering over Margo, as
he neared the door to the chapel. It was one of
those three bastards, hovering in a bathrobe—not a monk's robe with cowl pulled over
its head. It was one of those three bastards all
right, but it wasn't the dangerous one. It was a
female, judging from the long hair hanging in
tight, angry waves down its back—hair just like
Margo's.

Jared remained standing outside of the door
to the chapel until he was able to learn the
identity of the figure. This was important. If he
knew who it was, then this one could be
eliminated as the chosen one. Surely if this was
the chosen one, it would have been properly
dressed and ready for the kill.

"Aunt Margo," he heard the female say,

speaking in a wistful manner. "I'm not really afraid of Nathan. He's dead. He can't hurt me. And you're here to help if he should try, Aunt Margo."

Jared turned then and went back to bed. The female had spoken but had made no sense. Eve. It was Eve, the idiot, the least harmful of the three.

"Aunt Margo, I'm scared," Eve had said after touching Margo's shoulder and scaring her half to death.

"But not scared enough to stay out of my chapel," Margo said, rising to face Eve. The girl looked puzzled. Obviously Margo's words had gone through her head without penetrating her brain. "Nathan's here. See him?" she said, pointing to the skeletal corpse sitting in a chair near the altar. "Aren't you afraid of Nathan?"

Then she wondered why she'd done this to Eve; reminding her of Nathan probably heightened her fears. What was she trying to prove? Yet Eve didn't fear Nathan.

"No. He's dead, but the chosen one is alive. And now it's killing, and I'm dreaming about the murders, just like I was the chosen one myself."

"Oh, Eve," Margo said, wrapping her arms protectively around the girl, "you're not the chosen one. Please don't be afraid."

"But, Aunt Margo, it doesn't help knowing I'm not the one. I mean, I know I can't be the chosen one because I'm too stupid."

"Don't ever say that!" Margo said, holding her at arms length now.

"But I am, and the chosen one is smart. So it's not me. Still, when it murders someone, I see it, and I don't wanna see it," she wailed in protest.

"Eve, listen . . . a while ago, Jonathan told me how the child had called up the pets to save you from those men on the road. Jonathan and Joelle are seeing the same things you are through the child's eyes."

"That doesn't help," she said, "just 'cause they see it, too. Did he tell you the child went back and killed those five men?"

Margo couldn't speak. There was nothing to say that would change things. Her fears had been realized. The child had gone back and killed those men.

"The chosen one took those men to the woods behind the house and let the dead ones kill them."

"Please, Eve," Margo said, grabbing onto her for balance. She felt herself going, felt her knees sinking. She was about to faint. There was only one course open to her now, only one way to stop the senseless slaughter by the chosen one—an open challenge from Margo herself.

Margo had to take the chosen one on in an open battle of powers. She had to issue a challenge in front of Valerie's children, and hope the chosen one responded. This way, she'd discover the identity—and probably be killed!

But it didn't matter, not to Margo. She was

old and would die soon anyway, maybe a whole
lot sooner than she thought. Jared told her that
death was the only way for someone of her
stature to break the ties binding her to Satan.

So it wasn't as though she were about to take
a needless risk. At this point, she was as good as
dead anyway.

Joelle sat in her room alone, crying her heart
out, until Garth came to comfort her.

Joelle was sitting on her bed, listening to the
sounds of screaming echoing inside her head,
while a vision of five men, running from a bunch
of rotted corpses, danced in front of her eyes.
Even though it had taken place hours ago, it was
just too awful to forget.

The murders kept coming back to her,
haunting her and filling her with guilt because
she'd wished those men dead—and not without
reason. Those men had tried to kill her and
Jonathan and Eve, so wanting them dead as
payment for their crimes had been a natural
reaction.

But then it had really happened, and she had
seen the whole, gruesome scene—as though she
were the chosen one herself. Oh, that was too
horrible to even dream or think about. Being the
chosen one meant spending the next few million
years or so gathering bodies for the master.

It was not a job she wanted. Of course, living
that long was a nice thought, but the gruesome
details of the expected chores of the chosen one
put a damper on it. It made her wish it was

Jonathan or Eve. She loved them dearly and normally wouldn't have wished anything so bad on their heads, but, since she herself didn't have the stomach to carry out the duties that went with the job, she wanted nothing more than to be able to pass it on to someone else.

But what if it *is* you? she asked herself. What will you do to stop—

"Nothing. You couldn't stop it if you tried."

Joelle heard Garth's voice and felt her heart flutter. Wiping her tears, she found herself staring up at the only man who, until now, had made her think of love and romance.

She recalled the first time they'd met, when Eve introduced them, and how something unspoken had passed between them. Joelle felt drawn to him now as she had then, but she was troubled. "Where were you today? We needed your help."

"I was there."

"Doing what? Watching those men try to kill us?"

"Hardly. I was waiting for my orders from the chosen one. The child has found its powers, and I obey."

"And what if the child didn't do anything?" she asked, trying to keep her mind on the subject at hand and not on Garth as a man she wanted desperately. "The child could have been so frozen with fear—"

"No way. The child doesn't know fear. You were safe. You didn't need me." After he'd spoken, she noticed the way he was staring down at her. It made her feel funny inside.

What he'd said made her feel funny as well. He'd mentioned the chosen one, and how he was waiting for its orders. The chosen one told him to beat those men, and Garth obeyed. Joelle hadn't given those orders, so maybe she wasn't the one. But since she did think along those lines, she was still a contender, still in the running.

"You just said we don't need you. If that's true, then what are you doing here now?" she asked, feeling a bit sad. Maybe he'd come to say good-bye. "By the way, how did you get in? My door's locked."

"Doors don't stop me," he said, a huskiness in his voice that had been missing before. "Especially not when there's someone waiting on the other side of that door, and it's someone I want to see real bad."

"Are you talking about me?" she asked, leaning back on her elbows and crossing her legs in a sexy way—a pose she'd often dreamed of using someday but had never tried until now. "You mean me?" she asked again.

"Yes."

Joelle studied him for a moment—his tan skin and his light brown eyes. Garth must have known how she felt about him from the very beginning, or he wouldn't be here now. Yes, she wanted him badly, and yet, there was something different about him. Then it came to her, and to think she'd almost missed it! He had hair now, she noticed, a full head of it, light brown and curly. "I kind of liked you bald," she said.

"Sorry. When I make the transition, it's not

always under my control. Maybe next time."
Never taking his eyes from hers, he sat on the
bed next to her and boldly rested a hand on her
abdomen.

Garth had picked up on her feelings for him,
she thought, but there were a few more problems
between them, and they were spoiling the mood.
He'd already explained why she didn't see him
today when those men were attacking them, yet
she needed answers to the rest of her questions.
For one, what did he look like when he wasn't
human?

"Do you want me to show you?" he asked,
reading her mind.

Joelle was tempted to go ahead and allow him
to show himself in his natural state. But then, if
she saw the beast in him, would she still want
him afterwards?

"Probably not," he said, removing his hand
from her abdomen to rub the back of his neck.
"But I'll do it if you want me to."

"No, that's all right," she said. "I can live
with the mystery."

"What's the next thing holding us up?" he
asked impatiently, anxious to get on with this.

"Holding us up?" she said, repeating his
words, as the shock of reality dawned on her.
Joelle had been flirting with a man, and now he
was calling her on it. She didn't know if she
could carry it through. Playing at being sexy was
one thing, but actually being sexy was another.
"Holding us up?" she said again, her voice
nervous and squeaky.

"Yes. Holding us up, stopping me from servicing you or making love, as you humans like to say." Garth had again placed his hand gently across her abdomen. She wanted to rip it away, and she wanted to keep it there as well. "I know you're mixed up," he said. "It's only because you've never been with a man before and you're afraid of me."

"But you're not a man," she reminded him, feeling that this was her way out. Now she wouldn't have to reject him and come off looking like a tease. After all, she had been leading him on.

Garth started to say something, then stopped, removed his hand and rose to leave. Joelle watched him without saying a word. She watched him walk across the room and begin to vanish as he passed through the door without opening it. While she watched, many things came to her, the most important of which was the reality of the situation. She was in love with Garth.

She couldn't begin to imagine why, but she was. And because of this, she couldn't risk losing him. "I'm sorry," she said quietly.

Garth stopped and came back into the room, facing her with a strangeness in his eyes. "What?"

"I'm sorry," she said again, a bit louder this time.

"I can't hear you!"

He was making it hard on her, and, judging from his expression now, he was enjoying it. He wanted her to say it louder, loud enough for the whole world to hear.

"Say it again, and that'll be enough."

"Everything in multiples of three."

"You've done your homework, Joelle. Everything must happen in threes." He had his hands on his hips as though he were in charge here, and Joelle knew he was.

"I'm sorry," she repeated for the third time, adding, "and I'll never do it again."

"Good. Now, before we start, what else is bothering you?"

Joelle stared at him. "I want you to tell me the name of the chosen—"

"I can't. You know I can't. Is this going to come between us?" He was closer to her now, standing over her, legs spread slightly apart. "Tell me now."

"No," she said, reaching for him, pulling him down beside her, moving his hand to her breast in a way that she never dreamed possible. This was her first time. She should have been afraid, and she had been until a few moments ago, until she realized how much Garth meant to her. Now, he was bringing something out in her that she didn't know existed. Deep inside she was more passionate than most women dreamed possible.

Garth kissed her lips and her neck, caressed her body with his mouth. Getting Joelle ready didn't take long; she'd been ready from the start. When at last they both lay naked on her bed, and she was able to feel the heat of his penetration, she moaned because it hurt, and she moaned because it didn't hurt for long. She moaned because it was the greatest sensation ever.

"Oh, Joelle," he said huskily. "I'll never leave you. I'll always be at your side."

"Like Jared is with Aunt Margo?" she asked, her breathing heavy and labored.

"Yes. Just like Jared is with Margo."

After speaking, Garth smiled for a moment. Joelle had been silently critical of her Aunt Margo because of her relationship with a demon, and now Joelle was destined to follow the same path. He wondered if they'd last 50 years, and would he, Garth, use the same illusion Jared did to keep Margo looking young and desirable? Would he do that to Joelle?

Chapter Sixteen

MARGO STAYED IN the shower longer than was necessary, but the water was hot. It penetrated her flesh and soothed her. It made her forget about the world on the other side of the door, and she had to forget.

Her world had grown sour, nightmarish. In less than a week, everything she had was trash in her eyes—her power, her wealth, Jared. Yes, she had to be honest about this. Jared was her demon/man now, and she was a slave to his love. He was trash, but she was worse.

Her power and wealth had been obtained by calling up the foul dead, or rather, creatures who'd never lived before, to kill her father. They had skinned him alive before ripping his head off!

Margo buried her head in her hands and cried. This was getting to be a habit, she thought, but there was too much bottled-up emotion not to cry.

They skinned him alive before ripping his head off!

Her father had not been all bad. No, she had loved him once, before his mind was twisted by Nathan and the others. He'd been a good man, good to her. He took her everywhere—to the zoo, the beach, the park—anywhere she wanted to go.

He had read the funny papers to her on Sunday. He had bought her the first bike she ever owned, working overtime at his job for months to pay for it.

So why didn't she think of the positive aspects of their relationship before ordering his death?

Why didn't she listen to her mother?

Mom told her to find it in her heart to forgive him, but Margo didn't. She went and killed him instead, and now she realized that she'd put her hatred on the wrong head, that she'd laid the blame for her blindness on the wrong person, that she'd taken the wrong life. There was just no way to take it all back, no way to wish him alive.

Margo turned off the water. It wasn't helping.

After wrapping a huge towel around her body, she stepped up to the mirror to look at herself, to look at the person who'd spent the last 63 years in a dream world where everything supposedly was bright and wonderful. She had to look at that person. She had to see if the mark of the idiot was on her forehead.

But no, it wasn't evident. Her idiocy was still internal. Yet the revelations storming her brain, and tormenting her otherwise serene and naive life, hadn't struck without some sort of outward trace. Margo looked at the gray flaring at her temples, then leaned into the mirror to get a closer look at the crow's feet around her eyes and the laugh lines along the sides of her mouth.

She dropped the towel to look at her body and was barely able to see pouchy pockets of flesh, evidence of aging, marring her breasts and abdomen. The marks were heavy, as if she'd aged rapidly. The reason she could barely see them was because her eyes were failing her.

She was going blind again!

"Sorry, Margo," Jared said, suddenly standing in the doorway behind her. "There's nothing I can do to stop this—the blindness, the aging. I've lost the ability to keep up the illusion."

The illusion, he'd said. There was her answer. A week ago, the night he'd killed Aubrey and Tom Soames, Margo had been so damn vain about admiring her own reflection in the mirror while she was brushing her hair. She'd wondered then about her looks, and why she'd never taken the time to age.

Well, there was her answer. It was all an illusion, and now the veil was lifting. She was stripped of the facade of eternal youth. She was aging. She would be old soon.

And Jared! She'd wondered about Jared that night as well and why he'd stayed so young. Was that an illusion also? Would he age now?

"I'm a demon, Margo," he said, reading her thoughts. "I'll always be the same."

She closed the towel then as quickly as she could and buried her face in her hands. She was ashamed to let him see her like this. She was old, probably somewhere around 40, which wasn't really old when she stopped to evaluate her age in terms of years. Still, it was old to someone who'd never looked a day over 25 or so.

Tomorrow she might look 50. "Please go away," she begged. "Please don't look at me."

"We have to face this," he said quietly. "We can't hide."

"Yes, we can! Just go away!"

"I can go, but what about the others? What about Valerie's children? Should I tell them to leave as well?"

Margo dropped her hands and stared at him in the mirror. That was a good point. She had to face Jonathan and Joelle and Eve. She couldn't hide forever. "What do I say?" she asked. "How do I explain this?"

"Just tell them the truth," he answered, walking towards her and reaching out to touch her. She shivered as his hands enfolded her shoulders. "Tell them it was all an illusion. Tell them I've lost some of my powers."

"But why, Jared?" she asked, leaning against him to absorb the strength from his body. "Why?"

"Because your relationship with them isn't based on lies."

"No, I don't mean why should I tell them the truth. I meant, why did you lose some of your powers? Was it because of me?"

"Yes. You renounced your ties with your lord—"

"Fuck him!"

"Well, now he's doing the same to you. He took away my ability to keep you young and desirable, and he's taking away your gift of insight. Soon—"

"He'll take my life," she said, leaning harder against Jared, as if by doing so, she could stem the oncoming nightmare. "I love you, Jared," she said helplessly, knowing she had nothing with which to hold him now.

Not even the fragrance of Monkshood blended with Nightshade was enough to keep him from seeing an old woman where he hadn't before. The illusion was lost to her now. "I love you," she repeated and stepped away, knowing he could never love her back. He was a demon-man, incapable of feeling that kind of emotion.

"Where are you going, Margo?"

"To look out my bedroom window," she answered, as wistfully now as Eve would have.

"Why?" he asked, following closely behind, afraid she was about to do something foolish.

"Because I want to look at the trees and the sky and the world outside while I still can, before those things are lost to me forever."

"All you have to do is take it all back. Recant your renouncement."

"No," she answered stubbornly, wheeling to face him head on. "I'll let my hair go gray, and I'll let myself get wrinkled, and I'll even die a horrible death—probably in the jaws of his hounds! I'll do all this willingly because now I know the truth about him and about my religion. I can never go back in my thinking—not now, not ever."

"Your choice," he said, not sure she'd heard because she was standing in front of the window by this time, staring at her beloved trees, dead though they were. Jared was just as glad she hadn't heard, for if she had, she might have continued to stare at him.

And the last thing he needed or wanted was for Margo to see the few tears that were marring his vision. He'd spent too many years with her. He *was* almost human, and right now, he was mourning her fate.

Dennis Windsapple was shaving when the urge to see Margo Windsor became an obsession. Over the last month he'd noticed gray flaring at his temples; he was aging. Before he got too old, he was determined to ask Margo to marry him.

While she might not be interested in a middle-aged man with a pot belly, since she was young and beautiful and alluring, he had to give it his best shot.

And he had to forget about her boyfriend if he were to go and see her today.

Her boyfriend wanted him dead.

Then again, maybe Margo wanted him dead, too.

No! Margo felt something for him. After all, ten years was a long time to remain just friends. There had to be some underlying current of emotion streaming through Margo Windsor's heart for Dennis Windsapple, and if so, he planned on using that emotion to manipulate her into marrying him.

To hell with her boyfriend! If the bastard loved her as much as Dennis did, then he'd be asking her to make their relationship legal instead of shacking up with her like he was.

That's your edge, Dennis boy, he said to himself. You want to marry her, not just climb in bed and be done with it.

Margo just had to say yes. But there were five more men missing from town since yesterday morning. Word had it they went to see Margo and never came back!

He lifted the razor to his neck and realized his hands were shaking, and not just from the passions he felt for Margo Windsor. He was scared, afraid of becoming a statistic. The count was now 29 and climbing, even if you didn't include the grisly murder of Ben Anderson, the smithy.

No, he shouted inwardly. He wouldn't continue to think this way. He loved Margo, and he wasn't about to talk himself into being afraid of her now, not after ten years. Besides, wasn't he the one who was always telling folks how crazy they were whenever they tried to lay the blame for those mysterious disappearances at

Margo Windsor's feet?

He told them they were nuts! Only now he must be crazy too, along with the others, because his mind was heading in the same direction. All of those missing people had gone to see Margo Windsor and never came back!

But you will, he told himself. Margo likes you. Margo might even marry you . . .

At this point, he decided to put his marriage proposal on hold for a while. Of course, he'd still go and see her—but for what? To ask her about those missing people?

Why not? Margo and he had always spoken the truth between them, so it wasn't as though she'd be mad at Dennis for asking a few questions. In fact, she might even welcome the opportunity to clear her name. Chances were that Margo probably was unaware of what was going on around her.

Yes, that was it. Margo didn't know the truth. After all, Dennis had just now remembered the hatred directed at him by her boyfriend. He'd been standing out next to his car, ready to climb in, when he felt this rage assaulting his senses, and he turned and saw her boyfriend. It had to be him—her boyfriend. He was the one doing the killing while Margo was taking the blame.

Wiping his face with a damp cloth, he splashed on after-shave and studied his reflection in the mirror. He wasn't that old, at least not as old as he'd felt moments ago, and the gray didn't look all that bad. It sort of blended in with the rest of his hair and made him look distinguished.

He was halfway dressed and ready to go see his beloved Margo when he stopped and went to the phone. Dennis wanted to call his secretary. He had to tell someone where he'd be in case he was needed for bank business—or in case he didn't come back.

Loving Margo was one thing. Allowing that love to blind him entirely to the dangers involved in seeing her was another.

It was cold there in the dining room, or maybe it was just nerves. Margo sat with her back stiff and rigid and tried not to shudder. Valerie's children would be down soon. What would she say to them? How would she explain her aging, especially in terms they'd understand?

Previously she'd thought of telling them in a way that any teenager would have been sure to follow. "Jared was keeping me young by using the art of illusion." This was how she wanted to begin. From there, the rest would have been easy.

She would say, "The breakdown of the illusion is similar to a storm causing static interference over radio waves. You see, Jared was the transmitter. He sent out the waves of illusion. I was the receiver. And Satan is the storm breaking up the waves, destroying the illusion."

Now, sitting here waiting for them, aging by the minute, she didn't think her explanation was all that good. In fact, seeing them was a rotten idea. Why let them see her and spoil their image of Aunt Margo? Why not go into hiding until they leave and let them remember her as she was—young and beautiful?

"How would you pull it off?" Jared wanted to know. He'd just walked in but had quickly scanned her brain. "What would you tell them? What is your reason for staying in your room?"

"I'd tell them. . . . How could I tell them anything? I don't want them to see me."

"Right! Then I'd have to give the explanations," he said, sitting opposite her and studying her eyes behind those dark glasses. "They'd probably think I killed you if you didn't show up at least once before they left."

Margo stared back and said nothing. He was right. They would want to see her, Jonathan especially. "You'd better leave," she said. "They'll be down soon."

"I'm staying. They know I exist. What's the use of hiding?"

Margo smiled at that. After all these years Jared had finally gotten over his shyness, or maybe he didn't care if they saw him now. They never knew about him before, but Margo had told them about Jared only yesterday. So, like he said, why hide?

Margo heard them coming down the stairs and swallowed hard. "How old do I look now?" she asked.

"Forty."

"I looked forty an hour ago. I must look at least fifty by now."

"Don't worry about it," he said, rising to his feet when the door opened.

Margo saw them come in—Jonathan and Joelle and . . . some strange man she'd never seen before. "Where's Eve?" she asked. Only no one answered because they were in shock. When Joelle stared at her aunt's gray hair and the lines on her face, she turned white. Jonathan started to speak, but stopped. Then he stepped back towards the door as if he couldn't face this and wanted to leave instead.

The stranger was the only one who seemed to be able to handle Margo's appearance. Since she'd never laid eyes on him before, he wasn't able to notice the rapid change in her. "Where's Eve?" she repeated.

"Out back . . . playing," Joelle said quietly. "She said she wasn't hungry, and if we were gonna talk again, like we did yesterday morning, she'd rather go out and play."

"I see. Being out back is a lot safer than being out front near the main road," Margo said, thinking for a moment about what happened the day before with those five men. Then she started to ask the twins who their friend was, but Jared cut her off.

"Garth, I see you're still hanging around. Thought I told you to stay away from here." Jared's voice sounded hateful and menacing, and this puzzled Margo. She'd never seen this man before. How did Jared know him? "I told you to get lost."

"And I told you I couldn't."

"What's going on?" Margo asked, rising to stand near Jared who ignored her and continued to argue with Garth.

"There's only one bodyguard in this house, and that's me!"

Garth smiled and folded his arms in front of his chest. "And you're doing a swell job. You're to be congratulated, Jared. In fact, looking at your woman, I can tell you're on top of things—"

"You'd better stop there," Jared warned, but Garth ignored his threat and continued with his taunts.

"Maybe I should be servicing her. Hell, I can handle two!"

"Handle two?" Margo shouted. "Servicing?"

At that point, Joelle turned and angrily shoved Garth away. "Who the hell do you think you are? The house stud? You son-of-a-bitch!"

Margo realized the gist of the conversation and felt her knees buckle. This was another demon/man, another Jared, and he was to Joelle what Jared was to her. Would the nightmare ever stop? "No, Joelle! You couldn't be involved with him!"

"Maybe I'm missing something," Joelle said to Garth, ignoring Margo. "Maybe we're not talking about the same thing, so I'll give you the benefit of the doubt. When you service a woman, Garth, just what are your duties?"

"I hump her, and I keep her looking good," Garth said, laughingly. After hearing his answer, Joelle's face became a mask of rage. She raised her hand to slap him, but it froze in midair. "Watch it," he warned her. "We don't take to being hit."

"Don't threaten my sister, you bastard," Jonathan said, speaking for the first time since entering the room, his fists rolled into balls. "Joelle, what's this bullshit? Did you sleep with him? Did you?" But Joelle never answered. She put her head down to avoid looking at Jonathan. "Did you?" he raged at her.

"Look," Margo said, cutting in, "something awful is happening here. In fact, something awful has been happening all week. It's been a nightmare a minute, and it has to stop. Let's just sit down and talk. No shouting. Just talk. Especially you and me, Joelle. We *must* talk."

Margo didn't know why, but everyone listened to her. Now they were all seated around the dining room table waiting to talk this out—Jared and herself, and Jonathan and Joelle and Garth—three humans and two demons.

It was a farce, like something written by Moliere, only funnier because things like this didn't happen in real life.

"Well now," she said, trying not to laugh, but there was an edge to her voice bordering on hysteria which caused her to giggle a bit. "I see that Joelle has a fella. Tell me about him, Joelle."

Joelle had her head down, purposely keeping her attention away from Jonathan, who was glaring at her. "There's nothing much to tell. He followed us here from Philadelphia."

"All the way from Philadelphia. Well, I must say, that's a trip. And now you two are an item?"

"Yes," she answered quietly, almost jumping out of her skin when Jonathan pounded on the table with his fist.

"I can't sit here and listen to this!" Jonathan bellowed, getting up and knocking his chair over.

"You will sit and you will listen," Margo commanded, losing her temper. "We will all listen. We will be courteous to one another!"

Jonathan's mouth dropped open. He stared down at Margo, then pulled his chair upright and sat down.

"Thank you, dear," Margo said, before turning her attention to Joelle's fellow. "Mr. Garth . . . or should I call you, Garth?"

"Garth is fine," he said, focusing his eyes on Margo in a tantalizing manner.

He was trying to flirt with her, probably to make Jared angry, but Margo ignored his advances and kept talking. "Why did you follow them?"

"To guard their lives."

"I see. You mean to guard the chosen one. Isn't that really what you had in mind?"

Garth nodded silently and licked his lips in a lewd manner. There was no mistaking the message he was sending to Margo.

"Hey, look, bastard," Jared said, rising to his feet and knocking his chair over, "you wanna go at it?"

"Sure," Garth said, getting up. "But I can't understand your jealousy. You're a demon, same as me. No human emotions—"

"Stop it!" Margo shouted. "This is my home, and I will not allow this. Jared, come sit by me. Garth, you knock off the bullshit. I'm trying to talk to you, and I want answers. I'm not interested in your nonsense." This was exhausting, not that she hadn't gone through something similar before. When Valerie's children were younger, she was always breaking up fights between them, but this, this was terrible.

"Now . . . I want Garth to sit there, at the other end of the table, away from Jared, and I want him to tell me about himself and what he's doing to Joelle. I want Joelle to listen carefully, and I want Joelle to learn from Garth what he's really like. I want Joelle to understand why she's making a mistake getting involved with him."

"Did you make a mistake, Aunt Margo, when you became involved with Jared? Did you?" Joelle was half-shouting now, oblivious to Jonathan's anger.

Margo glared at her—with what little sight she had left—and decided not to answer. This conversation wasn't working out the way she'd planned. Rather than go on with this and listen to people fighting and arguing from one end of the table to another, she figured she'd try something else.

She sighed heavily and got to her feet. "I'm going outside to get Eve."

"I'll get her," Jonathan said tightly and started to get up, but Margo stopped him.

"No, I'll do it. I have to get away from this for a few minutes. I need a break. When I come back with Eve, we'll eat breakfast as though nothing happened, and while we're eating, everyone will concentrate on what's been said here. Then we'll talk, and we'll keep on talking until something's straightened out. Do you understand?"

She watched the silent nodding of heads around the table, then she left the dining room to get Eve. Once or twice on her way to the back door, she had to stop and lean against the nearest wall to keep her equilibrium.

The nightmare grew and flourished, and she was getting too old for all of this.

I'm going to faint . . .

Must get Eve . . .

Mustn't think . . .

Standing at the back door with the knob in her hand, she opened it, sucked in her breath and almost gave in, almost let herself go insane over what she saw.

Oh, Eve was there all right.

It had to be Eve. The twins were in the dining room!

Eve was talking to her friends.

Eve was dressed in a black monk's robe with the cowl pulled over her head, and her friends were the walking dead from the woods behind Margo's house.

"Eve!!!" Margo said, her voice high and squeaky.

Eve turned and pulled the cowl back for Margo to see that it was her. Then Eve smiled, and Margo screamed and screamed and screamed.

Margo stopped screaming as suddenly as she'd begun. Someone was there, someone had come running around the side of the house to see what the screaming was all about. It was so good to see Dennis Windsapple at that moment. Even with her sight failing her, she could make out Dennis' features.

It was just that he was looking at her, and he looked like he was in shock, but not at the sight of Eve or the dead ones. He was in shock at the sight of a Margo grown old.

All he kept saying, over and over, until Margo thought she'd go insane, was, "Is that you, Margo? Is that you, Margo? Is . . . ?"

Chapter Seventeen

DENNIS WINDSAPPLE WASN'T sure he was driving in the right direction, but he hoped he was headed towards Monkshood. As a rule Dennis didn't have this problem, having lived in the same area since birth. He knew the roads as well as anyone.

But today was special, Dennis thought, as he rode along a ribbon of highway with his radio blaring. His mind wasn't with it, to coin an old phrase, so he could have been going north, away from town, without knowing it.

Whistling to the tune of a rock song, he stopped every now and then to giggle. Having the ability to giggle made this a special day. Listening to raw rock on the radio—and liking it—made this a special day. Walking among the dead at old Margo's house—and surviving—made this a special day. He giggled again and ignored the saliva bubbling on his lips.

Driving along, he scanned the surrounding countryside and thanked God for being alive to appreciate what he saw. Then he thought about what he was doing and laughed. Would you be doing this now, Dennis boy, if you hadn't come so close to death?

The answer was no. Dennis, like most other people, never took time to smell the roses until the opportunity was almost lost, until he'd just about lost the ability to smell anything—but death.

Not only was this a special day, it was a beautiful one as well—sunny and a bit chilly, but not too chilly. And the sky was magnificent, blue as blue can be, dotted here and there with foamy, white clouds. Lord, it was beautiful; everything around him was beautiful.

But not everything that he looked at was alive; some of what he saw was dead.

The trees and bushes were dead; everything on the ground around him was dead, everything with the exception of those pretty blue Monkshood plants.

Dennis pressed his foot harder on the accelerator and again hoped he was headed in the right direction, but it really didn't matter. He was in no hurry to get home. No one was waiting for him at home, so why rush? Why not slow down and enjoy the scenery?

Because, you fool, if you slow down, they might catch you!

The dead ones, those Monkshood witches and warlocks, might catch you. And the others, the

29 missing people, the rotted corpses walking like zombies might catch you, too.

Pushing harder on the accelerator, he wiped his mouth with the back of his sleeve and smiled. He'd met an old friend today, one he'd never seen in the flesh, but an old friend just the same. He'd met Carl Ruttenberg, the devilish, fat tailor who'd been burned at the stake hundreds of years before with his baby tied down next to him. Carl had his baby with him today, carrying it in his arms.

Of course, Carl had no right keeping that hood tied over its tiny head, but Carl took it off when Dennis told him to.

But the baby's face was burnt, its features fused into a tiny lump of flesh!

Dennis was salivating heavier now and giggling louder and driving faster. Although he didn't want it this way, Dennis was leaving his precious Margo behind without asking her to marry him, and she might have, now that she was around his age—or older.

Dennis recalled the sight of her with her gray hair and her face all sagging and wrinkled. He glanced at his own face in the rearview mirror to see if his was sagging as badly as hers, but it wasn't. Therefore, he concluded, Margo was older than he was now, and Margo was a horror.

She had those dark glasses on, looking darker than ever against her whiter than white skin. Dennis never remembered her being so pale before; Margo always had good color.

Maybe she was dead, too!

No, she was alive!

And that kid with the robe on, that dumb, little Eve was alive, too, but she wanted Dennis dead. She wanted the dead ones to kill him, and she almost had her way, except that Margo stepped in and demanded she let him live.

Eve thought about it for a long time and finally agreed, only if Dennis vowed to keep his mouth shut about what he'd seen there today.

Dennis swore he'd keep it to himself, then he signed an oath in blood, using his own blood. Eve jabbed a finger on his right hand with her dagger and made him bleed, but then he couldn't write a thing with his blood running all over the place.

"Hell, kid, I'm right-handed," Dennis told her in a forthright but humble manner, and Eve, being so smart the way she was now, jabbed a finger on his left hand, enabling Dennis to scratch out an oath with his own blood. Eve even supplied the quill, and there was Dennis, scratching and dipping, scratching and dipping until the oath was complete. That oath said he'd rather die than tell anyone about what went on at Margo's, and keep the oath he would. "I swear, I swear," he shouted to no one in particular. He was in the car alone. There was no one to hear him, and no one to tell him that doing 80 on a narrow, country road was a bit on the foolish side.

"Yes, it is a bit dumb, Dennie boy. It wasn't too bad back there where the road was straighter, but there are a couple of bad curves up ahead."

Dennis heard the voice and giggled. He wasn't alone in the car as he'd originally imagined he was. Wiping the excess saliva from his chin, he peered in the rearview mirror and saw—Carl Ruttenberg, holding his baby, without the hood. Good, old Carl had come along for the ride.

"I was worried about you being alone," Carl said, as if he'd read Dennis' mind.

"Well now, that's just about the nicest thing anyone's done for me in ages, and to think you didn't want me to be lonely. Gosh, Carl, you're some kind of a guy. But, Carl, would you please put the hood back over the baby's face?"

"Of course, Dennis, I didn't realize it bothered you."

This was awful. Dennis had offended Carl, but he didn't mean to. "I'm sorry. No offense intended."

"None taken."

Such a nice, kind voice. A real, swell guy. "You know," Dennis began, jamming his foot harder on the accelerator in a sudden urge to get away from Carl and his ugly baby, "maybe we can find a plastic surgeon to fix the baby's face."

"Good idea!" Carl said and leaned closer, his breath caressing the back of Dennis' neck.

Dennis peered in the rearview mirror and saw a blackened mouth with a thick, black liquid oozing from it, a pair of nostrils flaring with revenge, and a pair of eyes, hot with hatred. Then he thought about how Carl was going to kill him, but he didn't know why.

"Because the chosen one doesn't trust you."

"I signed an oath—in blood!" Dennis pointed out, his voice laced with hysteria.

"It doesn't mean a thing."

"But Eve promised—"

"Not to kill you herself!"

Dennis turned back to the road and wondered how it would happen. He was doing 90 now, and the road curved ever so slightly up ahead. Naw! Carl asked him to slow down because the speed bothered the baby, so Carl wasn't about to force him off the road.

"Why did she pick you?" Dennis asked. He had to know. There were so many dead ones hanging around, so why Carl?

"Why not? I'm the one your ancestors burned at the stake, along with my baby. I have a lot of getting even to do. Besides, I've been on your mind quite a bit lately. My killing you is fitting."

"And just how will you do it? I have a right to know."

"The sentence is death by burning," the blackened mouth said as an equally blackened hand touched his shoulder and set off an inferno of flames.

Dennis saw the flames, but they didn't register at first. Actually, he figured it was his imagination. After all, why would Carl set him on fire when Carl was there with the baby, and they might get burned, too?

Yet the flames were real, the fire was real, and the pain was real. The only thing not real was Carl Ruttenberg and his baby; they were gone now. Dennis peered through the rearview mirror

again and saw an empty back seat—and flames
licking up around his head.

Then he quickly computed his chances for survival. His coat was burning now but not much,
he thought. This was a devil's fire, hard to put
out. Then he computed his chances for future
survival if he came through this alive. Not much,
he thought. They'd come after him again. Eve
would make sure of that.

Christ, the pain was awful now, so awful it
made him want to scream. His back and his hair
were on fire. Jamming the accelerator closer to
the floor, he got up to 100 and vowed not to
make the next turn in the road ahead, although
he could have if he wanted to.

If Carl had still been in the back seat with the
baby, he might have made the effort just not to
scare the baby, but Carl and the baby were gone
now. Carl had up and left, and there was just no
reason to try and stay on the road.

So much was happening. Eve was the chosen
one, Garth and Jared were fighting, and Joelle
had herself a fella.

Margo sat in the kitchen alone—she couldn't
face the others still waiting in the dining room
for her to return—and held her head to stop the
waves of motion and nausea that threatened to
make her faint. It was Eve, her baby, her poor,
brain-damaged, born-dead baby.

And she had to stop Eve. She had to. But she
was growing old, and she was going blind. She
was losing her powers along with Jared. So now,

how would she stop Eve?

There was just no way.

"Aunt Margo, I can't take much more of this."

It was poor, sensitive, scared Jonathan. He'd come into the kitchen to join her. She waited until he sat down, then locked her eyes onto his and covered his hand with her own. "I can't either, but we must be strong until this is over." That sounded good, she thought, wondering what she'd say next if he asked how. Telling someone to be strong was one thing, but telling them how to do it was another.

"My world's collapsed," he said tearfully.

"Mine, too." And I've lost more than you, she wanted to shout but didn't. He was looking for answers, not abuse.

"Joelle's shacking up with a beast, an inhuman thing, and Eve . . . I really thought it was Joelle. I thought she was the chosen one."

"I thought so, too," Margo said quietly. "She seemed to be the only one, out of the three of you, who could pull it off. You, Jonathan, are too sensitive, and Eve—"

"Eve's too stupid."

Margo heard the voice but didn't recognize the worldliness behind it. Eve had come into the kitchen behind Jonathan.

"You were the one who kept insisting you were stupid," Margo said bitterly. "Not us."

She watched Eve walk over to where she was sitting with Jonathan, a new wealth of knowledge and confidence apparent in her gait.

Jonathan grew tense at the sight of her. Sliding his hand from beneath Margo's, he started to lay it casually on the table, but then he grabbed Margo again and held on tight. Margo saw the expression on his face, the pallor of his skin, the fear in his eyes, and felt herself growing angry. Eve was frightening her own brother beyond belief.

"Is this what it means," she demanded of Eve, "to be special, as you termed it a while ago? Look what it's doing to your family."

"Sorry about that. There's nothing I can do to stop this."

"You can turn your back on it," Jonathan said, his tone full of hope.

"I can't, and I won't!"

"Eve!"

"Jonathan, do you know what it's like to be stupid? Do you have any idea what it's like to have people mock you because you're slower than they are? Turning my back on this honor will make me stupid again." Her eyes were trained on him now, only they looked funny. For a moment, Margo feared for his life. This wasn't Eve, his sister. Not now. This was Death in the flesh.

"I tried to take care of you."

"Yes. And I'm taking that into consideration."

"Bless you, child!" Margo said sarcastically before she could stop the words from passing between her lips. Eve turned away from Jonathan and stared at her now, only Margo felt no fear. According to Jared, Margo didnt' have long to live anyway. "Oh, thank you for not killing us."

"Careful, Aunt Margo. I will not be mocked!"

"Eve," Jonathan said, to draw her attention away from Margo, "how did this happen? How did you know it was you?"

Eve sucked in her breath and smiled. "I didn't—not until we took those pictures in the woods."

"I don't understand."

"I saw the dead ones in the woods without the use of a camera. I saw them before the photos were developed."

"How did you find out about the photos?" Jonathan asked. "We took great pains to hide them from you. We didn't want you upset."

"Garth showed me the photos to confirm what I saw. Anyway, the dead ones were all around us that day, following us through the woods. I was frightened of them at first, but they made no move to harm us. It was funny. You and Joelle never let on that they were there."

"I can't believe you actually saw them." Jonathan let go of Margo's hand and rose to pour himself a drink of water. "You didn't say anything."

"Well," she said, "I figured you'd accuse me of being crazy again, just like you did when Garth followed us from Philly."

"I apologize for that," he said sincerely. It wasn't fear speaking now, only shame.

"Anyway, you and Joelle never mentioned them, the same as you never mentioned Garth. Also, I was able to look beyond the illusion Jared set up for Aunt Margo's benefit. I knew she looked old, but nobody else did. So I began to think about it, how I was able to see things with the naked eye that you two couldn't. I put it all together and came up with the answer—I was the chosen one—and to make sure, I asked Garth."

"And Garth said yes?" Margo asked quietly.

"What a stupid question," Eve said tersely. "Just a few minutes ago I was outside with the dead ones, I was in control. Didn't that prove anything?"

Margo sighed heavily before answering. "I was hoping you were wrong."

"Well, I wasn't! You saw it yourself. You saw the proof. I control the dead ones, as promised!"

"Why were you picked?" Jonathan asked. "You have . . . had problems since you were born."

"Being born dead was a way of throwing everyone off the track. I mean, how could it be Eve? Right, Aunt Margo? Isn't that what everyone thought? Eve is no contender. She's too stupid. My lord, Satan, planned that part of it, and he planned it well. Let her be dumb and everyone will leave her alone! It was a form of protection for me."

Margo listened to her, heard the obvious and wanted to die. It was all too simple; had she used her head, she could have figured it out long ago.

The chosen one had to be protected at all costs until it was old enough to take over. What better way for the lord of lies to protect his own than through the use of deceit?

"I saw the murders as they were committed," Jonathan said. His face was marked with tears now; he was losing control again. "I saw them, those people you killed! Then I wondered if I was the chosen one, or Joelle, because we were there when your murders took place. And you let me go on wondering if I was the one."

"You only witnessed the murders because I had to borrow strength from you and Joelle. I wasn't sure if I had my full powers yet, or if I had to wait until the eve of Dagu's Nacht when my lord comes to see me. So I borrowed what little you two had to add to my own. That's why you—"

"Eve—named after the mother of creation," Margo said, her attention focused on nothing in particular. "I bet your lord, Satan, even picked your name. And it's fitting. You're the mother of . . ." Margo stopped speaking then and trained her eyes on Eve. There was something awful in her heart for Eve now, and she couldn't hide it. "No, not of creation! Of death and destruction and insanity—"

"Enough, old woman! You test my loyalties, and you push too hard. My name is fitting. I am the beginning of the end. The last thing you'll ever see on the face of this earth!"

Margo could see it happening now, long after it was over. Jonathan jumped Eve, but only because Eve was threatening his Aunt Margo and Jonathan was losing control. So why couldn't Eve make allowances? Why couldn't she just stop him by holding him at arms length? She had the power.

Why did she thrust his body through an inferno of flames?

Why did she make him walk ten levels in hell?

Why did she torture him before she was through with him?

Why didn't Jonathan fight her?

Why did he allow himself to go insane?

Margo sat for several minutes, although it seemed like hours, and held onto Jonathan. Eve was near the door, smiling, her face a mask of vengeance. Jonathan had been screaming, telling his Aunt Margo how bad it was down there.

First he mentioned something about smoldering flames and people who were locked inside of them. For a while, he was one of those people. "Oh, Aunt Margo," he said, "the heat was awful; my skin blistered and bubbled. The pain was maddening."

Then he mentioned great hoary beasts who stuck him with their talons and bit him with their teeth. They also pushed him roughly to the ground where Jonathan landed on top of a bunch of jagged rocks that put holes in his flesh. As if that weren't enough, they thrust a dagger into his navel and twisted it in circles, and another up inside of his rectum, tearing the tender membranes of his intestinal wall.

Finally he mentioned seeing Nathan, with some man whom Nathan introduced as his grandfather, Margo's father. His grandfather's eyes were blazing with insanity when he spoke to Jonathan. His grandfather was one of the lucky ones.

Jonathan was quieter now, his body wracked with grief, his tears soaking the shoulder of Margo's dress. As he cried, Margo stared at Eve and wondered why the others hadn't come running when they heard Jonathan's screams. Joelle and Jared and Garth were still in the dining room. They should have heard the commotion and responded.

"They have their own problems to contend with," Eve said, after scanning Margo's brain. "They're too busy for this nonsense."

"Nonsense?" Margo said. "Driving Jonathan crazy is nonsense? He cared about you, more than you'll ever know. You see, Eve," she said, her voice no longer soft and subdued from shock, "you were stupid, so you couldn't feel or sense the love they had for you. Now you're smart, but your intelligence appeared in the space of a second, allowing you to skip over years of emotion. Actually, you missed out on a lot. You'll never know what it's like to love someone and be loved in return."

"And neither will you, old lady. Oh, you can love. You can give it, but Jared will never love you back. He's incapable."

"That's true, but we're not discussing Jared and myself now. We're discussing you."

"Well, while you're discussing me, bear this in mind. Jonathan wasn't really hurt—not physically—not yet at least. The torture he suffered was only an illusion, like the one Jared used to keep you young."

"Should I thank your lord for small favors?" Margo asked bitterly. "Or should I thank you for not killing him, for just driving him insane?"

"Aren't you even curious about what's going on in the dining room?" Eve asked, changing the subject as quickly as she could. "Don't you care?"

"Of course I care. Unlike you, I care about others, but I'm with Jonathan now. He needs me."

"That's all right, Aunt Margo," Jonathan said, using the same, old, wistful manner that Eve used to have in her voice. "I'll be okay. You can go back to the dining room and see if everyone's alive."

Alive! She wanted to scream. Why wouldn't everyone be alive?

"I stopped there on my way back from hell," Jonathan said, sounding so much like the small boy he was ten years before. "Jared and Garth were fighting. Joelle tried to stop . . ."

The rest of his words were lost as Margo let go of him and ran past Eve. At least she was doing what passed for running at her age. She was slower now than she'd been days ago, before her age had caught up with her. She had to get to the dining room as quickly as possible.

She had to separate Jared and Garth, and she had to protect Joelle. Didn't Joelle know better than to try and stop two demon warriors from fighting? Margo, herself, had taken a chance stepping between them a while back, but Margo was fed up and hadn't considered the consequences of her actions.

Going the length of the hall as quickly as she could, Margo realized she was being pulled in two different directions at the same time. Jonathan needed her, and she'd left him behind with Eve. And Joelle needed her. This was awful. Surely Eve wouldn't harm Jonathan again, not when he was insane and helpless.

Eve couldn't be *that* cruel . . .

Or could she?

Turning in her tracks, Margo started back for Jonathan when she spotted him coming down the hall towards her. Eve was nowhere in sight. Grabbing his hand, she half-dragged him along until they were directly outside the dining room door.

"Aren't you going in there?" Jonathan wanted to know, his words spoken in the kind of singsong manner often used by toddlers. Margo's heart cracked a bit more as she remained silent. "Come on, Aunt Margo, let's go," Jonathan said, grabbing the knob and forcing the door open. Somehow he knew she couldn't do this herself.

Margo was afraid to look inside, but she had to.

There were no sounds coming from within, other than the sound of Joelle's sobbing. Joelle sensed Margo's presence and ran to her, burying her head against Margo's chest. "He's gone," she said, her body shuddering with emotion. "He's gone."

Margo felt a tightness across her chest. Who was gone? Which one? Scanning the room, she saw the lower half of a body sprawled on the dining room floor. The upper half was hidden by the table.

"You were gone for so long," Joelle wailed. "They started fighting, tearing at one another like animals and growling. It was awful. And Aunt Margo . . ." She stopped then and looked into Margo's eyes, searching for the courage she needed to say the rest. "Aunt Margo, Garth's gone—disappeared!"

Margo sucked in her breath with a sigh of relief. It was Garth. He was the one who was gone. That was Jared lying on the floor back there. Had she not been so nervous, she would have recognized his clothing.

"Garth kept teasing Jared about you. I was watching the door, hoping you'd come back before it turned ugly."

Margo released her and walked around to where Jared was lying. When she got to him and stood over his body, she knew at once that he was as good as gone, too. He was mortally wounded.

Falling to her knees, she lifted his head and cradled it in her arms. Jared opened his eyes then and smiled as blood streamed from between his lips. Margo wanted to rage, to scream, but she was dead inside. The one thing she'd been living for all of these years was now being taken away from her—Jared, her love.

"How can I live without you?" she asked without thinking.

"You must and you will," he said, his breath heavy and labored. Then he raised a hand and covered her lips with his fingers before she could speak again. She was about to admit that Jared had been right all along. She should never have allowed Valerie's children to come here. The loss she'd suffered because of their presence was just too great to bear.

"Don't say it," he mumbled. "You'll have them after I'm gone."

"Have what?" Margo asked, her voice choking with emotion. "Eve is the chosen one. Jonathan's insane. And Joelle's in mourning for a—"

"Demon/man. Just like me."

"Jared, no," she cried, caressing his lips with her own. "Don't say it. I love you, I'll always love you."

"I have to go back," he said. "I'll die here, just like Garth did, without help from my own kind."

Margo heard his words and felt her heart swell with relief. "You mean you won't die? You can come back to me?"

"No. Things will never be the same between us once I return home."

"Oh, Jared, don't say that. They will be. You'll see."

"No, Margo, it's better if I stay there. I'll be a

demon again in every way, in appearance and personality. I won't be the Jared you've known all these years. Your husband will change me. He'll force me to stay. Believe me, you wouldn't want . . ."

As Jared spoke, the metamorphosis began. He was changing in front of her, turning into a beast. "I have no control, Margo. I'm sorry," he growled, his voice thick and husky and inhuman. "If I'd been able to assume my demon form before I had that fight with Garth, I wouldn't be as wounded as I am now, but my powers are limited. I couldn't. Please, Margo, take the twins and leave."

"I can't," she said, cringing at the sight of him now. She was afraid of him, but she couldn't leave. This was still Jared, her Jared. "I won't—"

"Leave!" he shouted. "They're coming for me now. I don't want you hurt."

"Jared, no," she moaned as a pair of hands encircled her shoulders. It was Joelle, and Joelle was forcing her up and away from Jared. Margo was almost hysterical by this time. She couldn't leave him.

"Jonathan, help me!" Joelle screamed. Between them, they dragged Margo from the dining room just as the room became filled with smoke, while the squawking and squealing noises of several demons filled the air.

Once outside, separated forever from her Jared, Margo threw her head back and cursed the forces of darkness. She cursed her husband as well, her lord, Satan, and she cursed Eve, because Eve was standing in front of her now, smiling.

But it wasn't a happy smile. It was one of vengeance.

"I'll kill you!" Margo raged. "I'll stop you and send you where Jared's going—back to Acheron, you bitch!"

"We'll see," Eve said quietly, still smiling. "We'll see who gets sent there first. You or me." Then she turned her back and was gone, leaving an hysterical Margo Windsor alone with the task of comforting the twins—one insane, the other in mourning over the loss of *her* demon/man.

Jared had been right.

She should never have allowed them to come here.

But there was just no way to change things now.

Chapter Eighteen

"CAN'T YOU DO something to help him?" Joelle asked Margo once they were safely locked in Margo's bedroom with Jonathan. "You healed us when we were beaten. Can't you do the same now?"

Joelle seemed to have gotten over Garth and was more concerned about Jonathan now. Then again, maybe she only shelved her grief for the time being because Jonathan needed her so badly. "I can't do a thing to reverse his insanity," Margo answered sadly.

"But why? He's so helpless." She started crying again, slurring her words until it became impossible to understand her.

"Joelle, I could cure him if his mind were lost, like amnesia, but I need a whole mind to work with. Jonathan's psyche is damaged. I'm as helpless as you. Besides, my powers are weakening."

"Could Eve do it?" Joelle wanted to know.

"Yes, but she won't."

"This is her brother," Joelle insisted. "She has to. She has no choice."

"She's not the same Eve. She's the chosen one now, completely devoid of emotion with no conscience or ties to humanity."

Jonathan spoke up then, saying he was tired and asking if it were time for his nap. Joelle clutched his hand in hers and led him over to Margo's bed, where she made him lie down. "Don't leave me," he begged in his little boy voice, and Joelle assured him that she wouldn't.

Margo stared at the scene unfolding before her and wanted to kill Eve! Jonathan was the baby now. Eve had done this to him. And Joelle had lost her love. It was a good thing Valerie was dead. Valerie could never take this.

Jonathan was snoring softly before Joelle left his side to whisper to Margo. "What do we do now? There's so much to straighten out."

"I don't know what you have in mind as far as straightening out goes. The most important thing now is stopping Eve," Margo whispered back.

"But Aunt Margo, if we can't . . . Do I take her home with me when we leave? What do I tell my father?"

Margo had never considered these questions, but Joelle had a point. If they couldn't stop Eve, if they couldn't reverse the process or make Eve walk away from her so-called honor, then what? "I don't know what to say, but I really can't imagine Eve going home with you as though nothing happened here. She's special now, not one of us, no longer a family member.''

''In other words, she won't go home with me. Daddy will just die.''

''No, he won't,'' Margo said firmly. ''Your father's a strong man. He'll accept what is.'' She stopped speaking at this point and wondered why the two of them were whispering. Eve could hear every word they were saying, no matter where she was at the moment.

Joelle left her side then and sat at the bottom of the bed. She placed a hand over Jonathan's foot, the one protruding from the bottom of the spread, and wiped her face to stem the flow of tears. ''I feel stupid saying this, but I miss Garth even though we were only just starting out.''

''We haven't got time for this,'' Margo said harshly. She missed Jared. He was her life, her breath, her love, and she wanted no reminders, not when getting rid of Eve was the most important item at hand. And by that—getting rid of her—Margo wasn't thinking in terms of just chasing her away. Margo wanted her dead and gone forever!

Margo wanted to send her to Acheron, but Margo didn't have enough power to do so, despite her threats. And Eve wasn't stupid now. Eve knew about Margo's waning powers. ''We'll see who gets sent there first,'' Eve had said to Margo. ''You or me.''

''Was she really outside speaking to the dead

ones from the woods when you went to get
her?'' Joelle asked. Margo nodded silently.
"She controls them now, doesn't she?'' Again
Margo nodded silently. Then Joelle was quiet
for a moment, her brow tightened by anxiety.
"Do you think she'll use them to kill us?''

"I don't know,'' Margo said and went to sit
beside her.

"I'm scared, Aunt Margo,'' Joelle said and
let go of Jonathan's foot, clutching Margo as
she did. "Eve can use the invisible pets to kill us,
and we can't stop them. Or she can wait until
we're asleep and use the Walk of the Dead.''

"I don't think Eve will do either of those
things,'' Margo said lightly, though she wasn't
sure. Eve was a different person now—look
what she did to Jonathan—and she'd threatened
to destroy Margo. Still, there was nothing to be
gained by speaking the truth and adding to
Joelle's fears. "Why don't we take a nap
ourselves?'' Margo suggested, suddenly tired
herself.

Too much had happened this past hour. She'd
lost too many people in such a short space of
time—Eve, Jonathan, Jared. "Maybe once we
rest, the answers to our questions will come
easier.''

"I'll wake Jonathan.''

"No, this bed is big enough to hold three. It's
important that we stay together for the time
being. We need each other—at least I do. I can't
stay here, in this room, alone.''

"Anything you say, Aunt Margo.'' Joelle lay

down between Jonathan and Aunt Margo, but she didn't go to sleep right away. There was one more question, and it had to be asked. She knew it would hurt—herself as well as Margo. It would be a reminder of Jared. Still, it had to be asked.

"Where do you think Garth is?"

She felt Margo tense up beside her and wished she hadn't said another word, but she just had to know. "According to Jared, he's dead, isn't he?" Margo said softly.

"I think so, but he disappeared into thin air. I mean, he was badly injured and all. He must have gone somewhere to heal."

"Maybe . . ." Margo's voice broke then, but she took a deep breath and went on. "Maybe he was taken home, where Jared is."

"I hope not."

"Joelle," Margo half-shouted, "wake up! He's a demon! He's sworn allegiance to Eve. We're fighting her. We don't need him, too!"

"I never thought of it that way. I hope you're wrong, Aunt Margo. He promised to stay with me always."

Margo decided to let her live with her illusions. After all, Jared had allowed Margo to exist under an illusion for close to 50 years. Joelle was entitled to the same.

As for Margo, she hoped Garth was gone for good. She could see the truth even if Joelle couldn't. Garth, if he was still here, was a threat, just like Eve!

Margo remembered closing her eyes and drifting

off into a troubled sleep, but she couldn't remember waking up or getting to her feet to stare down at the twins who were lying close together. Jonathan and Joelle were holding hands, as if by doing so they could guard one another from Eve's wrath.

Margo was restless, and she knew why. It was because of Jared. He wasn't there in her bed where he belonged, and he never would be again. She left the bedroom and leaned against the outside wall for strength, wishing it was his body she was leaning against. Oh, how she missed him. The emptiness. The loss. There were no words to describe how she felt.

No, stop this! She couldn't have him back no matter what she did, so she had to be strong and accept what was. The twins needed her now, Jonathan surely, if not Joelle. Joelle would find another to love before long. Joelle was cute and wouldn't have many problems in that area.

Standing alone in the hall, Margo considered going to her chapel, but she had no one to honor with her prayers. While she could've prayed for Jared, it was useless. He was back home—with her father and Nathan and the rest.

Nathan! That was it! Nathan! And Jared!

Why hadn't she thought of it before?

That was the answer!

Eve was as good as gone!

She had to wake the twins and tell them the wonderful news. She'd found a way of stopping Eve—

"Really, Aunt Margo? Did you find an answer?"

Margo heard the voice coming from behind
her but didn't turn to face Eve—because it
wasn't Eve. That voice never came from Eve.
Carefully wrapping her hand around the knob to
her bedroom door, she started to turn it, to open
the door and make her escape, but the body
behind the voice anticipated her move.

A large black hand, with stubby fingers and
knuckles heavy with hair and tumors, laid itself
against the door in front of her, while the body
of the beast sort of hovered over her. It was big,
whatever it was, probably eight feet or more.
Margo was scared, but only because she was
almost blind and helplessly old.

"Can I help you?" was the only thing that
came to mind.

"You can turn and look at me, old woman.
This way you'll never forget who I am or what
my purpose is here. I guard the chosen one.
Garth is gone. I'm the replacement."

Margo didn't want to turn, and Margo didn't
want to look, but she had to. He had her by the
shoulders now, forcing her to face him. Oh, my
heart, she thought, and tried to close her eyes
against the horror to stop the pounding in her
chest. He *was* close to eight feet tall, and he was
black all over, his body thick and shiny and
heavy with scales—demon armor.

He had no neck. His head was like a huge,
black boil on his shoulders, and his few teeth
were spaced out and jagged.

"The better to eat you with, my dear, in case
you forget and try to harm the chosen one. I

should kill you now. In fact, I should kill you
and those two bastards inside, but waiting
makes the game more interesting. And, by the
way, your husband sent me.''

"Yes, ten years ago," Margo said, surprised
that she could even speak. She didn't know why
she knew the truth about this creature, except
that some of her insight was still intact. "He sent
you to Philadelphia. You're right. Garth is
gone, and you, the beast that paraded as Garth,
are here now."

The black demon's lips parted in what could
have passed for a smile. "You're a pretty smart
old bitch for figuring that out. I applaud you.
And Margo, say hello to my lay, Joelle!''

Margo sat up in bed and covered her mouth to
keep from screaming. Jonathan and Joelle were
still lying next to her. Her screams would have
only added to their fears, so she kept quiet and
crossed her arms in front of her chest to quell the
shaking in her body. What an awful dream! And
to think she actually imagined she'd been awake.

Rising from the bed, Margo grabbed her robe
and slippers. She needed a good, healthy shot of
brandy to steady her nerves. Walking slowly to
the door, she stopped for a moment and
wondered if she was taking a chance by going
downstairs. Eve might have been in the den, or
that creature . . . In fact, he might be outside in
the hall at this moment, waiting for Margo to
venture out.

No, it was only a dream, and, as far as Eve is
concerned, this is still your house! Looking over

her shoulder to check on the twins who were still
asleep, she opened the door . . . and tried not to
scream. He was out there, standing guard, but it
was only a dream. He didn't exist, so why was he
there?

"To guard Eve, you old fool!"

Margo slammed the door and leaned against
it. It was Garth again, without his disguise. She
never dreamed he was that hideous.

"Aunt Margo."

Joelle had awakened and was sitting up in
bed.

"Is anything wrong?" Joelle asked.

"No, honey, go back to sleep."

"Why are you just standing there? Did you
want something from downstairs? I can get it for
you."

"I just wanted some brandy, but I can live
without it. Now, I want you to go back to sleep.
We're going to have a busy day tomorrow." She
stopped talking then and crossed the room to her
bed. "Listen, Joelle," she whispered, "I have a
plan, but I can't say much about it."

"Why not?" Joelle asked, rubbing her eyes,
still half-asleep.

"Because Eve is everywhere, remember! All I
can say is that it came to me in my sleep. I was
thinking about Jared and about Nathan, and it
came to me. Now, in the morning—"

"In the morning? What time is it?" Joelle
followed Margo's gaze, saw the darkness outside
of her window and knew they'd slept all day and
into the night. "I should be hungry. We haven't

eaten, none of us, yet I couldn't eat if I tried."

"Depression does that to you. Anyway, in the morning we'll all go down to breakfast together as though nothing happened, and we'll enter into the first part of the plan. Okay?"

"Okay, Aunt Margo, anything you say."

"And Joelle, no matter what I tell you to do tomorrow, you must do it without asking why, no matter what it is." Joelle nodded silently. "And remember, Eve might be your sister, but you mustn't think of her that way. She's one of them now, and she's a threat to our lives."

Margo heard a low throaty growl coming from the hall and climbed into bed next to Joelle. Jonathan was still asleep. Joelle drifted off again, but not Margo. Margo had to stand guard over the twins to protect them from the black, demon warrior outside of her room.

Margo wanted to tell Joelle about the demon in the hall—about Garth—but she decided not to. Joelle had been through enough; she never could have faced seeing Garth as he really was.

"Yes, Aunt Margo, I'm going to kill all three of you, starting with the twins."

Margo was out in the kitchen—at Eve's command—making breakfast. Jonathan and Joelle were in the dining room. The demon warrior was nowhere to be seen. Margo figured he was shrouded in his veil of invisibility since he never would have left the chosen one alone.

After Eve had spoken these words, Margo turned and faced her. She couldn't believe she was hearing this.

"You and Joelle were wondering about it last night, weren't you?" Eve asked, her lips drawn into a thin, cold smile of death.

"But why?" Margo already knew the answer, but she had to hear it from Eve. She had to hate Eve enough to pull off her plan. Eve was still her baby. She could look at this evil, vile creature and still remember the old Eve, the one she loved. "Why kill the twins? Why not just me?"

"Because it's fun, and because the power is mine to do with as I please. There's quite a thrill in being able to choose who lives and who dies. Now that I do the choosing, I plan to use it at will. After all, everyone talks about overpopulation, but nobody does anything about it."

Eve was speaking as though she were discussing the weather. Margo remembered how Jared had been worried about one so young wielding such power.

"And Daddy's next," Eve said, on her way out of the kitchen. "I'm gonna kill him the same as you killed your father. Forget whatever plan you had in mind, Aunt Margo. I'm just too strong to defeat."

Margo wanted to kill her on the spot, but Eve was right. She was too strong to defeat. Margo would have to use trickery to destroy Eve.

Opening the door to the kitchen, Margo listened and dared not think about her plan until she heard Eve speaking to the twins. Eve was in the dining room now and too preoccupied at this point to scan Margo's brain and learn the truth.

She went over the plan in her mind once again

to be sure it would work.

Margo had remembered the night before that
Nathan wanted to be buried in those woods
behind the mansion because they were on
hallowed ground. As such, Satan's troops
couldn't follow him there to drag him to Hell.
The evil ones were afraid of treading on
hallowed ground.

Jared also couldn't enter those woods for the
same reason. He told Margo that he'd often
stood on the outskirts of those woods and flung
bodies in there because he dared not enter a
place that had been blessed by the God of the
Christians.

That's when the wonderful scheme came to
Margo. She planned on sending the twins to the
woods where they'd be safe from Eve; as the
chosen one, Eve couldn't go there now. Once
the twins were on safe ground, Margo planned
to lure Eve into chasing her into those same
woods to suffer whatever fate would befall a
demon when entering hallowed ground.

Of course, Margo had considered that this
was the home of the dead ones, but if Eve didn't
have time to summon them for killing, the twins
would be out of danger until Margo got there.

Now, if only the plan would work!

Margo and Joelle didn't eat much, but
Jonathan ate like a condemned prisoner. His
sickness didn't seem to have much affect on his
appetite, Margo thought, as she watched a plate
full of food disappear in minutes flat.

After breakfast, Margo stared at Eve, who was at the head of the table hovering over them like a vulture, and suggested that Jonathan and Joelle go for a walk in the woods behind her house.

Joelle started to refuse until Margo looked directly at her, passing an unspoken message with her eyes. That message said, "We've already discussed this. You promised to do whatever I told you to do without asking me why."

"Come on, Jonathan," Joelle then said, taking her brother by the hand as though he were a child. "Let's go look for some squirrels to chase."

After they were gone, Eve spoke to Margo for the first time since joining them at the table. "Strange that you're sending them there. The dead ones live in those woods, but somehow I can't imagine you forgetting about the dead ones." Her brow was knotted in deep thought by this time. "While I don't know what your plans are, I want to thank you for making my job easier."

"Easier!" Margo said coldly.

"Yes, easier! The dead ones won't have far to go when I send them after Jonathan and Joelle."

"And what about Garth?" Margo asked, still with that coldness in her voice. Margo desperately tried to distract Eve before she could send the dead ones after the twins. "I know he's still alive!"

"You've seen him?"

"Yes, parading around in his natural state, as a black, demon warrior. What about him?"

"I don't understand," Eve said and smiled, never taking her gaze from Margo's face as though she were trying to stay one step ahead of her elusive aunt. "What do you expect me to say?"

"Will you send Garth after the twins as well?"

"Certainly. And if Garth's lucky, he might even get it on with Joelle again before he kills her."

Margo listened to Eve's hatred being vented as lewdly as possible, but kept her temper. This was to be a battle of wits. The last thing she could afford to do was to lose her temper, therefore losing the fight as a result. Yet Eve said something then, and Margo lost it despite her efforts not to.

"In fact, Garth is after them now."

Margo heard those words and rose from the table, heading for the back door as quickly as she could. Garth was after them! She hadn't counted on this part of it. Garth was supposed to have stayed with Eve, no matter what, while Jonathan and Joelle made it safely to those woods.

How come people never did what you expected of them? How come they always made it so hard by doing whatever the hell you least thought they would? How come?

* * *

Joelle was halfway to the woods with Jonathan when a demon warrior blocked their path. Only two things saved her from falling apart. She was used to seeing demons from her coven days, and she didn't know he was there to kill her.

She didn't know he was Garth, either.

"Who are you?" Jonathan asked, hiding behind Joelle.

"I'm your ticket to Hell," the demon answered.

"Is he gonna kill us?" Jonathan asked, turning to Joelle.

Joelle tightened her grasp on his hand and didn't answer. Frightening Jonathan even more at this point would have been disaster. Jonathan would have run from this menace, and Joelle wanted him by her side so that she could protect him.

"You, protect him?" the demon asked, laughing. He'd read her thoughts, and now he was using those thoughts to torment her. "How?"

"Well, I'm not sure, but maybe I can conjure up another demon to help us," Joelle said, ignoring the laughter coming from this hideous beast. "Maybe I can call up Garth. He was supposed to protect us from harm."

Joelle listened to her own words hanging in the air and was horrified when the black horror in front of her went through a rapid metamorphosis. First he changed himself into Garth, then back to the beast again. Composing herself as quickly as she could, she decided to torment him back.

"You're not Garth," she said. At this point she really didn't care that he was Garth. Margo's words from the night before had returned to haunt her. Garth was, and is now, here for the protection of the chosen one. He was no friend to her, and no lover.

"If I'd made love to something as hideous as you, I'd remember it. No, it wasn't you. You must think I'm an asshole to believe you." She watched the jaws of the great beast working in anger. Good, she thought, he's angry. Now he'll lose control.

"I'll never lose control," he spat, reading her thoughts again.

"Joelle, I'm cold," Jonathan whined. "Let's go back to the house."

"It's not safe there," she hissed. Jonathan was breaking her concentration.

"It's not safe here either," he whined. "That thing's gonna kill us."

"No, he's not," Joelle said, falling back against Jonathan when she spotted an army of rotted corpses coming out of the woods behind the beast. Eve was taking no chances. Eve wanted them killed before they could carry out Margo's plan, whatever that plan was.

Taking his eyes from Joelle for a moment, the beast turned and saw the dead ones. Then he laughed. "Reinforcements, not that I need them. I can kill you two without even thinking about it, without even using half of my powers."

* * *

Margo was breathless by the time she saw the twins on the road ahead. Garth was blocking their path to the woods. Then she saw the dead ones coming from the woods and heard Eve's footsteps coming from behind her, and she knew they were trapped.

She was not concerned with her own fate. Hell no, she was as good as dead anyway. It was Jonathan and Joelle that she was worried about.

"Worry no more," Eve said, reaching her side, grabbing her arm, forcing her to walk ahead and stand beside the twins. "You'll all die together. There'll be no one left to worry about."

Joelle turned and faced Eve, her face frozen with a look of complacency. Joelle was still playing the game of torment to confuse both Garth and Eve. Eve saw Joelle's smugness and became enraged. "In one minute, sister dearest, that shit-grinning expression of yours will be replaced by one of fear."

"Eve, please," Margo pleaded, "spare the twins. I'm a prize catch—the bride of Satan. Kill me. The master will be pleased."

"You'll all die!" roared Garth. "Not one will be spared!"

The dead ones had formed a circle around them by this time, giving Joelle no chance to defeat the warrior by confusing him. Quickly her mind settled on another plan. After all, Margo's plan had seemed to fail, so now it was her turn. Facing the dead ones, Joelle spoke directly to them. "Which of you are Aubrey and Tom Soames?"

None of them answered at first. Their eyes were dull and glassy as though they were hypnotized. Joelle scanned their rotted faces and tried to pick out the Soames' boys. Eliminating the dead ones dressed in antique clothing—those were the Monkshood witches and warlocks—she looked at the others and repeated her words.

Still no answer.

"So you died for nothing," she hissed, "and now you will allow your deaths to go unavenged."

"Silence!" Eve raged. "I'm in charge here. You will say nothing!"

Joelle was afraid of Eve, but Joelle figured she was as good as dead anyway. So why not make an attempt to save Jonathan and Aunt Margo and herself? "See this bitch?" Joelle shouted, pointing to Eve. "She's responsible for the deaths of Matthew Soames and five other men from town. And him," she said, pointing to Garth. "He killed Aubrey and Tom Soames and all the rest of those so-called missing people."

"Jared killed them!" Garth raged indignantly. "Not me. I was in Philadelphia with you."

Joelle knew he was speaking the truth, but demons thrived on lies, as did their master. "Liar!" she raged in turn. "You killed them. You told me so yourself. You bragged about it."

"You're the liar," Garth said, stepping closer to Joelle while the crowd of dead ones mumbled, shuffling their feet and seeming to come to life.

"He was my lover," Joelle shouted, playing to the crowd. "He told me when we were alone."

"Liar!" Garth said, lunging at Joelle while Margo threw her aside and stepped in Garth's path. Margo had been quietly standing by up until now, figuring Joelle knew what she was doing, but she had only tormented a beast into attacking her. Yet Garth was seized by the dead ones before reaching Margo.

Joelle's words had brought them out of their trance and angered them into acting against at least one of their murderers. Garth was dazed at first, but then he recovered and swung his arms at the dead ones.

Joelle knew it would be quite a battle. Garth was a powerful demon, but the dead ones were beyond feeling pain and beyond giving in as easily as they would have if still alive.

Then she turned to the Monkshood witches and warlocks. "This bitch is the reason you were burned at the stake. She's a witch, and you were innocent! You died for the likes of her!"

Eve tried to get Joelle by the throat as the Monkshood witches and warlocks surrounded her.

At this point, Joelle grabbed Jonathan and Margo and headed for the woods, but Jonathan was crazy and uncoordinated. He didn't seem to know how to run, and Margo was too old to run. But run they must. They had to make those woods before Garth and Eve were free of their captors.

Jonathan fell once or twice, and Margo was

out of breath, but the woods were there, ahead of them, like an oasis in the desert. "A few feet more," Joelle shouted, "and we're on hallowed ground. Garth told me about this place."

She'd no sooner spoken those words when Garth appeared on the road in front of them again. Hissing like a beast gone mad, he lunged for Joelle, while Margo let go of Joelle's hand and lunged back at him. She wanted to keep Garth busy while Jonathan and Joelle made it to the woods.

Slamming into him was like running into a freight train. Margo fell to the ground from the force of the blow while Garth hovered over her, waiting for her to regain her composure so he could kill her. Killing her while she was down was just no fun.

Margo shook her head and started to get to her feet, but Garth raised a hairy foot to kick her back down. His foot was in mid-swing when Margo spotted it. Ducking from the force of his attack, Margo managed to throw Garth off balance. Garth fell forward, stumbling, trying to catch his balance.

Jonathan, seeing a chance to help, growled and rammed Garth from behind, locking his arms around the demon's waist. As he did, both of them stumbled forward while Jonathan shouted, "Leave my aunt alone. Leave my aunt alone," over and over until he was so enraged he couldn't think.

He finally stopped when Garth flew so far forward that he landed in the woods—and was no more. Jonathan stared at a screaming, flailing ball of fire and went back for his sister and his Aunt Margo.

Joelle, meanwhile, had Margo almost on her feet when Eve came rushing up from behind them and tried to grab Margo by the throat. Jonathan saw this and reached out in time to drag Margo and Joelle to safe ground, while begging Eve not to follow. Somehow, for one fleeting moment, sanity had reached out and taken hold of him—and he knew that Eve would perish if she followed them into the woods.

But Eve was too angry to listen. Eve had a mind of her own lately and wouldn't listen to anyone. So, as Jonathan watched, Eve entered the woods, entered hallowed ground as Garth had, and exploded in a raging ball of fire.

The prophecy had come to an end.

The chosen one was dead.

Tears flowed heavily from their eyes. Jonathan cried openly, as did Joelle and Margo. As they cried, they mourned for poor, brain-damaged, born-dead Eve. And while they mourned, all Hell mourned with them.

The air around them came alive with the howling and wailing of thousands of saddened beasts. Wind from the four corners of the universe rose and assaulted the trees, bending them almost to the ground like twigs, and everything else in its path as well, ripping bushes up by their roots. The earth shook beneath the feet of the mourners as Satan raged and vented his fury, unwillingly accepting his defeat.

While they watched, Eve was reduced to a stinking, festering pile of blackened flesh. And the dead ones—the 29 missing residents of Monkshood, along with the Monkshood witches and warlocks—returned home to their woods, no longer victims of the evil things perpetrated by men in the name of religion!

"Aunt Margo," Joelle said dazedly, "how come the dead ones can live here and not get blown up when they enter these woods?"

The answer was simple. They didn't kill willingly; their minds had been taken over by the evil around them and manipulated towards destruction. All the evil was gone now, so the dead ones were safe—at least for a while.

Chapter Nineteen

MARGO WINDSOR SAT alone at her dressing table and tried to brush her hair, but it was such an effort. She was so old and so blind.

Palming her brush, she felt cold plastic against her hand. The golden brush inlaid with precious stones was gone, and she wondered if her wedding ring had gone the same route. Had it turned to trash as well? Searching as best she could, she found her jewelry box and . . . *heard the front door open downstairs.*

The ring felt like cheap metal. It was rusty, too, as rusty as her marriage. Dropping the ring, she ran the brush from front to back, hoping she'd have time to finish 100 strokes before . . .

Someone was climbing the stairs. . . .

. . . her company arrived here in this room. Tonight was the night; she was sure of it. After all, her money was gone. Earlier in the day, a man had come from the bank to tell her that she had only a few dollars left, barely enough to exist. Of course, he blamed the mysterious disappearance of her wealth on Dennis Windsapple. Dennis had supposedly embezzled all her money.

The footsteps had reached the bottom of the stairs on the second floor. . . .

Then Dennis committed suicide, the man said. Drove his car off the road and into a tree. Killed instantly! It was strange though that Dennis' body was all charred and burnt, even though the car he was driving hadn't caught fire on impact.

The footsteps were on the top landing now, across from her room.

"Sorry," the man had said. "We'll make up the loss. We're insured you know." And Margo smiled, mainly because the man from the bank didn't know the truth.

Someone was crossing the hall to her room. . . .

Her money hadn't been embezzled by Dennis Windsapple. It was taken back, retrieved by her husband because of broken marriage vows. Margo had renounced her ties with the master beast and was paying for it now.

Someone was turning the knob on her door. . . .

And damnit, Margo so wanted to leave her money to Jonathan and Joelle and . . . oh, she'd almost added Eve to the list. She missed those kids, but the twins were better off back home where they belonged with their father.

The knob was turning, turning . . .

In fact, their father had finished his assignment—taking pictures of old rundown buildings, as Eve had called it—ahead of time and had come for his children. Margo had taken him into the den, after he'd gotten over the initial shock of seeing her as old as she was, and had explained the whole story.

Turning, turning, turning . . .

Jonathan Senior broke down once or twice, but he mostly accepted it since he knew about the prophecy. Then he took his children home.

The door was opening . . .

But not before promising to have Jonathan and Joelle come and visit some time real soon. Margo agreed, only because she didn't have the heart to add to his grief. Margo wouldn't be here when they came back.

The door was open . . .

In fact, Margo wouldn't be here after tonight. She listened to the sound of someone breathing heavy and the sound of his hounds—and knew her time had come. The twins knew what her fate would be and wanted her to run to Philadelphia with them.

The hounds were growling, anxious to begin.

Margo had refused to run because her husband's men would have caught up with her no matter where she went. And why endanger their lives? Why put them at risk?

"It's time," someone said.

And Margo felt her heart crack almost in two because that someone was Jared. There was no mistaking his voice, but it was so cold and impersonal. She should've expected this; he said he'd change. She still loved him so.

"I'm ready," she said as he set the hounds loose, and while she waited for the hounds to tear her apart, she listened for him to say more, because he wasn't finished yet.

"And by the way," he said, *as she knew he would, "your husband sent me!"*

874-0528

[Tammy]